Spilled Milk

Based On A True Story

K.L. Randis

SPILLED MILK
Based On A True Story
Copyright © 2013 by K.L. Randis

Cover Design Copyright © 2013 by K.L. Randis
All rights reserved.

The following is based on a true story. Author K.L. Randis testified at a criminal trial against her father, who was sentenced to prison for his crimes. He was sentenced to up to sixteen years in 2004. For the comfort and healing of the author's family, characters, places and incidents are used fictitiously, and any resemblance to actual persons, living or dead, business establishments, events, or locales is entirely coincidental.

Printed by Createspace

ISBN: 978-0-615-83560-0

SECOND EDITION

To Grandma Eileen and Grandpa George,
For believing in me.

And to my husband,
For always letting me write "just one more page."

Prologue

They never gave me a polygraph. I imagined myself strapped to a machine with a series of questions being rattled off. The proctors would nod their heads and mark the sheets as it fed out the results. Everyone wanted to know the truth, yet they asked the wrong questions over and over. "Are you okay?" "Do you need a break?" "What can I do?" No one would want to hear the real answers.

My hand closed around the organic chemistry note cards in my pocket. *How do hydrogen and chlorine react in the presence of an alkaline?*

The corner of my mouth twisted upward. Realizing it was inappropriate to laugh, I forced a serious face before anyone noticed. There I was, sitting in the District Attorney's office with stupid organic chemistry note cards in my pocket.

My mom sat against the adjacent wall from me staring off into space, a behavior I often mimicked myself. I never questioned the origin of my ability to transfix my eyes on an inanimate object while my brain sputtered into shutdown mode. It was a welcomed retreat at times.

Deep crevices muddled the brilliance of my mom's eyes and I wondered what she was thinking. Her weight shifted from one side of the chair then back again. It was a common dance she did to relieve the pressure in her lower back. The only interruption to her gaze happened when a man or woman wearing a suit entered the room.

I wondered if she even knew what organic chemistry was. "You would need this oxidizer. These two elements react like this, see?" I would draw a little diagram. "Simple."

"Oh, I don't know Brooke. You'll never need that anyway." The look on her face, the way her lips spread into a smaller, thin line told me she didn't want to hear about the things she refused to understand.

I was nineteen years old and a sophomore in college. The room could barely hold ten people and it was cement gray, just like I imagined when I thought of a courthouse waiting. A secretary sat in the corner checking her email, only stopping to pick up the phone or take a long, hard swallow of her mega-sized WaWa coffee. She was the only one in the room that looked at ease, while everyone else sat in an awkward silence waiting for Heather to come in and tell us what was next.

I hate this room. My butt is asleep. Yes, Miss Secretary, can I help you? I'll just stare back.

Mismatched posters held to the wall with ripened shards of tape. My uncle's chair had one leg slightly shorter than the rest and his mindless rocking helped pass the time.

My aunt picked up a pamphlet sitting next to her and opened it. It returned to the table just as fast. STDs and their warning signs were not her choice of reading material.

Heather shuffled through the door with wide eyes, banging her briefcase against her knees. "Okay, good, everyone's here then."

She was my designated victim advocate. Her job was to guide me through the court hearings so I could understand, usually having to explain things to me more than once. The flood of information I was expected to absorb about the judicial system failed to hold any meaning to me.

Heather didn't try to sugarcoat anything. She was blunt. "This is what the judge means," followed by, "Any questions?"

Hundreds. Thousands even. I solved chemical reactions with ease but tripped over the things Heather tried to drill into my head. She was worn too.

"I don't know how you're doing this," Heather had said just a week earlier, her emerald eyes glazing over. "I give you a lot of credit kiddo. They really tore you down in there and you kept your own. I know I keep saying this, but it'll be over soon."

I *would* get an Irish victim advocate. Her hair bounced around her face, blazing in a fireball of red glory while highlighting the doubt in her eyes as she tried to soothe me. I took it with a grain of salt, smiled, and accepted the one of many hugs that generally came my way after a debriefing.

2

She would often make some kind of remark about how us both being Irish was the only reason we would ever consider fighting so long and hard but that, "We make a great team, don't we?"

"You'd better come see me when all of this is over," she said. "You know, if you can ever handle coming back *here*," she motioned, flicking her hand into the space surrounding us.

She was right. I hated that room, the entire place: the smell of burnt coffee, the weird sounds the elevator made as we hurried down to courtroom three. I wanted to forget it all.

I had lost track of how many courtrooms I had testified in sometime after the first year of going there. Heather kept me grounded.

The security guards knew me well and were always happy to see me. The woman guard would greet me with a smile. "Ah, back again today?"

I would force a half-smile while scanning the lobby area. She would read my face. "He's not here yet, honey."

I relaxed and focused on getting into the District Attorney's office. The faster the better.

We parked behind the building and came through the less utilized handicapped entrance. Mom had rods and screws molded to her spine from a work injury years prior. She was a walking tin man, awkward gait included, guaranteed to set off the annoying alarm on the metal detectors. They waved a wand over her instead. She would nod and apologize for the inconvenience to the guards, but the smirk on her face absorbed all the pitied glances thrown her way.

Stroudsburg was a crumb-sized speck of a town in nowhere Pennsylvania. Coming into the building through the back threw off any news reporters trying to overhear conversations between everyone that walked in with me.

"Well then," the guard would say, lowering her voice. "Let's hope I don't have to see you anymore after today." She would wink as I crossed the lobby to Heather's office.

"Doesn't my lawyer look like David Caruso? You know, the guy on CSI Miami? He's got reddish hair," I said to Heather, moving a hand over my own unruly mob of wavy hair. She checked him out and raised an approving eyebrow.

Even though he was my lawyer, I only exchanged a few words with him throughout our time together. Heather was the one to keep me updated on the important things and she would relay any information back to him that I needed him to know. Whenever I would enter his office his eyes would say, "I'm sorry you're here again".

I sometimes imagined him making those slam dunk speeches I saw on CSI. Secretly I wanted to witness the kind of closing statement that would leave the courtroom gasping, *I knew it! Case solved!* He remained quiet and collected though, boring even. I grimaced. I never wanted my life to end up like a TV show anyway. This was real life, *my life.*

The majority of my extended family showed up on the last day of court. I understood the drive from Long Island, New York to Pennsylvania was a long one. I didn't expect the support *every* time we had a hearing. That last day was important, though.

There was comfort in the waiting room, a sense of familiarity. Family stared at me and waited for me to cry, to think, to breathe.

Secretaries and lawyers, rushing in late to meet their first clients of the day, analyzed all of the people around me as they passed through. They only acknowledged the older adults, as if I were a commonplace child. I ignored them and studied my note cards, their eyes skimming over me as they wrongfully assessed my age and the reason I was there. They tightened their lips in pity.

Must be a custody hearing. Poor kid.

Chapter One

Wow, he can hold his breath for a long time.

My brother's head bobbed halfway under the surface of the kiddie pool. I traced the outline of Barbie's face on my bathing suit and waited for him to come up. Adam could hold his breath longer since he was seven, a whole year older than me. His mouth must have been bigger and could hold more air.

Oh well, I won the first two times we played who-can-hold-their-breath-the-longest. I guess he can win this one.

I poked his back between the shoulder blades to signal that I had come up for air and his head sank toward the bottom, rising again like a lazy balloon. He didn't budge.

"Come on Adam, you win. You can come up now."

The way his body drifted made the hairs on my neck feel funny. I stiffened a little.

Where's Dad? Does he see this?

Oh, there he is talking to the neighbor, probably about boring things. It's funny our neighbor's name is Cornelia. Good thing she's old, it sounds like an old name. I wouldn't even play with someone with a name like that, it sounds like the name of a vegetable or a disease. They're nice neighbors, I guess, but their dogs are mean. Maybe 'cause we tease them through the fence. I should tell Dad about Adam. If he yells at Adam to get up he definitely will. How is he holding his breath that long?

I climbed over the side of the pool and avoided dog poop as I crossed the lawn.

"Dad?"

I knew I shouldn't interrupt his adult conversation. This was important though; Adam couldn't stay underwater all day since we still had a fort to build. It was his turn to steal food from the pantry so we could hide and eat it. Sneaky older brother, I wasn't stupid. He always backed out of stealing food and then I would be forced to do it.

Not this time.

My dad kept talking to Cornelia about how Long Island wasn't what it used to be and how much he hated bills. "New York is an expensive place to live, I know, but how am I supposed to raise these kids and eventually send them to private school on one paycheck? Not to mention Molly didn't plan on breaking her back and disability only pays so much.

"Dad, I have to tell you something."

Cornelia looked down at me and smiled. *She's a pretty lady to have a disease for a name.*

Dad gave me the stare, the one that said "go away". I don't think I'd ever really seen his eyes because his glasses were so thick but I knew they were blue, like mine. My mom's were blue and all of us kids had blue eyes, so his had to be too. His were different though. His eyes never laughed.

"Yeah, what?"

Better make this fast. "I have to tell you something."

He blinked at me.

I pointed toward the pool. "Adam won't get up. And he already won the contest so…"

My dad was halfway across the yard before I even put my hand down. By the time I started running after him he already had Adam scooped up in his arms, face up on the ground beside the pool, and his beard pressed against his lips. They were the color of blueberries. Cornelia started screaming about an ambulance but I didn't see one. All I saw was Adam lying on the ground in his Ninja Turtles bathing suit.

What a faker. He doesn't have to fake to get attention, I already know he won.

Adam started coughing and water came out of his mouth at the same time he started crying. "Daddy!" he gasped. His white knuckles grabbed at Dad's shirt. I started crying too because it seemed like the right thing to do and I didn't realize that Adam was really in trouble until just then.

My dad helped Adam to his feet. "That's all I need, another bill for an ambulance. It's not like I have insurance or anything. Brooke, get next door and tell Cornelia she better not call an ambulance. He's fine."

Cornelia didn't look happy but I did as I was told and ran back home. Adam was still sucking in deep swallows of air as tears slid down his cheek and a Popsicle stood hostage in his left hand. My dad sat at the kitchen table, his hands shaking as he sipped his water.

Look at him, my dad. He just saved Adam's life. I bet he would save mine too if I needed it. I bet he would do anything for us.

My feet stuck to the grimy kitchen floor as I crossed the room and grabbed my dad's arms to open them so I could crawl into his lap. I wrapped my arms around his neck and put my cheek against his scruffy face. He always smelled like machines. Mom said it was because he worked hard all day, putting them together and fixing the broken ones.

"Let's not tell Mom about this, snuggle bug." He pulled me into his chest with one arm and took another sip of his water.

Adam's near drowning would be the first of many secrets I would keep for my dad. "I won't, Daddy."

I put my head on his chest. I knew why he didn't want me to tell. Mom would be upset that she missed Dad saving Adam's life. She would have wanted to see it happen too, like I did, so she could remember all her of life how great he is, like I will.

Chapter Two

I was seven.

All I knew about a CB radio was that Mom and Dad met on one and after a week of talking they decided to meet up at Jones Beach. It took them over an hour to find each other since New York's beaches that stretched the length of Long Island were often packed on the blazing summer weekends.

My aunt had already landed her beau-to-be and had a wedding planned for that October. Not wanting to be outdone, Mom moved in with David after a few short weeks of dating. They wed in September and planned the house, the two kids, and the white picket fence. Three kids, two bug infested apartments and a cramped unkempt ranch on a desolate dead-end street later, I finished a glass of milk and readied my next question.

"So, what's a CB?" I asked.

After I watched a cartoon about two giraffes in love, I realized I didn't even know how my parents met. The giraffes flirted through a lyrical orchestra of words and sing-alongs. I imagined that's what my mom felt like when she fell in love.

Mom looked up from the tea bag she had fished out of her mug, trying not to burn her fingers. "Uh, it's a way people used to meet each other. You would talk over the radio and get to know people you wouldn't normally meet. It was a new kind of technology then. Everyone was doing it," she assured me. "I wasn't the only one."

I remained motionless. *Keep going.*

She took a sip of her tea. I stared at her.

"Why? You doing a book report or something?"

"No."

I watched the ash dangling from her cigarette threaten to drop onto the table before turning away. It was always the same. Unless there was a reason, questions were to be kept to a minimum. She went back to her tea, ending the conversation. I left to find Adam.

He was cross-legged on the floor playing with his K'Nex set when I walked into the living room. I leaned against the neglected grand piano and cleared my throat. "You'll never guess how Mom and Dad met." My arms folded across my chest and I shifted my weight. "Mom just told me."

"Through a CB," he said, without looking up.

"Not-uh." *Why does he always know everything?*

He stared at me.

"How do *you* know?" I said.

We were fifteen months apart in age which meant everything was a competition; who could read all the Disney books the fastest, ride their bike further or know all answers to the universe both large and small. I studied Adam as he focused on jamming a long yellow connector into a blue corner piece.

Ha, that's not gonna fit. He needs the green connector. Stupid.

He would sit there for hours in his solitude and craft the most magnificent things: ferris wheels, cars, and the Empire State Building. Sometimes I would play with him, but building houses and cars that were destroyed by Dad's work boots got boring.

"I found an old box in the garage a few months ago. It looked like a radio so I took it apart because it looked broken," he said. He shifted onto his knees to search for another piece.

"So how'd you know that's how Mom and Dad met then?" My eyes glanced over the holes in his sneakers. His t-shirt swam around arms no thicker than sticks.

Adam had a way of making me feel like I should always know his exact thoughts, and that it was some great inconvenience for him to have to explain anything. I shifted from one foot to another, raised my eyebrows, and sighed loud enough to wake a sleeping baby. He fished around for a random piece, skipping over the green one I knew he needed.

Over the years I learned that as long as I was quiet and let him think I was seriously concerned about not having a clue to what he was talking about, he'd save me and let me in on the thoughts running through his head.

After a minute Adam pushed one of his sleeves up above his shoulder blade. There was a white scar the size of a grain of rice on the back of his shoulder. He rubbed it thoughtfully before his eyes met mine. "I showed Dad how cool the inside of the box was, there were all these wires and stuff. He told me I broke the CB him and Mom met on. She was keeping it, I guess. He pushed me into the wall. Mom's garden scissors cut me."

"Oh."

Mom tripped over a toy fire truck as she entered the room. "Hey— *Adam*," she said, looking at all the scattered pieces on the floor. You could barely see the spinach colored carpet beneath the toys, random pieces of clothing, and clutter everywhere. The cramped room could barely hold the piano, sofa, and TV. "I thought I told you to put this away? Now let's go. Put this away, *now*." She picked up a toy, decided she didn't know where she could relocate it to, and put it back down again. "We're not going anywhere unless this room is spotless. You have five minutes."

Adam practiced his lawyer skills. "Mom, I *only* have to finish this one piece."

"Where we goin' Mom?" I asked.

"Grandma's. Grandpa's making dinner so once Thomas wakes up from his nap and after Kat eats—Adam I said *now*." She shoved a pile of plastic pieces into a heap with her foot.

"But Moooom," Adam said. "It's not fair. All I need to do is this *one piece*."

The thought of going to Grandma's was exhilarating. My knees hit the floor beside Adam and I searched for the part he needed. His eyes widened. "Hey! Hey Mom she's messing up my stuff!"

"I'm helping."

"No you're *not*. You don't even know what I'm looking for!"
Mom is going to yell in two seconds. Where IS it?

I locked eyes with the green connector and reached for it. The structure now complete, I looked toward Adam. His head dropped and he turned on his heel. "I knew I needed that piece. I didn't need your help to find it."

"Can we go now?" I asked.

Mom hustled Adam, Thomas, Kat and me into the minivan. We spent ten minutes driving down Southern State Highway before we pulled up in front of my grandparents' impressive, white Victorian home. Engraved columns hovered around the garden on the side of the house and the lawn was zebra striped from a fresh cut; it meant

Grandpa was expecting us. He was nowhere to be seen, but if I had to guess he was probably in the backyard skimming the swimming pool. Oak trees that lined the property kept him busy during the fall and summer months between his weekly pool and grass preservations.

My seat belt was unbuckled and I jumped over the seat in front of me before Mom put the van in park. The metal door handle fumbled in my hands before I rushed it open and jumped off the platform of the van onto the grass.

Grandma came to the front door before I could call out to see if Grandpa was still lingering in the garden. "Grandma!" I said, and ran full speed to the front porch.

"Hey, sugar!" she said as I tackled her waist. She wrapped me in a soft hug and pulled me closer. Her perfume danced around my face and she tightened her grip.

"How's my girl?" she asked. Grandma's hugs were always so genuine, so warm.

Before I could answer, Mom was walking up the porch steps and handing Kat over. "Careful, she's doing the projectile spit up thing again," she warned. Grandma held outstretched arms and took the baby while Adam zigzagged around her. Thomas waddled behind him, stopping to put a dandelion in his mouth.

"Hi Grandma!" Adam called out. He dashed into the house and I heard the wooden toy chest creak open in the front room. My grandpa had built him a custom toy box when he was just two years old, but my mom said the stain he had used on the cedar wood gave Adam an allergic reaction. Grandpa had spent weeks building it, even detailing the top in bright white letters that spelled out his name. Now it was tucked under the window of their front room, waiting for us whenever we came over.

My grandma moved us into the living room. "I just had the carpet shampooed, sorry if it's still damp. Just put the diaper bag on one of the flowered couches, Molly."

Symmetrical paintings depicting the ocean floated above each couch. I wandered over to the wood stove and looked up at the mantle filled with pictures of family, grandkids, and knickknacks from the beach.

I sunk into a couch and stared up at the ceiling that seemed to go on forever. The room smelled and felt like Grandma. "My goodness, look at how big everyone is getting," Grandma said. She put Kat on the living room floor. "I *think* that somebody's birthday is coming up, but I can't remember who." She met my eyes with a smile.

"Me! It's my birthday Grandma. I'm turning eight." I smiled.
She remembered.

"Oh it *is?*" she exclaimed, bringing her hand to her forehead. "Well I guess we'll just need to go to Toys R Us while everyone else swims then."

"Oh Mom, no," Mom started, shaking her head, "not necessary." She handed Kat a stuffed bear and pulled a pill bottle out of her pocket. Two oval shaped, cream colored pills fell into her hand. With a fluid motion she popped them into her mouth and threw her head back.

Now you see them, now you don't.

I had heard my mom repeat the story of how she hurt her back thousands of times. She had worked as a nurse's aide at Great Side Hospital in lower Manhattan. Her shifts were sporadic, and having four small children at home made it difficult to juggle everything.

She managed to generate a significant income working around Dad's work schedule. They had asked her to work a double shift a few weeks before Christmas and she obliged, making a quick last-minute call to the babysitter.

A heavy-set man had just come out of surgery for gallstones and she assisted in transporting him to his room. The registered nurse left the room suddenly, telling my mom not to move him until she came back with more help. She hurried out before my mom could protest otherwise.

The man groggily tried to shift himself from the cot to the bed on his own. His weight fought against him, and he began to slip in between the two beds. Mom acted on instinct and pushed against the cot to catch him between the two beds instead of letting him fall to the floor.

Two nurses walked into the room a second too late and scrambled over to help just as Mom fell to the floor from the pressure. She herniated and ruptured seven discs in her back; doctors were sure she would never be pain or painkiller free for the rest of her life.

She had saved her job by doing the right thing and she saved the hospital from a major lawsuit. In return, she became a permanently disabled mother to four children, eventually succumbing to such intense chronic pain after five back surgeries that she started collecting social security disability and had to leave her job permanently.

I remember one day I watched a girl run off of the school bus and her mom swooped her up and swung her around in a tight hug, backpack attached and all. The mom kissed her head as she set her down, eyes bright and chatting about how her day was. My eyes welled up. I came home and accused my mom of not loving me.

"Why can't you pick *me* up?" I cried. "I'm the smallest one in my class, I'm little!"

Mom started crying too. "Oh, Brooke, I'm sorry. I just...can't." She gripped the edges of her back brace with white knuckles.

I couldn't even sit in her lap as I sobbed. My only comfort was to stand next to her while she sat at the kitchen table and bury my face in her shirt until I had nothing left to cry.

That day I learned to let go of things like being picked up and feeling hugs that squished my bones. Instead, I focused on giving those things to Adam, Thomas, and Kat. I wanted to feel that closeness, even if I was the one who had to initiate it.

"Oh no, no, I want to. I insist she pick something for her birthday," Grandma beamed, watching my mom swallow her pills. She turned to me. "You ready, sugar? Let's go."

We talked about the beach and my upcoming birthday as she merged onto the highway. "So, tell me everything, what grade are you going into?" she asked.

The only time I stopped talking the entire ride was to ask her what she thought about the rule of checking out *only* three books from the library at a time. I was pleased to find we shared the same opinion of it being totally unfair.

As we pulled into the parking lot of Toys R Us she asked me what I wanted. "I'm not sure," I said. I tapped my foot and waited for Grandma to turn off the car. The store was full of beautiful dolls, board games, and costumes. I was headed right for the notorious pink aisle all of the girls at school talked about.

Grandma held my hand as we crossed the parking lot and gave it a little squeeze as the double door opened in front of us. "Whatever you want," she said. She meant it.

I sped past the clearance toys and stuffed animals. The Barbie aisle was a short distance from the outdoor play section. Grandma strolled close behind me. "Oh, look at *this* one," I said. Princess Barbie was off of the shelf and cradled against my chest. Swim

Team Barbie stared at me. "Or *this* one. Grandma she has a bathing suit, she can swim with me."

Grandma laughed. "She can! Whatever one you want, take your time."

Each doll's face and features had to be considered along with the extras each doll came with: a stroller, an umbrella, and binoculars. There were so many. I lined up three choices next to each other and studied them. School Teacher Barbie won; she came with a blackboard and real chalk. "This one," I said, and handed it to Grandma.

"Excellent choice."

She took my hand and headed toward the registers. I let her cruise me around passing people and aisles so I could study my Barbie's clothes inside the box. A toddler down one aisle threw himself on the ground in protest over a matchbox car. The checkout lane was a few feet in front of us when I saw something. I tugged on Grandma's hand. "Wait. Grandma, can I look at something?"

She checked her watch. "Sure sugar, quick though. Grandpa should have started the grill by now."

An end aisle with a clearance display caught my attention. I picked up a small book with Disney's Aladdin and Jasmine on the cover, turning it over in my hand. A jingle from the side forced a smile. A small, silver lock clasped the front and back of the book together. My eyes widened. "Grandma, I want *this* instead."

I handed it over and Grandma flipped it from front to back. She checked the price, a mere $3.99, and gave me a crooked smile. "This?" she asked. "Do you know what it's for?"

"It's a journal," I said. I saw them on TV and read about them, but I never had one. It was a real journal, with a lock to keep all thoughts and secrets forever bound to the person who wrote in it. "Please, Grandma?" I asked. I tried to read her face.

She looked at the Barbie in one hand and journal in the other. She thought for a minute, and then bent down until her blue eyes were level with mine. "If you *really* want it and *only* if you promise to write in it every day, until it's completely full," she bargained.

My heart skipped. "Every single day," I promised.

"Okie dokie." She stood up and tucked the Barbie on a nearby shelf, shaking her head. "Of all the things in this store, it doesn't surprise me." She put the journal on the conveyor belt and paid with a crisp five-dollar bill.

We got back to the house just as Grandpa was pulling burgers and hot dogs off of the grill. I rushed inside, eager to show Mom and Adam my present. "Look what Grandma got me!" I gave it to Mom and wiggled in next to Adam on the patio bench to eat a cheeseburger.

"Oh?" Mom said. She flipped it over. "Mom, you took her to Toys R Us and got her a book?"

"It's what she wanted," Grandma said. She shrugged, taking a seat next to Kat and Grandpa. "She's the birthday girl."

"It's not a book *Mom*, it's a *journal*," I corrected. Lemonade dribbled down my chin. "Grandpa, Grandma got me a journal and I have to write in it every day. I will too, I'll write on every page."

"Mmm," he said in agreement, putting ketchup on his burger. "Good."

Grandpa wouldn't have been a very good journal keeper. He didn't talk much. It's usually what he didn't say that said a lot.

After dinner Adam and I swam in the pool while the adults poured drinks into glasses shaped like tennis balls. Grandpa's brow was pressed together as he stood next to Mom's chair. He was telling her something important, I knew, because he shook his finger at her as he talked. Grandma brought us ice pops a short time later and we sat next to the adults to eat them.

Grandpa still had a perplexed look on his face and tried to give Mom some money. "You need it, just take it Molly," he demanded.

Grandpa didn't like it when Mom turned down his ideas. She gave a brief rebuttal before he stuffed the bills into her purse. He mumbled for a few more minutes and finally excused himself from the table to check his tomato plants.

When it was time to leave I thanked Grandma again for the journal and tucked it under my arm. "Remember your promise," she said, winking at me and giving me a final hug. I couldn't wait to get home to write in it.

We pulled up in front of our unimpressive ranch. Dad's car was absent from the driveway. "I'm putting Kat to bed," Mom called over her shoulder. "Adam, help Thomas inside and clean up these toys before your father gets home. Brooke, load the dishwasher would you?" Kat slumped over Mom's shoulder like a hefty rag doll, puffing out breaths of air.

I lugged a kitchen chair over to the sink. Once I was level with the countertop, I picked dried spaghetti off of plates and splashed water inside the cups that had sour milk. The liquid soap container weighed down my arm but I finally managed to pour some into the square tray of the dishwasher. The sink was empty ten minutes later, and I used my shirt as a towel.

The front door opened and I heard heavy boots in the hallway. Dad was home.

Chapter Three

I was nine when my best friend across the street let me write in her journal. My Aladdin and Jasmine one had every page filled and my mom refused to get me another one.

"I don't have the money for that crap, Brooke," Mom said. "Write on a piece of paper."

Since Alyssa hated to write and since we were best friends for life, she let me use the one her mom got for her.

I was playing Barbies with Kat in the kitchen when Alyssa's mom called. Mom rolled her eyes when Meredith's number flashed across the caller ID and she steadied her voice before she picked up.

"Oh hey Mer, what's—?" Mom's silence as she listened forced me to look in her direction. She twisted the cord around her finger and turned her back to us. "Mmmhmm? Yeah, Brooke likes journals."

My face tingled with heat when Mom paced two short steps towards the living room. She spun and looked in my direction, the receiver glued to her ear. My mom—usually the one chatting away on phone calls—was unable to utter a single syllable. Instead she darted her eyes at me with an open mouth.

I prayed that Alyssa's mom was asking if I could come over for dinner or to play. The banquet my Barbie was attending with my sister's teddy bear was no longer interesting and I half listened, pretending to be fixated on brushing Barbie's hair.

"What do you—I mean, can I see it?" Mom's voice heightened. The thud in my chest was nothing compared to the knots that started to form in my stomach.

What did I do?

Mom grabbed her tea and headed for the door after slamming the phone down. "Brooke, watch your sister."

My legs weren't fast enough to chase her. "Mom, what's—"

"No!" She screamed when she saw me trying to follow. "You get back at that table and you watch her until I get back. GO!" She disappeared through the front door and I paced the kitchen. Hours went by. Maybe it was minutes. I wish I had known Alyssa's number by heart, I would have called her.

After Kat and I put our Barbies back in their bin, the front door opened. My mom's quick footsteps in the hall made the hairs on the back of my neck stand up and I looked for a place to hide. With knuckles clenched, I readied for the screaming to start. *Whatever she says you did, just apologize. Apologize and offer to clean up the kitchen.*

Crumbs that lingered on the kitchen table became my focal point so I didn't have to see her face when she entered the room. I moved them around with my finger until I felt eyes on me. Mom's eyes. I couldn't look at her.

Silence.

Please say something.

I had to look. My eyes darted up, briefly, to catch my mom standing with her back to the counter and her one hand covering her eyes. It was what she did when she was about to explode. She buried her face, building up, maybe asking God for forgiveness for the terror that was about to reign over the kitchen.

"Brooke." Her voice was solid, calm.

"Yeah?" I flicked a crumb. *Should I start screaming first? No, she would drown me out.*

She moved her hand down her face, dragging her fingers past her eyes and cheeks. When she pulled her hand away I thought for sure her skin would come with it.

"Let's go. Kat, you too. *Now.*"

Alyssa was nowhere to be found as I sat on her couch staring at the journal I had been writing in for weeks. I couldn't look up. *How was I going to explain this?*

"Brooke, honey," Alyssa's mom started. "Do you know what sex *is?*"

There isn't a right answer to that question, lady.

My toes curled in my shoes. There was a hole in the big toe of my right sock. I wiggled it. My lips pressed hard against each other in a hushed war with my head. *Say nothing, Brooke. Journals are secret, they shouldn't have looked.*

"This picture." Mom slammed a cold finger against the page in my lap. "Where did you see this? How did you draw..." She trailed off. "Where did you get ideas to draw pictures like that?"

Alyssa's mom squinted at me. "Did she maybe see this on TV Molly? I know those late shows can be full of garbage like this."

"Is that it, Brooke?" Mom's voice was alarmed. "Did you see this on TV?" She played the unknowing parent role. "Did you see this when you weren't supposed to?"

My head suddenly felt like it had filled up with sand, the heaviness barely allowing me to look in their eyes. They were curious, frightened. They didn't know what to think, those eyes.

"Well, Brooke?" Mom's voice reached furious status. "You didn't draw these pictures from nowhere. You didn't learn the word sex and penis from your books at home. Did you think we wouldn't find this? What would make you write and draw these things? This is Alyssa's journal, not yours! Do I need to look at the journal you have at home?"

"No!" Tears fell into my lap. "I saw it on TV," I lied. I couldn't let her read my journals at home. "I watched a show I shouldn't have watched. I'm sorry. I'm sorry Mom, I didn't mean to get Alyssa in trouble."

"Alyssa's not in trouble." Mom flipped the journal closed and threw it across the room. "YOU are!"

"Okay, all right, let's just—" Alyssa's mom motioned for my mom to sit down.

"You listen to me." Mom lowered her voice as she moved towards me, the smell of cigarettes flaring in my nostrils as she shook her finger inches from my face. "If I ever, ever see you draw or write things like this again, I swear to God..."

Her threats were promising. She would call all the family and all the neighbors about the bad thing I did. She would maybe even call the school, tell them I was a horrible child who drew bad things in journals, and that I shouldn't be allowed to go there anymore.

I would have to spend all my time at home with her and Dad, not allowed to write in journals, always labeled the bad child. My brothers and sister would be allowed outside to play and allowed to read books. Not me, though. I would be banned from those things for being the bad child that drew pictures of penises and sex in a journal that wasn't mine.

Meredith stood to coax Mom into the kitchen for tea. Mom's tears overpowered my own and Meredith tried to console her by putting a hand on her shoulder and shaking her head in a reassuring motion. "I can't take it anymore, these kids," Mom ranted. "Why would she embarrass me like this? Why do I even bother?"

"I won't write those bad things anymore," I said, though no one heard me. They had already walked into the kitchen, leaving me alone. The journal was scooped up off of the floor and was flung into the closest garbage can. My sleeve served as a makeshift tissue as I whole-heartedly vowed, whispering with my eyes clenched, "I won't ever write about these things again Mom. I'm sorry. I'm so sorry."

Chapter Four

"Mom told me what she found in Alyssa's journal yesterday," Dad said. He cleared his throat and craned his neck to see if Mom was standing in the kitchen. She wasn't. "I don't know why you would need to draw the things you did."

Yes, you do.

"But I know you're a smart girl, and something like that won't ever happen again. Right?"

We sat there in silence. I wished Thomas would burst through his bedroom door and ask for cereal or that the dog would come to the back door wanting to be let back in. His voice hissed the last part, *"Right?"*

How can he sit across the table from me drinking his coffee as though this conversation is perfectly normal? My fingers pinched the skin between my eyes as I strained to figure out if I was awake or still asleep. *Is he really saying this to me right now?*

"Good," he said, accepting my silence as confirmation. "In that case, I think we need to talk about your bedtime being changed."

"Dad, I said I was sorry." I spoke carefully, pleading.

He held up his hand. "I think a girl your age deserves to go to bed at… I don't know, nine o'clock every night. No more eight-thirty. What do you think?"

I hated the smile that spread across my face. A half an hour increase meant a lesser amount of time I had to spend in my bedroom at night.

"Aunt Jean and Uncle Bruce are here!" Adam screamed, running around the corner and almost into the kitchen table.

"Shut up, I don't need you running around here like a goddamn wild animal." Dad pushed his newspaper away and stood up to adjust his bathrobe. "Sure, just stop on in anytime," he mumbled. "Molly, get in here!"

Mom appeared from the bathroom as she threw her head back and popped two white pills into her mouth. I had trouble swallowing medicine when I was sick, but Mom could swallow multiple pills *and* without water.

"What? Dave, whatdya want?" Her words slurred. "I'm right down the hall, not across the street." The comment made me cringe as I waited for Dad to take offense to it but two heavy knocks on the front door diffused the moment.

"I'll get it," I said, sprinting towards the door.

"Brooke! Honey here, take these bags." Aunt Jean handed me two grocery bags full of food. "Go, go, you know where they belong. Molly! How are you? So good to see you."

The yellow plastic scuffed along the ground as I fought with the weight to get it into the kitchen in one piece. Adam and I spent the next fifteen minutes dragging yellow bags inside as Mom put on tea and Dad changed out of his robe. I loved visitors.

"Dave, how's work? Keeping you busy?" Uncle Bruce outstretched a rigid hand.

"Doesn't need to. I got four kids at home to do that for me."

Uncle Bruce smirked at the comment. "Yeah, Jean is about ready to pop any day now." He rubbed his own middle section. "Can't wait to meet the little guy."

"Mmm." Dad chugged the last of his coffee.

"I can't believe how tall Adam is getting," Uncle Bruce continued. "Where's Thomas? I must have missed him when we walked in."

Dad didn't even try and guess. "Brooke, go find Thomas."

It was a statement more than a demand. Thomas had spent most of the day out front poking ants with a safety pin, so I had a pretty good idea of where he was. I left the chatter of the kitchen and pushed open the front door.

Alyssa was walking up to the house as I let my eyes adjust to the sun. We had a bet going on how many people were living in the blue house three houses from mine. Last time we counted there had been over twelve people. This time I was betting on at least fifteen and Alyssa thought maybe there would be eighteen.

"Spanish families live like that, all of them together," Alyssa taught me. "This way they have more money and more people to do the chores."

"Ohhh," I nodded. "Maybe that's what my parents are trying to do, keep having kids, make a Spanish family."

"Maybe," Alyssa said. "Aren't you Irish?"

Slurpees from the 7-11 convenience store were riding on our bet and I was expecting an update. My quest to find Thomas was forgotten and we paid little mind to the police car that pulled up in front of the house ten minutes later. Then I noticed that Thomas was sitting teary-eyed in the back.

The policeman was tall and he brushed the sweat off his forehead as he went around to the passenger side. He opened the back door and said something in a lowered voice. My throat tightened.

"Is that..?" Alyssa asked, staring through the summer haze. She craned her neck to get a better view of the kid sitting in the back seat. A piece of hair fell from her ponytail and she tucked it behind her ear, her eyes never leaving the street.

"I think...ohhhh no, that's THOMAS!" Alyssa gushed, her wide eyes shooting towards me.

"Something's wrong," I said, heading into the house to get Mom.

"Yeah something's wrong. Thomas is in the back of a cop car. Where's his bike? Didn't he ride his bike to 7-11? Hey, where you goin'?" Alyssa's voice trailed behind me.

I had already reached the front door and was pulling it open before I could answer. The look on Thomas' face...he wasn't in trouble, I knew. Something bad had happened to him. My motherly intuition always heightened when I knew Adam was about to cry and when Kat was scared. The bond I had with my siblings made it seem as though I could read their minds.

I spared Mom the rush of confusion that was bound to set in and gushed out—before anyone could pose any questions— "Thomas is outside in a cop car! Come quick!"

Panicked voices, mainly Aunt Jean's, followed behind me as I turned on my heel to head back outside. "What? Thomas? What are you talking about?" The only footsteps I didn't hear following were Dad's.

I opened the front door and almost fell off the front step in a flurry of curiosity. If I stood far enough to the edge of the house I would be able to listen to their conversation without Mom telling me to go inside. I chose a place under the boys' bedroom window and sat on the ground, putting my finger to my lips as a non-verbal cue for Alyssa to keep quiet.

Thomas had been crying. Luminous trails where tears slid down his dirty face reflected in the sun. Mom had buzzed his hair a day earlier and his white scalp was bright against his tanned skin. At eight years old, only a year younger than I was, he had at least fifteen pounds on me. He kept his head down, but the second he saw Mom he broke down into a fit of sobbing.

"Are you okay? Thomas what happened?"

"Ma'm, are you this boy's mother?" The officer stood in front of my mom, nodding his head in Thomas' direction.

"What's going on?" Mom demanded. Her eyes revealed no room for patience.

"Ma'm a clerk from the 7-11 called 9-1-1 because they saw your son get assaulted. Two teenage boys held a knife to your son's throat for his bike. They got away on it, and a good Samaritan tried to follow them, but they had a truck at the corner and they threw the bike into the back and took off."

I turned towards Alyssa and her eyes were as wide as mine.

"I'm sorry." Thomas sobbed while wringing his hands in his shirt. "I'm sorry they took my bike, Mom."

"*How* many times have I told you that you go to the store *with* someone? See what happens? You think you can just go anywhere? Well, you CAN'T."

At this point several neighbors had gathered outside. They pretended to water dead flowers on their porch or sweep the stoop—anything to have a reason to be outside at that exact moment.

"Ma'm?" the policeman tried again. "Your son was just assaulted. Would you like us to escort you to the hospital? Have him checked out?"

Mom bent over and did a sweep of Thomas' neck. "You said they held a knife to his throat?" she asked, looking for a wound.

"Yes Ma'm, a pocket knife is what the clerk said."

"Well, he looks fine. Go on, get inside and wash your face."

Thomas pushed his way through blurry tears and rushed inside. The police officer lingered.

"The store doesn't have security cameras, so we're going to take what testimony we have from witnesses and see what we can do about getting his bike back. At least we have a description of the truck and a partial license plate, but I wouldn't be surprised if nothing pulled up. This kind of thing is happening more and more around here."

"Thank you," Mom said, uninterested. "He just got that bike, so if it's not found then maybe it'll teach him a lesson."

The officer looked over at Alyssa and me sitting off to the side. His eyes softened. "We'll let you know what turns up, Ma'm. I'm sorry for the scare."

Mom lit a cigarette as the officer made his way back to the car. The mumbling under her breath had grown to a loud whisper by the time he turned his key in the ignition, and as he drove away Mom finally noticed the flock of neighbors standing around watching.

She puffed and exhaled a steady stream of smoke. With her exhale came a round of tears that let the neighbors assume that something terrible had happened. *Poor Molly, poor Molly and her troubles. So many kids, so much stress.*

Mom crushed the butt into the concrete, wiped away a tear, and made her way into the house to give Thomas hell.

Chapter Five

"We're running away," I told Kat. She watched me stuff two shirts into a suitcase. "We're going to Grandma's house. I know the way, we can walk there. I have two suitcases. This one is yours." I pointed. "Put some pajamas in there, no toys. We'll sneak out the window after everyone goes to bed. Okay?"

Kat nodded and walked over to her dresser to start packing.

I was going to be twelve that summer. While I finished packing my suitcase, I remembered back to when Mom had the first of many surgeries meant to repair the damage to her spine. I was seven then, and Dad started to tuck us in at night since Mom couldn't do it anymore. She wasn't able to do much of anything with rods and screws in her back. Always a heavy sleeper, my sister would be tenderly snoring after a few minutes of Dad rubbing her back and I would try not to fidget in the bed we shared while I waited for my turn.

I don't remember how long it usually took me to fall asleep. I don't remember when my back rubs turned into chest rubs, and then stomach rubs. By the time Dad was spending close to forty-five minutes in my room at bedtime I would pretend to be asleep, squeezing my eyes shut so hard I would see white. *You're sleeping*, I convinced myself, *and everything is fine because you're sleeping. Everything is fine.*

I couldn't call out. Mom was passed out from her pills. Kat could sleep through an earthquake. The boys' bedroom was on the other side of the house. There was no one.

Kat was a heavier sleeper and Dad knew this. He had spent a long time on the side of my bed one night. That time it had hurt and I held my stomach when he got up to walk away, afraid I would throw up. He crept to the other end of the bed and sat down next to Kat.

Just as he was about to reach over I jumped up, kicking my legs and using my arms to hit the waterbed.

As the bed rolled and shook, Kat startled awake and started crying. Dad bent down and tried to console her. His eyes struggled to see me through the shadows of the room but when they met with mine, I threatened him with a clenched jaw and silent tears.

Don't you dare touch her. My pajamas were soaked as my chest heaved. *Don't you dare lay a single finger on her. I'll tell. Try me.*

My message must have been clear. After Kat's cries subdued, he walked to the bedroom door and crept out without saying a word. I lay back down and put my foot against my sister's leg so I could monitor if there was any movement on her side of the bed, as I always did. *I'll protect you, baby sister. I'll protect you.*

Mom couldn't protect us anymore. Even if she wanted to, she couldn't. Those white pills masked her ability to function and there was too much pain for her to notice. The heaviness of the new role I played in my family was suffocating.

I didn't want it.

It became an unspoken arrangement from that point on. If I didn't fight, if I kept his secret, he wouldn't hurt Kat. I figured that if he was hurting me, he couldn't be hurting her. It was the only way I knew how to protect her.

I had to protect her.

When bedtime rituals became painful, I made the decision to run away. Kat would need to come with me. I thought about taking my brothers too, but I noticed that after Dad would spend time in my room he would take it easier on them the following day with his physical attacks. Adam and Thomas would seem calmer too, since they didn't have to run from his outstretched hand or his belt. He roared a little less. Maybe *I* was the problem. If Kat and I disappeared, maybe he would be nicer to them. My plan had to work.

I controlled the harmony and the balance. I shivered watching Kat close the latches on her suitcase. I didn't want to think about the next morning when everyone woke up and we were missing. I hoped Adam and Thomas would protect each other if Dad started to hurt them once we were gone. Maybe they would run away too.

Mom had come home earlier that afternoon from a doctor appointment. She was scheduled to go in for another back surgery, but they would need to wait because she had something called shingles. She was talking on the phone in the kitchen and I heard her saying that it was something deadly.

It was my deciding factor.

If Mom was going to die, I had to get out before she did. I didn't have a choice. I couldn't imagine living in a house alone with Dad.

That night we had cereal for dinner since it was in the middle of the week. "Fridays are paydays and Saturdays are food shopping days, if there's enough money after Dad pays the bills," Mom would say.

Kat and I were quiet as we exchanged knowing glances across the kitchen table. By this time tomorrow, we would be at Grandma's eating chicken or mashed potatoes. Maybe both. Dad was working the overnight shifts all week. I lived for overnight weeks. Soon Kat and I turned off the lights in our bedroom.

We kissed Mom goodnight.

We waited.

At ten o'clock I slid off my bed like a snake and sat on the floor, pulling on my sneakers.

I listened.

The house was quiet. I moved to the edge of Kat's side of the bed and put my hand on her shoulder. "Hey, we gotta go. Put your shoes on," I whispered.

I sat on the floor and pulled the suitcases out from under the bed. They were heavy but it wasn't too long of a walk. Maybe twenty miles, or thirty. It only took Mom ten minutes to drive there, so I figured it would take us about twenty minutes to walk there. I didn't know for sure.

"Are we gonna tell Mommy?" Kat stood with the suitcase in her hand. The moon illuminated her fluffy blonde hair. Her pupils resembled our cat's eyes when he sat to watch the birds and I could tell she was scared.

"I don't think we can." I leaned in closer to whisper. "Mom can't know where we're going 'cause Dad might ask her and then he'll know where we are."

"Why can't Daddy know we're going to Grandma's?"

The shadows from the night-light hid my face. "He just can't," I said. I thought for a minute. "Okay, let's tell Mom. Just so she's not worried. So she can come visit us if she wants."

Kat nodded.

The door to Mom's bedroom creaked as we tiptoed inside and stood by the side of her bed. Pill bottles were lined up on the nightstand next to her; some of them she didn't bother to put the tops back on. The glowing TV let me watch her breathe in and out, her mouth open enough to fit a piece of paper, lips cracked and blistered. She chewed on ice chips perpetually because of her dry mouth.

"Mommy," I whispered, nudging her shoulder. She lay motionless and I looked at Kat. She shrugged. "Mommy, wake up."

The clock read eleven-something. Her nightstand was so littered with pill bottles I couldn't see the rest of the display.

I picked up her hand and watched it drop like a brick onto her bed. We didn't have time. Sitting on the edge of the bed, I crouched down next to her ear. "MOMMY!" I yelled.

She startled awake, grabbing at the air in front of her. I pushed Kat back against the wall to avoid her flailing arms. "Ohh, what? What happened?" She sat up in bed and I wasn't sure what to say. Her hand was on her chest. "What are you two doing out of bed?" She checked the clock. "Go back to bed."

Kat scrunched up her face and her bottom lip started to quiver. "Mommy, we have to show you something."

"Yeah Mommy, we have to show you something." I pointed. "It's in our room. Come look."

I grabbed Kat's hand and started towards the door as I heard Mom throw the blankets off of her. She answered back, rubbing her eyes, "What is it? A mouse?"

Mom pushed the door open and flicked on our bedroom light. Kat and I stood next to our suitcases holding hands. Mom looked from the floor to the open window. "What are you two doing? It's freezing out, close that window."

"Mom," I said, carefully. "We are going to Grandma's. We're gonna run away now and we just wanted you to know. So you didn't worry."

"Yeah," Kat finished. "You can come with us if you want Mommy, you just have to get a suitcase. We only have two."

Mom folded her arms across her chest and stared at us. She lowered herself onto the bed. "Wait, I don't understand. You're running away? From me?"

"Mom, we have to."

I don't know who started crying first, but all at once we were in a group hug. "My babies. Oh Brooke, I am so sorry. Is this what you want? This is really what you want?"

I nodded through cloudy eyes. "Yeah, Mommy. We need to go."

She stared at the open window. "Oh, Brooke. I am so sorry. Please stay home, please stay. We can make things better here. If you ever want to run away to Grandma's house just tell me, we'll all go together. Your brothers too, we'll all go."

I didn't need to explain?

Maybe she knew. Maybe she realized when Dad wasn't in bed and when he savagely tore after my brothers when they did something wrong. Maybe the pills didn't make her as numb as I thought they did.

"Okay, Mommy," Kat said on our behalf, wiping her nose on her sleeve. "We'll stay. We can run away to Grandma's later."

Mom looked at me. "Okay, Brooke? We'll all run away together someday, we'll all go together."

I looked at my feet, then at her face.

I believed her.

"Okay, Mom." I forced a smile.

She helped us unpack. When Mom got to the bottom of my suitcase she pulled out a black and white marble notebook. "What's this Brooke?" Mom turned it over. The front read:

Brooke Nolan's Journal
*PRIVATE ** KEEP OUT*

"Can I read it?" Mom bit her lower lip. "I won't tell anyone, promise." She smiled.

I hesitated. "Sure. I need it back tomorrow." I used composition notebooks as journals since Mom and Dad wouldn't buy them for me. They were the first things I packed. I couldn't live without them.

* * *

The sound of a glass breaking in the kitchen woke me the next morning.

Adam must be unloading the dishwasher.

I wiggled under the covers, stretching my arms and legs before I sat up. My toes brushed against the firm skin of my journal. It had been nestled at the foot of my bed. I opened it up to the last entry.

Watermarks stained the page as I touched the spots and listened to it crinkle. Mom's unique uppercase writing and run-on sentences sprawled across the pages at the end of the last journal entry I wrote.

Dear Brooke- I love you with all my heart. I love all of you. But you have an extra special place in my heart. You are so smart and aware of everything and I don't know what I would have done without you (and your brothers and sister). They don't understand yet, but I know they will someday and then they will say my God how did she do it and I am going to have to say with a huge help from your sister Brooke. I am so sorry for all the times I yelled at you. I had no idea the burden, stress and strain I am putting on you. You're only a child and this should not be. My God, help me to make Brooke's life a whole lot better. I promise I will try to help you Lord, please help her, she's only 11 years old. With all my love. I'm sorry for getting your book wet but I was crying.

That week my brothers, Kat and I played in the living room when Mom and Dad came in to tell us some big news.

"We're moving!" Mom exclaimed. She clasped her hands together. "We're going to Pennsylvania. It's about three hours from here and there is so much room to play and run around. There are farms and woods to explore and you guys can build your own tree houses. Best of all, I found the most beautiful house, it's perfect." The sparkle in her eyes told me she loved this house already. She loved Pennsylvania.

Dad looked at me.

"What about school?" I tried to hide the desperation in my voice. "School isn't over yet, it's almost Christmas. We can't move."

Dad leaned forward. "We're moving the day after Christmas. You'll be on break, so you won't miss anything while we switch your schools."

Adam and Thomas started talking about the bears they were going to hunt and Kat asked if she could have a pink tree house.

I looked out the window.

Three hours away?

We didn't know anyone who lived in Pennsylvania. All of our family was there in New York. They should have just told us we were moving to Mars.

Mom smiled while she listened to the boys talk. Her eyes met mine and suddenly went soft. Her smile retracted and I noticed wrinkles outlining the corners of her eyes.

My face pleaded with her to remember the promise she made days earlier. I begged her to remember. Whether she knew it or not—as she looked away to soak up the excited chatter—she had failed me. My shoulders slumped to the ground and I fought with the screaming voices in my head. I guess we were never going to run away to Grandma's house.

Chapter Six

At first Mom didn't believe me when I told her I was dying.

"You're twelve. You're not even close to dying." Mom poured her tea and sat down at the kitchen table. "Didn't you just invite Cristin to come over? If you're not feeling good then maybe she shouldn't come over."

"It's not that I don't feel good, my stomach just hurts." I pressed my hand into the lower right side of my stomach. "Right here. It just started hurting. Can I use your heating pad?"

"Go ahead." She turned on the TV and dropped a dollop of milk into her tea. "While you're up there, bring me my pills?"

Dad sat at the kitchen table listening. "Why don't you try and use the bathroom, Brooke?"

The new house in Pennsylvania boasted four bedrooms that quadrupled in size compared to what we had in New York. All Kat and I had in our room was our bed and a small vanity my cousin handed down when she got tired of it.

We struggled to fill all the space. We needed two couches, a real dining room set, and dressers since there was room for them. Most of the furniture was mismatched and thrown together. The best part about the new house was the three bathrooms.

Three.

One upstairs, one downstairs, and one in my parents' room.

Kat and I could get ready for school in the upstairs bathroom while the boys got ready downstairs. It was heaven.

I clicked Mom's medicine cabinet open and pulled four bottles off the top shelf. White, cream colored, and pink pills slid into my hand as I counted out the different dosages. I squeezed my hand around them. The heating pad Mom used for her back was dangling over the edge of the bed and I picked it up as I headed to the door.

I had managed to make a friend only one week after moving—Cristin—and she got her period for the first time two weeks after we started hanging out. While the unfamiliar pain crippled my stomach I tried to smile through it, knowing I was finally going to get to hide tampons in my book bag too.

I stood at the top of the stairs and gripped the handrail. *Jeez, this period stuff is no joke.* My stomach felt tender to the touch and I shuffled one foot in front of the other. Cristin walked through the front door as I reached the bottom of the stairs. Her voice seemed muffled. My stomach flipped over and I caught my breath.

"Hey, what's up?" She eyed me. "My dad just dropped me off. You okay?"

I shook my head and doubled over, clutching the pills in one hand and the heating pad in the other. Cristin raised her eyebrows and took the heating pad. "I'll go plug this in. Living room okay?"

I couldn't talk. I nodded my head and forced a smile. Sweat formed around my eyes and lips as I trudged into the kitchen. Mom's eyes were glued to the TV. A stabbing blow dropped me to my knees and I cried out. "Ah, Mom, it hurts!"

"Brooke?" Mom rolled her eyes, "Oh come on, Brooke. Do you want some ibuprofen? Do you want…"

The kitchen spun into a white cloud. I could hear Mom screaming for Dad as my head hit the kitchen floor. Pills scattered across the linoleum. Mom's breath engulfed me and it was the bitter combination of smoke and teabags. "Hang on, Brooke! Call 9-1-1! Oh my God. David call 9-1-1!"

I woke up, confused and in a white room surrounded by a curtain. Monitors hummed and needles pulsed under my skin on both hands.

"Brooke? Brooke, honey, you need to wake up."

It was a masked ninja. *How did he know my name?*

"Brooke, I'm Dr. Destachio. You need to wake up, sweetheart. You're just coming out of surgery now."

A nurse to my left pushed the bed and I realized I was being whirled into a room. Suddenly pain radiated through my stomach and up into my throat. My body shook in waves. "Pain…Pain medicine, please. Please."

Dr. Destachio smiled. "You got it, kiddo." He fumbled a tube going into my right hand. "There you go. Gave you some good stuff. I'll be back to check on you soon."

I didn't understand what was happening but I couldn't stay awake long enough to talk to anyone. Mom was there at one point but the weight of my eyelids wouldn't let me see her. I heard voices; Dr. Destachio's voice.

"If you would have waited any longer..." He trailed off. "Her appendix ruptured as we were removing it. She was very lucky."

Mom choked out some words and I imagined her crying. "We called 9-1-1 right away. I knew something was wrong when she told me she had a bad stomachache. She's a little stubborn to see doctors but I told her it was important we get her to the hospital."

"You did the right thing. If she needs anything just let us know."

I woke up hours later and squinted while the sun turned my room bright orange, then eerily fading to black. A voice echoed from the TV. Mom shifted in the oversized hospital lounger and flipped through Dr. Phil re-runs.

"Mom?" I didn't recognize my voice.

Mom shimmied out of the chair and set her tea on the table next to her. She lowered herself to my side. "It doesn't hurt," I said, following her eyes to the tubes sticking out of me.

She smiled and reached across the bed, tucking a Precious Moments doll next to my face. Angelic, teardrop-shaped eyes stared back at me. It smelled like a hospital doll. "Daddy got you this when you were in surgery. So she could look over you."

Over the next few hours the doctors wanted me to eat some crackers and walk around so the gas used to fill my stomach for surgery would loosen up. It hurt to walk, to sit, and to laugh at my grandpa when he called me on the hospital phone. He told me if I scared him like that again *he* would put me in the hospital next time.

"Well, we'd like to keep you here another day, Brooke. Your appendix was severely infected. We just want to make sure nothing got into your bloodstream to make you sick." Dr. Destachio flashed his crooked front tooth. I glanced at my mom shifting in the seat beside my bed. She was in pain when she did that. "Unless you're really feeling okay enough to go home. You'll just have to take it extra easy the next couple of days."

The hospital was a vacation. I had slept more in two days than I had in years. I had a team of attentive adults all catering to me. I never wanted to leave.

"If it's okay, I want to go home." I struggled to say the words but I knew Mom needed to be in her own bed. It only meant more pain for her if she wasn't.

A nurse helped me into a wheelchair while Mom brought the car around to the front of the hospital. Dad stood at my side. I flinched when he slid his hand to smooth the top of my hair. "You're very brave. And you were a very good girl while we were here." I pretended not to hear him as I watched a young mother get into the car in front of us with her new baby.

I struggled to get into the van but soon we were pulling onto the highway and headed home. The Precious Moments doll sat at my side and I picked her up. I noticed a cord attached to the bottom as I flipped her over. Soft lyrical music filled the air when I pulled it, and my stomach sank. Dad smirked and watched the outside scenery float by.

Was this some kind of sick joke? I thought, listening to the tune radiating from the doll.

Mom glanced at me in the rear-view mirror and softly mumbled the words to the song, the irony of the nursery lyrics resonating down every back road towards home. "Hush little baby, don't say a word…"

For two weeks I was untouchable while I healed from surgery. Mom put a little bell next to my bed and all I had to do was ring it for a snack, pain medicine, or for the remote. Kat ran in to help me most of the time, which she was happy to do as long as I didn't show her my wound.

As I healed I caught up on schoolwork and looked through Seventeen Magazines that Cristin dropped off. She spent most of her afternoons entertaining me from my bedside. I yelled at her a lot to stop making me laugh since it felt like my insides would spill out when I did.

Soon I stopped taking the pain medication the doctor prescribed and ibuprofen was enough to make me comfortable. I put the pill bottle on top of the TV in my room just in case I needed it. Walking around was easier. I was allowed to go back to school after two weeks of recovery time but my days dragged. I daydreamed out the window, waiting to hear the bus, wanting Adam, Thomas, and Kat to come home.

Mom was out at the grocery store. Dad was working overnights and usually didn't get out of bed until around five. When my bedroom door creaked open, I rolled over in bed expecting to see Cristin.

"Yeah, Dad?" My heart raced.

No one was home.

He held a white cup in his hand. "I made this for you, honey." The bedroom door closed behind him. My breath became shallow.

"I'm okay, thanks though." I supported my stomach underneath my sheets as it rumbled.

I can't. Not now...please.

He didn't blink as he crossed the room, hand outstretched. "It's chocolate milk. Your favorite."

I took the cup, searching my head for a distraction. "Thanks. Um, Dad can you check and see if Mom is home yet?" I gripped the sheets. He needed to leave.

"She's not home, snuggle bug. Drink that up so I can bring the cup downstairs."

I mentally cheered myself on. *Okay, Brooke, chug. Chug faster. The faster you drink the faster he's gone.* The contents disappeared behind my milk mustache. I outstretched an arm. "Done."

He sat on the futon next to my bed. "Good girl. See? I thought maybe you were thirsty."

I stared at him. *Why wasn't he leaving?* We locked eyes. "You can bring the cup downstairs now, Dad. I'm done." It wasn't a suggestion.

He must have sensed my resistance. "I will."

The room began to spin. It was slow at first, but then so fast I closed my eyes and moaned. My body floated above the sheets. Heaviness engulfed me, the sensation not allowing my arms to leave the bed.

"My...head. Why's my flace...Flace? Face. Whaaaat." Words slurred out of my mouth. I wasn't sure Dad could even hear me. I rubbed my eyes and the room began to shrink. My eyelids were bricks. As I drifted, I tried to focus my attention. My eyes set on my TV. I studied the square box, the red buttons...my pill bottle was gone.

Brooke, stop it. Stay awake. Sleep later. Stop it, stop.

A suffocating weight was on top of me, pulling down my bottoms and the sheets.

I smelled cologne and spicy aftershave.

My eyes wouldn't open as I struggled to see what was going on. Prickles of cold made the hairs on my arms stand up and I shuddered. A violent force of pain shot between my legs and up through my stomach.

I cried out.

Consciousness came and went. The room spun and I tried to focus on something, anything. I remembered my bell. My outstretched hand fumbled across the bed. I grabbed air, sheets, and the side of the bed. *Come on, come on.* The smell of blood gagged me. The bed fell beneath me and I was falling, falling.

* * *

When I woke up the room was dim and the hall light was on. Voices lingered from my parents' room. "I'll tell you, it was a good goddamn thing I was home." Dad was talking to Mom.

"I don't understand, David. She just…fell in the shower?"

"I was dead asleep. All of a sudden, BAM, I hear something loud. I ran into the bathroom and Brooke was laying at the bottom of the shower, passed out cold."

My hand reached for my hair. It was wet.

"Why was she taking a shower? I mean, I helped her take one this morning."

"Damn cat peed on her bed. She must have laid down in it before she figured it out and got it all over her. I threw the sheets out, disgusting mess that made. Brooke's clothes too, piss all over them. I can get her new pajamas. I threw those out too. I didn't think she needed to go to the hospital, figured she just turned too fast or the wrong way and sent some pain through her. It'll teach her. She'll be fine Molly, I checked on her a few times."

"Jesus" was all Mom said. Then there was silence and the TV was all that echoed through the corridor.

The walls of my throat stuck together, my chest heaved, and I struggled to hold back my sobs. I lowered my hand between my legs, praying that it had all been a nightmare, a twisted and terrifying lapse of reality. When my fingers rolled over swollen and broken skin, I cried so hard that it rocked me to sleep.

Chapter Seven

Mom leaned against the shopping cart as we maneuvered our way through the sea of people in Wal-Mart. "The pain in my back makes me walk on my toes. The doctor said it shortened my Achilles tendon, so I need to have surgery to make it longer. I can't believe I need another surgery. Never a dull moment." She stopped and picked up loose-leaf paper from the shelf. "Didn't you need this?"

I looked at the price. "No," I said, dismissing her with a wave of my hand. "How long is the recovery?"

"A week. Maybe two. He didn't say. Why?" She shook her head at the notion that I had a problem with her recovery time. "It's a serious surgery Brooke, you can't rush things like that."

I turned my eyes toward the fluorescent lights hovering above our heads. The thought of being alone in the house for longer than one night terrified me. It was always a catch twenty-two scenario. If I stayed with a friend, I risked Dad lurking on one of my siblings. If I stayed home, I was subjecting myself to the unknown and to him. Every time, I chose to stay. I chose peace of mind knowing my siblings weren't hurting. It was the right thing to do. I was older and they needed protection.

I threw a pack of paper towels into the cart. "Just wondering."

"So who's this Judd character you've been hanging out with? Your father doesn't like him. You meet him in school? He's in eighth grade too, right?"

"Yeah, I met him on the bus. We're in the same grade. And Dad doesn't like any guy I'm friends with."

"Friends?" Mom cocked her head and raised her eyebrow.

"Yes. Friends. Guys and girls *can* just be friends."

"Uh-huh. Well ask this *friend* to come over to our house. I don't like you always going over there, I don't even know if his parents are home."

"They are."

It wasn't a total lie. His dad worked on their fifteen acres of farmland. Technically he was home, even if he *was* somewhere in a field, miles away.

"I got a one hundred on my project," I said, shifting the conversation.

"What project?"

"My Spanish one."

"You're taking Spanish?"

I rolled my eyes. "Yeah. And I got a one hundred on it."

"I don't know why your brothers and sister can't work more like you. I don't even know that you have projects until they're getting handed back to you with a grade on them."

I smiled. Mom had the patience of a two-year-old when it came to helping with homework assignments. I would ask for the supplies I needed and would hand back a graded project weeks later. As long as it didn't inconvenience her, she didn't care.

It also didn't take me long to figure out that if I asked Mom to hang out at Judd's house, she would usually say yes if I had a ride there already set up. Again, it was no inconvenience to her. I could then use her answer as leverage when Dad would raise an eyebrow—as I got ready—asking where I was going.

But I already had permission.

It was set in stone.

I could go.

Judd was taking a lighter apart and I was sprawled across his bed flipping through channels. "It's like you use my house to sleep or something," he said, focusing on the little pieces he was collecting in his lap. "Don't you sleep?"

"Yeah," I said, stretching my arms above my head. "I sleep here."

"Haha."

"You know what's haha? Your hair. What is it, white now? Doesn't get much blonder than that."

"This is deep." He ran a hand through his crew cut. "Nobody else can pull this off."

"Mmmhmm. You hungry?" I climbed off the bed and made my way to the door before he answered.

"Nah. I'm eating a big dinner tonight so I'm saving room." He rubbed his non-existent stomach and a hollow sound erupted from underneath his shirt.

We were both picked on in school about our weight, or lack of weight really, which is how we became friends. We stuck together. He towered above me when he stood up. I challenged his decision to not eat, crossing my arms in front of my chest. "Are you really not hungry or do you just not want to eat?"

He smiled. "I'll have a little I guess."

Judd ate two grilled cheese sandwiches and a bowl of tomato soup. I knew better than to bring this to his attention, so instead I just asked if he wanted more. "No, but why do you eat so weird?"

I looked at my plate. "What do you mean?"

"You pull everything apart. It's like a war zone filled with grilled cheese casualties." He flicked a crumb from my cheek. "Can't you just eat everything instead of picking it apart like that?"

I bit my lip. "Yeah, habit I guess."

"Who taught you to eat like that?"

"No one," I shot back. "Leave it alone."

It was a vicious cycle. Most of the time there was barely any food at home. My brothers and I would start to steal Pop-Tarts and other food from the pantry when it was there. If we were sent to bed without dinner or there just wasn't anything to eat, we would dig into the stash in our bedrooms, stale or not.

Then Dad bought a locking system for the food cabinets. Food was disappearing and he would be enraged when Mom would ask him to go to the grocery store more than once a week. He brought the key to work with him. I could get food when Dad got home just by asking. So I asked every day, just to fill my siblings' stash.

On the rare occasions there was enough food for dinner several nights in a row, the experience was always overwhelming. Six bodies crammed around a table, and everyone tried to get the seat furthest from Dad. His hands would shoot out across the table faster than a whip and catch someone in the face because of something they said or did. We were not allowed to get up from the table until he was finished eating and our plates had to be clean too.

Dad never hit me.

Never.

I would often claim a place next to him at the table to give my siblings distance between him. Most of the time, I just couldn't bring myself to eat sitting next to him. My stomach danced and dipped throughout the meal.

I adopted a way of eating where I would rip whatever I was eating into little pieces. If I pushed those pieces around my plate enough, it appeared like I ate. When there was no food in the house, I couldn't eat. When there was enough food, I couldn't eat. And everyone wondered why I was so skinny?

Judd reached over and picked a piece of crust off my plate and shoved it into his mouth. He chewed graciously, wiped his mouth with his bare arm, and smiled the wide-toothed grin that always seemed to get him into trouble.

"Like you have any room to talk about the way a person eats," I said.

He ruffled my hair and threw his arms around my neck for a fake chokehold. I fell to the ground to psych him out and laughed when he reached down to help me, socking him in the stomach just hard enough to get him to back off.

"Whew, all right muscles." He groaned getting up from the floor, smoothing his hair. "The guys should be here soon, are we goin' swimming?"

"Yeah," I said. I took Judd's outstretched hand to help me up. I followed him into his room and he pulled a bottle of vodka from the back of his closet. He kissed it with puckered lips. "I'll bring the refreshments."

After a few guys from school showed up we walked through two fields behind Judd's house and shimmied in between electric fence wires that held the cows in. We were just small enough to fit through the middle section, but Judd would hold them apart for me with sticks anyway. "Careful, go slow Brooke." The worried tone in his voice always made me smile. We crossed the last field and I ran the rest of the way when the guys started to push each other into cow pies.

"Whose house is this again?" I dropped the stereo by the poolside and gazed at the bugs floating on the surface of the in-ground pool.

"Uh, my aunt's, or something. Kind of complicated. My parents technically bought it, but my aunt will be moving here sometime soon I think." He plugged the stereo into the speaker system of the garage that was right next to the pool. "But for now, it's our pool."

Two of the guys jumped in right away. I grabbed the skimmer. "Brooke, this is Mack," Judd said, pointing to an overweight kid. "And this grimy dirt bag is Chalky." Judd grabbed Chalky by the shirt and propelled him into the pool.

He sputtered as he came up. "Hey Brooke, nice to meet you. Want to make out?" He winked at Judd, provoking him.

Judd dove into the water after him and they choked and fought each other for several minutes. Soaked, Judd pulled himself onto the ledge of the pool. He reached over and grabbed the vodka bottle and took a gulp. His face twisted. "Ah, anyone else?"

Mack raised his hand and Judd chucked the plastic container across the pool. I decided to take my clothes off before I got thrown in. My shorts and shirt were already damp from the boys jumping in, but I shoved them into my bag and turned around to hurry in.

I stopped. All three boys stared at me, motionless. I looked down. "What?"

Judd said nothing. A slow smile spread across his face.

"Am I missing something?" I checked to make sure the sides of my bikini were tied tight.

Chalky broke the silence. "So, hey Brooke, you work out?" Mack doubled over in laughter as Judd raced after Chalky in another attempt to drown him.

I skimmed my hands across the top of the water as I sat on the steps. The guys talked about their four wheelers and girls they planned to go after when school started. Judd winked at me and I splashed him in the face.

"Want?" Judd pushed the vodka into my hand.

"Yooo Paulie baby, took you long enough!" Mack suddenly called out. A boy I wasn't familiar with rounded the corner of the garage and made his way down to the pool.

Judd glanced over. "Brooke, this is Paul."

Paul nodded his head in the direction of the guys and set his bag down. "Wasn't planning on a nature walk before I went swimming. How many fields did I just walk through to get here?"

I laughed, too eagerly. He was taller than Judd, but still around the same age as us. He cruised over to the edge of the pool, planning his entry. He refused to look at me but acknowledged the guys one by one with a slight head nod and a derogatory comment.

I tried not to stare at his face, instead tracing its shape all the way up to his golden hairline. My cheeks betrayed me as I blushed, and I lowered my eyes to the vodka bottle in my hand. Pretending to be interested in the name on the bottle—Absolut—I entertained myself by coming up with words that rhymed with the name of the liquor. *Cowboy boot, expensive suit, that boy is cute...*

"You going to share or should I have brought my own?"

His voice was velvet. When I looked up it caught me off guard that Paul had his shirt off and was standing right next to me. His cologne swirled under my nose as he crouched down to be level with my eyes.

"Well?" he asked, opening his palm.

I couldn't look away. I didn't want to. He had no acne, no visible scars or uni-brow to stare at. Even his teeth were straight and pearly. There was nothing to focus on except his eyes. Deep, green puddles of color pulled me in and begged me to keep looking.

"All yours," I said, holding the bottle out by the neck. His hand wrapped around mine to take it, and he paused. My hand and heart smoldered and my lips parted into an unwelcomed grin.

His eyes moved over my face and down my neck. A smile spread across his face as he raised his eyebrows and stood up. "All mine, huh?"

My heart took off like a bullet. Paul walked away and I slid into the water for a distraction. I couldn't look away and I had a hard time following conversation after that. The few times I caught Paul looking in my direction I turned my head the other way to pretend I didn't see. It was agonizing.

Judd walked me back to his house as it started to get dark, the rest of the guys swimming and hollering behind us. "Why do you have to leave so early?" He tried to cover up the disappointment in his voice.

"Mom had surgery yesterday. Remember the foot surgery I told you about? She'll be there a week, maybe more. I just need to be home, you know, to take care of things."

"Stay," Judd said, turning to me. "Take care of *me* instead." His voice implied he was joking but there was a seriousness in his face when I looked at him.

"Yeah, you need taking care of all right," I agreed. "Besides, you have your buddies to entertain. I'll probably see you tomorrow, okay?"

When I got home I started dinner right away even though I knew Dad wouldn't be home from the hospital until much later. I boiled water for macaroni and pulled hot dogs out of the freezer. Adam had watched Kat and Thomas all afternoon. After everyone ate, I scrubbed the kitchen down and put a movie on in the living room so I could catch up on some of the summer reading I had been neglecting. I curled up on the sofa with Thomas and Kat while Adam clicked away at the computer in the kitchen.

A few hours later, Kat and Thomas were upstairs getting ready for bed when the front door flung open and Dad barged in. The noise startled me and my book crashed to the floor as I jumped up to see what was going on. Dad stormed into the kitchen and he chucked his things down on the counter. Adam was right in his path.

The attack was immediate. "What are you still doing on the computer? There are TWO cups in the sink and you're sitting on the computer like there is nothing to do? You need a special invitation to keep this place clean? Huh? DO YOU?"

Adam was fast, but not fast enough, as Dad approached him and overturned the chair he was sitting on. My throat tightened.

"Get moving! Get this place picked up now!" The chair was airborne and sailed across the room hitting Adam square in the chest. He sank to the ground, hitting his head against the wall behind him, a faint blood streak following him down.

"Dad! Stop!" I rushed to Adam's side and pulled the chair off of him.

"Stop? You want me to stop? I haven't even started!" He grabbed a cup from the sink. "What the hell is a dirty dish doing in my sink? I work all day, have to sit at the hospital all night, and this is the crap I come home to?"

The cup whirled past my head and exploded on the wall behind me. Glass shards propelled in every direction, coating the vinyl floor with luster. Adam and I tripped over our own feet rushing toward the stairs. Dad ranted and bellowed behind us.

"Get back here and clean up this mess. GET BACK HERE!"

I slipped and frantically grabbed at the banister to help me up. Adam clutched his chest where the chair had hit him. I prayed Kat and Thomas were hiding in their closets like I taught them.

Heavy footsteps chased me. I rushed inside my room and fumbled to lock the door. Dad was seconds behind me and I scanned the room for Kat. She was nowhere to be seen.

Good girl.

My bedroom door busted open with one blow and I screamed, covering my face. When I dropped my hands he was inches from my nose.

"You think you can lock this door on me? HUH? You think you can keep me out? This is MY house, MY house." He shoved me against the wall.

I glanced around him and saw Adam, shoving Thomas down the hallway into his bedroom.

Keep him safe, Adam.

Dad turned away and grabbed the bedroom door with both hands and pulled it off the hinges. Adrenaline screamed at me to run, but I squeezed my hands at my side trying to plan an escape.

"Go ahead, try to lock the door now. You better get your ass downstairs and clean up that mess. Do you hear me? DO YOU HEAR ME?"

Standing my ground, I uncontrollably flinched and nodded. I had to redirect his anger. Adam and Thomas hid down the hall. He'd be after them next.

"Sorry Dad, I'll clean it. They were my cups."

Please believe me.

He eyed me up and down as his chest heaved from struggling to chase us up stairs. I watched the blood start to drain from his face and he started to look away from me—a sign he was backing down.

"Get it cleaned up. I don't want to tell you again."

He shuffled the door to the side with his boot and made his way down the hallway. I closed my eyes listening to the sound of his footsteps, praying. It seemed like an eternity before I heard the sound of a doorknob turn, then silence. He had gone into his own room. I checked the clock. It usually took about an hour for the tension in the house to start winding down. I knew Adam and Thomas would stay in their room until then.

When I opened the closet door, Kat was sitting in the far back corner. I clicked the light on and welcomed her into my arms. We had both learned to be expert silent criers, and her face was stained with the remnants of fear.

"I'm sorry." I stroked her head. "I'm sorry, I should have made sure the sink was empty."

It was only day two of Mom being in the hospital, and she still had more than a week of recovery.

I tried to push away the thought of how hard it was going to be over the next few days as I focused on cleaning up the shards of glass that littered the kitchen floor.

* * *

Hours later, Kat puffed little breaths of air as I slipped into our bedroom. Careful not to wake her up, I stared at the open space where my door should have been. It was my lifeline and the only way I could prepare myself. Now I wouldn't hear if Dad came into my room in the middle of the night.

And I didn't.

I glanced at the clock with a half-opened eye as I was being carried.

Two in the morning, what's going on? Ohhhh where is he taking me? This is all a dream, all a dream. He'll go away if you're sleeping. This isn't happening if you're sleeping.

The plastic smell told me I was in his bedroom and on his waterbed. I tasted blood as I bit my lip and twisted my face. The room was a black hole. Not even the stars were brave enough to watch, as they cowered behind overcast skies. Pain shot up through my body as I contorted my back. My cheeks were on fire and the room began to spin. I grabbed at the sheets and the weight of his body pushed me deeper into the bed.

I couldn't breathe.

I heard something like a doorknob turning, but began to drift. I saw my body, lying there on the bed, getting crushed and prodded. I was above the scene, accepting the calm waves that washed over me as I separated myself. Soon I was flying, high above everything left behind. I left the shell of my body and I didn't look back.

I couldn't look back.

When I woke up Kat was standing at my bedside with a plate, nudging me. Sunlight bathed the room in gold and I shifted my weight. "Ohhh," I cried out.

The pain between my legs and in my stomach was unreal. I squished my eyes together instead of screaming so I didn't scare Kat. She put the plate on the floor next to the bed.

I smelled peanut butter and jelly.

"Adam said you should get up Brooke, because you've been sleeping for two days."

"Two days?"

Kat nodded.

I tried to remember everything that had happened but a wave of nausea forced me not to. The pain must have been so intense that I passed out, I knew that much. I limped into the bathroom and refused to look in the mirror while I undressed.

Hot water ran down my body and nursed the pain away. It washed away the blood and tears. It rinsed my soul. I scrubbed my arms, chest, neck and legs. Water pellets rushed at my face, pouring over me and pooling at my feet. I watched red-tinted remnants go down the drain and when I thought I was finished I washed a second time, just to make sure that nothing was left of the other night.

I changed clothes and pulled a sweatshirt on over my head. My bedroom door had been replaced, perfectly new, like nothing had happened. Adam and Thomas flicked through channels in the living room as I descended the stairs. "Jeez, Brooke. You're the only one who's allowed to sleep for two days and not get in trouble for it." Adam shook his head. "Judd called you six times. Tell your boyfriend he doesn't need to call so much, it was making Dad mad."

I poured a glass of water and steadied myself. Dad walked into the kitchen and I gripped the side of the counter. I opened my mouth but nothing came out. His face was composed, comical even. He stared at me.

"You okay, snuggle bug? Must have not been feeling well to sleep that long, huh?" He picked up a glass and took a lengthy sip. "I told Mom you must have had the flu or something since you threw up in your sleep." He lowered his voice. "You're feeling better now though, right?"

I couldn't process what he was saying. I knew I wasn't crazy, I wasn't. How could he stand in front of me pretending nothing happened?

This can't be normal. I squeezed my legs together for confirmation that the other night had happened, that I was dragged from my bedroom in my sleep, and it wasn't just a nightmare like I wanted it to be.

Pain shot up through my thighs and stomach. My lips parted to scream at him and tell him that he couldn't do this but I caught sight of my siblings sitting in the living room. The idea of resisting him and my siblings being his next target was unbearable. I was their only protection, the only one who knew what he was capable of. My shoulders slumped and I stared at the ground. I didn't have a choice.

To care for them, I couldn't say a word.

I lifted my head and watched his gaze run over my face. He was waiting for confirmation that the secret we had was still protected, still safe.

"Right," I whispered. I failed at trying to cover the defeat in my voice. "Whatever you say, Dad."

Chapter Eight

Freshman year of high school is when I got my first job working as a telemarketer. Technically I didn't have my working papers, so I invented an imaginary year that I was born on the application to make myself old enough. The hiring manager scanned me several times when I handed in the application, and he asked if I had ever been in sales. I told him I could sell the Brooklyn Bridge if he taught me how. I was hired on the spot.

"Brooke, where ya goin'?" Judd pushed one of his friends aside and jogged over to me. "You want to come over? School's over soon, I want to get the pool opened."

"I can't. I work till nine." I pushed my Honors English book into my locker and pulled out a three-ring binder.

"You always work. And you always study." He picked up a heavy science book, made a face, and put it back in my locker.

"Yeah, maybe you should try it sometime," Cristin said, suddenly appearing to open the locker next to mine. "Then you wouldn't have to cheat off my tests all the time."

"Ahh come on Cristin, you know I'm not looking at your answers. You're just so…so beautiful. I can't help staring at you in class."

Cristin rolled her eyes and I covered my mouth to stifle the laugher.

"Besides, if I wanted to really impress the parentals, I would sign up for Honors classes like Miss Perfect over here and copy off *her* answers." He nodded at me.

The blow to his arm probably didn't hurt like I wanted it to. "You *wish* you could keep up with me in those classes," I said.

"Yeah okay, later uglies." Judd turned on his heel and fled after Mack, who was mocking him from across the hall.

"You going to work?" Cristin threw her book bag over her shoulder.

"Yep. If I get top rep of the week again it'll be a nice paycheck."

"Good." Cristin eyed me. "Then we can go shopping before you disappear behind those clothes. What are you? A size one?"

"Double zero," I corrected. I pulled my bag over my shoulder and gripped the books that wouldn't fit in my bag close to my chest. "Gotta go though, see ya tomorrow."

I navigated through the chatter filled hallways toward the front of the building. Two girls in cheerleader uniforms stood on chairs to tape bright pink flyers to the announcement board. They walked away and I paused a moment to read it.

~*~ Tryouts! ~*~
Fall Football Season Cheerleaders
Saturday, June 5th, 11:00 a.m.
In the 'Big Gym'

"Don't even bother."

A girl I recognized from gym class interrupted my daydream.

"They always pick the same girls," she said. "Unless you're in with their little cliques, you don't stand a chance. It's stupid anyway."

I nodded. I didn't belong to any clubs or sports. The little time I did have—not occupied with home life—I worked to make money or study. Sure, it was going to help when I applied for college but I felt like I was missing out on something. I never got a chance to do something because I wanted to. I did things because I had to. Without thinking twice about it, I ripped the flyer off the bulletin and stuffed it into my book bag.

Mom picked me up from work a little after nine that night. "What took so long?" she huffed, turning the key in the ignition.

"Had to fill out a lot of paperwork. I booked a lot of appointments."

"Oh, that's good. Did you reach the daily goal? What is it, two appointments a night?"

"Yeah. I made twelve."

I demolished a bowl of cereal when we got home, mentally prepping a conversation with my mom about tryouts. "Mom, I wanted to see what you thought about me trying out for cheerleading."

She didn't look at me. "I don't have the money for all you guys to do after school things."

"I'll pay for it," I offered. "You won't have to pay for it I just wanted to see what you thought."

"I don't know Brooke, as long as I don't have to pay for it and you continue to help out with things around the house when they need to get done. I don't care." By *things* she meant money and cleaning. I was pretty sure I could juggle everything.

"I'll keep my job and I'll pay for it. Tryouts are in two weeks but I would need to get a physical." She sighed with the force of a cough and looked at me. It would mean she would have to make the appointment, pick me up from school, and wait the hour at the doctor's office to bring me home.

"...Or I could just do the physical the school offers. It costs more but...Yeah, that's what I'll do." I dumped the milk from my bowl into the sink. "Need to study, goodnight."

The only time I took off work was to study for midterms or finals. So when I told my boss I needed the Saturday off for tryouts he laughed. "Ha. Brooke, if you have another exam I understand, you don't have to lie about why you need off."

I wasn't sure why, but the remark offended me. "I'm not lying. I really am going to tryout for cheerleading."

My tone changed his response. "Oh, yeah. I know. Um, sure. That's great, that's fine. You need to do stuff like that anyway, you know? Go be with the kids your age."

"Should I *work* like the kids my age too?" I looked around the office at all the middle-aged women talking away on their phones. He had given me a two-week trial period to prove myself and I blew away office records ever since. "I mean, I don't *need* to be the top operator for the fourth month in a row. Maybe I should give someone else a shot." I smiled.

"Very funny." He sunk into his leather armchair. "Keep doing your thing, go do your tryouts, just make sure it doesn't impact your numbers here."

I nodded.

I spent the next week worrying about how I couldn't even do a cartwheel. A few other girls I knew wanted to tryout too, so at least I knew some of the people who would be there.

"Have you been stretching? I know they do a lot of jumps and kicks so be sure you're stretching." Sonia whispered her advice to me between classes. "Most people diet too, but you don't have to worry about that."

"Yeah, you don't have to worry." Carmen adjusted the glasses on her nose. "Have you ever done cheerleading?"

I shook my head. "No, I just thought it would be something fun to do. I'm not banking on making the team, I know they choose a lot of the same girls."

"We'll all make the team, I'm sure." Sonia smiled. "They can't always pick the same girls. And we're pretty enough, how hard could it be?"

Mom dropped me off the Saturday of tryouts. I spent an hour that morning trying to figure out what a cheerleader looked like when they practiced. I settled on a pair of navy blue shorts and a white cami with a light blue sports bra underneath. My hair was pulled into a tight ponytail and—at the suggestion of Sonia—I didn't shave my legs for two days.

"Why not shave your legs?" Mom rounded the corner of the school and came to a stop.

"I don't know. Sonia said it was something they checked though. She told me not to put lotion on my legs either." I ran my hands across the stubble.

"Okay well, you'll call when you're done?"

"Yeah, Carmen has a cell phone. I'll call." I kissed her on the cheek and grabbed my water bottle and gym bag.

Sonia and Carmen were already inside. "There are *so* many girls here," said Sonia, scanning the lobby outside the gymnasium. The sea of girls sprawled all over the floor stretching and chatting was a little intimidating. At eleven o'clock sharp, a bulky red-faced woman opened the gym doors.

"Attention, girls." The lobby fell quiet. "I'm Coach McDade. It's going to be a long day, so listen carefully. Girls will be put into groups of ten and assigned a team captain who is already a member of our cheerleading team. They will teach you two cheers, a dance, and how to do three kinds of jumps." She paused to eye some larger girls sitting on the wall. "Cheerleading is strenuous. Make no mistake that you will be pushed both physically and mentally today. You will ache in places you never thought possible."

Several of the team captains standing at her side smiled and whispered to each other. "With that being said, our fall football season only has twelve openings. There are six spots for the junior varsity team and six for the varsity team. Auditions will take place today at four o'clock sharp. Good luck to all of you."

A team captain with bright yellow hair stepped forward as the coach turned and disappeared into the gym. "All right girls. When I call your name, step forward and follow your team captain."

Carmen and I were put into the same group with a team captain named Lucille and Sonia wound up with the bright yellow-haired team captain. The groups dispersed and found quiet spots for each team to practice.

Our team captain bellowed out commands over the next several hours. We jumped rope and ran in place. Lucille taught us toe touches, X-jumps, and hurdler jumps. When it seemed my calves would explode we moved onto learning the dance routine. It was only a two-minute soundtrack, but with everything else we had to learn it only left an hour of practice to learn the entire fast-paced routine.

Sweat dripped from my forehead and Carmen looked like she was ready to call it quits. Finally, the team captains rallied all the groups together in the lobby and by four o'clock the first group of girls were lead into the gym. There were five teams in all, and everyone looked exhausted. My team was the last to be called inside.

Lucille led us into the gymnasium and we were called out in pairs to stand in front of Coach McDade and three other staff members I didn't know. The first two girls to tryout were last season's football cheerleaders. They finished their jumps perfectly and nailed every section of the dance routine.

The next two girls went and it seemed like the judges didn't pay attention to any girls that weren't already cheerleaders. Carmen was up next, along with a red-haired eleventh grader. She struggled through her jumps but she picked up most of the dance routine and finished her tryout with a smile. She winked at me as she slipped through the gym doors to wait for me outside.

"Brooke Nolan and Chrissy Stires, you're up."

I took my place and flashed my biggest smile. I was sure I looked like an idiot.

"Brooke Nolan. Have you ever tried out before?"

"No, I haven't." My throat tightened immediately after realizing that I basically just gave her permission to not watch a single thing I did over the next two minutes.

"Okay girls. First, toe touch."

I clasped both hands together, pushing them up over my head as I swung my hands around and left the ground. When I landed I saw one of the staff members nudge the person next to her to look in my direction.

Wow, are they really going to make fun of me as I'm standing right here?

After our jumps were done, they called us one by one to do a chant and cheer. I messed up the words to the cheer but I recovered and smiled through it.

"No matter what, smile every second," Sonia warned. She exaggerated the point, forcing the corners of her mouth to dangerous heights. "Don't stop smiling!"

Music blared through the speakers as the music for the dance routine started. My calves threatened to turn to jelly just as I finished, but I noticed that every staff member—including Coach—was looking at me when the routine ended. One judge leaned in towards Coach and whispered something in her ear. She nodded.

"Very well, one more thing." Coach said, nodding to Lucille. "Bring your bases in here, Lucille. We want to see Brooke try a half elevator." Lucille raised her eyebrows and looked in my direction. "Now, Lucille." Coach waved her off.

"Brooke, do you know what a flyer is?" Coach asked, not bothering to look at me.

Blood rushed to my face. "Uh, no, I'm sorry. I don't."

She smirked. "A flyer is the girl that goes up in the air." She pointed towards the ceiling as three girls followed Lucille back into the gym.

"Girls, I'd like you to put Brooke into a half elevator." The girls eyed me. "Walk her through it, tell her what to do."

Lucille broke the awkward silence. "Come on you heard her, let's go."

Two girls were on either side of me and one girl was behind me. The girl behind me clasped her hands around my waist. "Damn girl, don't you eat?" she hissed into my ear.

Lucille took control. "Okay, now put your hands on their shoulders and go up on your toes. When we say cradle up, push off on your toes and into their hands. Lock your legs otherwise you'll fall."

"Or kick us," said one of the bases.

"I'll stand in front of you to make sure you don't fall forward. But don't fall forward," Lucille cautioned.

"We'll raise our hands chest high once your feet are in our hands. Push off hard, lock your legs, got it?" said the girl to my right.

I nodded. I was going to die.

My palms pushed into the shoulders of each girl on my side and I felt the back base grip my waist. I shifted my weight onto my toes and prayed I didn't smash my face off the ground.

"Cradle UP!" Lucille bellowed.

I jumped into the girls' hands, pushed off, and looked down. I shouldn't have looked down. My legs flailed underneath me and the back base all but took a kick to the chest as she caught me coming down.

"Ah sorry. Forgot to mention…and don't look down either," said the side base as she smiled at the impatient coach. "Also, put your hands in a T when you get to the top."

"Again," Coach insisted, crossing her arms over her chest while shooting a smug look to the staff that had whispered in her ear.

Okay Brooke. Push off, lock your legs, and don't look down.

Don't look down.

Don't look down.

"Cradle UP!"

I pushed off and landed in the side bases' hands. In a swift movement I felt the rush of air and then everything stopped. My hands out in a T at my sides, I assumed my feet were undoubtedly planted firmly on the ground and that I had missed their hands entirely.

Then I opened my eyes.

Coach and the judges were open-mouthed staring at me. I stared down at them.

Wait, I'm staring down *at them?*

Four hands secured my ankles in place; I had locked my legs and was standing several feet off the ground in a perfect half elevator. A wide grin spread across my face. What a rush!

"Cradle her." Coach flailed her hands at me. "Cradle her, then."

Lucille looked up at me, eyes wide. "But Coach, we didn't teach— I mean she doesn't know how to—"

"CRADLE HER!" Coach bellowed.

Lucille looked up at me, agony in her face. She mouthed *sorry*.

"Cradle!" Lucille bellowed. "One, TWO."

Hands disappeared beneath my feet as the side bases pushed up and sent me flying higher into the air. Instinctively I threw my arms back and my legs shot out in front of me. When I opened my eyes again, the side and back bases had crazy smiles on their faces while they held me safely off the ground.

Lucille was ecstatic. "Wow! Did you see that Coach? She did it perfectly. Did you see that Coach? She cradled just like she should!"

They raised my torso until my sneakers touched the ground and two girls patted my back. "All right, Brooke! That was awesome!"

My heart was still in my throat as I looked at Coach sitting in her chair chewing on her hair. "Well, Brooke." She picked up her pencil and wrote something down in front of her. "Seems as though you're a natural."

"What happened to you in there?" Carmen and Sonia demanded as I finally walked through the gym doors. I told them what happened and they stared back with the same open mouths the judges had. "You did a *stunt?* Well I guess it's a good thing you didn't shave your legs!"

"What does that have to do with anything?" I asked

"I figured, you know, because you're so skinny that if you made the team they would want you to be a flyer. You can't shave your legs before you stunt because otherwise the bases can't grip your legs as you go up. It's too slippery." Sonia beamed at me. "Aaaah that means you totally made the team!"

An hour later Coach appeared in front of the gym doors with a list in her hand. "A lot of girls here today showed great talent and promise. Unfortunately, we only have six spots per team this year, so if you hear your name, congratulations, you've made the team. First we'll start with varsity."

Coach rattled off names of mostly junior and senior girls who shrieked when they heard their names. The other girls looked around, nervous that there were only six more spots to be claimed.

"Junior varsity will now have the pleasure of adding the following girls to the team for the fall football season."

Carmen and Sonia gripped either of my hands. "If you're name is called, you've made the team. Margaret B., Sara T., Joanna N., Riley D."

There were only two names left.

Coach eyed the group of hopefuls. "Also, Lily P., and Danica R."

Our hands loosened as I realized with Carmen and Sonia that none of us had made the team. I looked at Carmen who already had tears falling down her cheeks and at Sonia who was shaking her head in disbelief.

The girls who made the team cheered and hugged each other as Coach put the list in her pocket. "I know a lot of you had great expectations for today. And I appreciate all your hard work. Please try again next season, as we're always looking for new and great talent."

"Yeah right," Sonia whispered under her breath.

"One more thing." Coach cracked her knuckles and cleared her throat. "I also want to congratulate Brooke Nolan for becoming the newest flyer on the JV team. We needed six cheerleaders, but didn't realize we needed a new flyer until she demonstrated exceptional talent during her audition." She looked at me. "Congratulations, Brooke. Welcome to the team."

Sonia tackled me and Carmen shrieked in my ear as they hugged and danced around in a circle with their arms wrapped around me. "You did it! You did it! You made the team, Brooke!"

Embarrassed at their celebration, I realized that I wasn't sure I wanted to be part of the team now that Sonia and Carmen weren't.

"And don't even *think* about quitting because we didn't make it," Carmen said, reading my thoughts. "You will be *awesome*."

Chapter Nine

"I think Paul likes you."

Cristin and I made our way through the packed annual West
End Fair. I was enjoying the bits of freedom before cheerleading
practice started. I wasn't looking forward to getting up at four thirty
in the morning to meet at the high school, but Coach insisted it was
better to work out and practice before the sweltering summer sun
came up.

"Really?" I looked back at Judd, Paul, and Chalky following
behind us. "I don't know, he hasn't said much to me since I met
him last summer. He was even in my health class this year."

"I think he's shy. But he keeps looking at you."

Dodging a kid with a balloon, I shrugged my shoulders.

"Have you even had a boyfriend since you moved here?" Cristin
pressed.

"Eh, no. Not really."

I thought about Dad and what he would say if I told him I was
dating someone. Since Adam wasn't into dating yet—and he was a
year older than me—I couldn't imagine it would go over well.
Work, school, and cheerleading would take up most of my time
anyway. I didn't think a boyfriend would be very patient with
waiting for me to cook dinner or clean the house before we could
hang out.

Sometimes I felt older than what I actually was.

We filed through the amusement rides and stopped every couple
of feet to talk to people we knew from class. Judd and Chalky put

moves on several girls we talked to while Paul lingered in the background of their conversations.

"Well it's nine thirty," Cristin chimed in, looking at her phone. "My mom is meeting me out front. Am I driving you home, Brooke?"

My mouth opened to answer her and Paul was suddenly standing at my side. "My mom will take her home."

The same cologne he used the previous summer engulfed me. It was the only thing he'd said all night and it was pretty forward.

"Are you, sure? I mean, I've never met your mom…"

"It's fine." Paul gave Cristin a head nod. "Go ahead, I got her." *You got me?*

Cristin raised an eyebrow and tried to stifle a smile. "Okayyy if you say so Paulie. See ya later Brooke." She wrapped her hands around my neck and whispered quick words of girlish encouragement in my ear.

Cristin disappeared into the crowd and Paul turned toward me. "So, you want to walk around a little while these fools try and play their A-game?"

He nodded in the direction of Judd and Chalky. They were engrossed in conversation and didn't even look up when Paul put his hand on my shoulder to steer me around a group of people to head towards the concession stands.

"So, we had health together." Paul scuffed his sneakers across the gravel as he pretended to check out everything in sight, except me. He acted so odd.

"Didn't think you noticed. I sat right behind you the entire time." I said. "You never said a word to me."

"It was first period, I didn't say a word to anybody. Not really a morning person."

"Oh."

"And I noticed."

"Huh?"

"You said I didn't notice," he pointed out. "But I did. I noticed you."

He shifted his gaze to mine and lingered a second too long. "Not like you noticed me." He swayed closer to me and nudged my shoulder. "I don't blame you. Everyone notices you though."

"Oh, shut up." I laughed and nudged him back. "Who notices me? I'm not exactly Miss Popular. I haven't even had a boyfriend since I moved here," I said, echoing Cristin's comment.

"Oh?"

We stopped in front of the display of John Deere tractors and he opened up the door to one of the larger ones. "After you." He nodded in the direction of the cabin.

Making sure no one was looking, I hopped up into the seat and he shut the door behind us. Crowds of people passed by, but unless you knew we were up there, no one could see us. We both shifted and put our feet up on the dashboard.

The warmth of his body danced near my skin. "Yeah, I don't really see you with other guys," he said. "Except Judd. You guys got a thing?"

"Me and Judd?" I said, laughing at the thought. "No, nothing there. He's my best friend and everything, I just…" I shrugged. "I just don't think of him like that, you know?"

Paul leaned forward and put his right arm behind me to inch closer. His emerald eyes glazed over my face and I raised my eyebrows when his fingertips brushed my hand.

"That's good… *If* that's what you want, I mean." His hand was wrapped around mine and I could feel his breath on my nose. "Look, I know we haven't really hung out and stuff…alone. But I like you. A lot."

Thankful that the cabin could only let in two, unimpressive streams of light, I tried to calm the blood rushing to my face.

"Will you go out with me?" he asked.

I opened my mouth but nothing came out.

Paul's lips brushed against mine. Both of us were afraid to move and I froze. He formed his lips around mine and laid a soft kiss on the corner of my mouth.

I remembered to breathe.

"Paul, wow." He leaned away to wait for my reaction. "I think…" I started.

Don't embarrass yourself.

"I think I like you too. We don't know each other, really. You know? Maybe we should just, hang out a few times? See what happens?"

I never had to reject anyone before and I wasn't sure if what I said was the right thing. I didn't want to push him away, because the feeling was definitely mutual.

Looking up I cringed to see his eyes go soft, but he nodded his head in a few slow motions. "Yeah. We should hang out. You're right." A sigh escaped as he smiled and brushed a piece of hair from my face. "I'd like that. Maybe we should head out now?"

Paul's mom looked me over with a raised eyebrow as I hopped into the backseat of their minivan. Paul asked her to take me home. "So, you're fifteen like Paulie? You guys have classes together at school?"

Paul groaned. "Ma, come on."

"Just want to know who she is honey. I'm Gina. Nice to meet you Brooke."

Paul squeezed my hand as we pulled into my driveway. "You need me to walk you inside?"

"Oh, no. Don't." I knew I said it too fast and looked at Gina staring at me from the rearview mirror. "It's fine. I just need to walk to the door, no biggie. I'll see you later."

Paul and I talked over AOL instant messenger for the next week, as I got ready for cheer practice to start. He wanted to hang out but I wasn't sure how I could explain hanging out with *just* Paul to my dad. Going to Judd's was different because there were always one or two other people there.

Practice for cheerleading was no joke. We ran the bleachers, did several sets of intense jump rope cardio, and lifted weights. I never thought of cheerleading as a sport, but I guess when my life depended on having physically fit girls underneath me to catch my fall, it made sense.

Coach blared into her megaphone from the bleachers as we ran laps and did push-ups. "Let's move it girls! If you stop, we go again. If you slow down, we go again. Your choice, move it!"

I struggled to keep up with the words and movements of the cheers and chants. Only one other girl who made the JV team had never done cheerleading before, but she had a cousin on the team who worked with her after school. The girls were not exactly inviting, especially because I had taken over a flyer position that technically was not up for grabs. I had replaced Jessie, and she became the side base for my stunts.

"I don't know why Coach makes you fly all the time. You've never even done this before. You can't learn this stuff over night." Jessie rolled her eyes and looked for confirmation from the other bases. "Right girls?"

The other base girl nodded her head in agreement but my back base snorted. "Lay off it Jessie, she's a natural. If you can do it, anyone can."

"All right ladies, laps! Then you're done," Coach said. "I want three laps from all of you. Go!"

Since I was an avid runner, I cruised around the track for lap one. A cramp snuck up on me during lap two and I pinched my side.

"Told you not to drink so much water, Brooke." Kendra jogged next to me and wiped the sweat from her face. "Gets me every time!"

Bolts of pain shot through my stomach as I struggled through the third lap. I had fallen behind all the other girls and I knew if I stopped Coach would make me run more. Halfway around, I couldn't breathe and stopped in the middle of the track.

"Move it, Nolan!" I could hear Coach's megaphone across the field. "More laps for everyone if you don't make it around."

I eyed the finish line around turn three and crumbled as a blaze of pain ran up through my stomach and to my chest. "Aaah!" I yelled out and dropped to my knees clutching my side.

The varsity captain reached me before Coach did and I was embarrassed to see everyone standing around me.

"What's wrong, Nolan?" Coach brushed the girls aside and moved closer to me.

"I don't know, my stomach feels like it's falling out."

The longer I sat there the more the pain subsided so I convinced Coach not to call an ambulance and to call my mom instead.

Mom and I sat in the doctor's office as he pushed off my stomach muscles and I yelled out in pain.

"Well I know you had your appendix out, so my guess would be it's a hernia. It only hurts when you strain yourself, right? To run, or do other strenuous things?"

"Yeah," I replied. I thought the cramps were from drinking too much water or not having enough stamina.

"Well I think we need to do exploratory surgery to see what's going on in there. It's a lot easier to tell when males have hernias because more often than not it will protrude through their stomachs with a bump. For girls it's harder to see unless we check it out internally."

Coach was not happy with my diagnosis because it meant I would be missing almost five weeks of practice. I wasn't happy because it meant I was going to be vulnerable again after surgery.

Dad was happy.

Surgery was scheduled to take about an hour. The anesthesiologist came in and put an IV in my left hand. "I'm going to give you some really good drugs." He moved some of the tubes around and when he was satisfied he looked at me. "Goodnight, Brooke."

Four hours later, I woke up with the same unrelenting pain in my abdomen as when I had my appendix out. The clock on the wall of my hospital room read six twenty-three p.m., and since I should have been in recovery before four o'clock I assumed something had gone wrong during surgery.

"You actually had a hernia on *both* sides." The doctor pointed to either side of my stomach. "Laparoscopic surgery is a beautiful thing. You have two scars the size of your pinky nail on each side, and the same size scar in your bellybutton where we made entry. I'm going to extend the time you have off from cheerleading to eight weeks since we had to repair both sides." He took note of my face. "Oh, don't worry sweetheart, resting at home is the best thing for you at this point."

And it was. For the first three weeks.

Mom got tired of waiting on me and the only time Kat came into our bedroom was to sleep. I was alone most of the day while the summer sun blared through the windows. Sweltering heat or not, I covered myself head to foot with blankets as a shield as I lay in bed, waiting.

Dad came in a few days after I was able to walk around enough to shower. I thought if I forced my body to stay limp enough, he wouldn't be able to move me and give up.

Blacking out was becoming a welcomed necessity to coping. I slipped past the reality of heavy breathing and pain and sought refuge in black space and dreamland.

My prescribed Vicodin kept me numb over the next few weeks. Mom told me when I was finished using them to give her the rest of the bottle for safe keeping. I nodded and watched her throw back her usual cocktail of pills. Maybe she stayed numb for a reason too.

"Dad is working the overnight shift. Why don't you come in and sleep with me tonight?" Mom suggested.

"Okay."

"First come in here, Brooke. I have to show you something."

I followed her into the bathroom and she pulled a white thermometer out of her pocket, handing it to me.

No, not a thermometer.

"Mom, you're pregnant?" The white stick flashed the word PREGNANT across a small screen. My hand pressed against my forehead. "How did you find out?"

"Remember when I fell last week when I was sleeping on the couch?"

Do I remember last week when you were so high on pills you passed out on the couch and got up hours later, only to fall on your face? Yes, Mom. I remember.

"Yeah, what about it?"

"I went to the doctor. Turns out I broke my nose but they couldn't send me anywhere to operate because they did a blood test and I was pregnant. I haven't told your father yet. I'm three months already."

"Oh. Well, congratulations!"

She hugged me and shoved the pregnancy test back into her pocket. "I'm going to tell him tomorrow. I wanted you to be the first to know."

We both crawled into her bed and she clicked the TV on. The news came on and after a few minutes Mom muted the TV and turned to me. "Brooke, I want to ask you something."

I gulped. "Okay?"

"I saw something that I wanted to ask you about. I really need to know the honest truth."

Oh God.

She put the remote down. "Do you know any kids at school that do Oxycontins?"

Wow, not where I thought this conversation was going.

I struggled to switch brain tracks. "Uh, yeah. I mean, I think so? I'm not sure. Why?"

"The news was saying that people are selling them for twenty-five dollars a pill. I could really use the money. You know your father doesn't give me much and I don't know what else to do since I can't work. Do you think you could find people to sell them to? They said a lot of high school kids are using them."

"You want me to sell your Oxycontins? Don't you need them?" The news had been covering a ton of stories about the controversial painkiller, but I never considered my mom selling it to make a profit.

"They give me a lot of them. I have Vicodin and Percocet too, so I could use them instead for my pain. Plus I'll need to cut back because of the baby now."

"Could we ask Grandpa and Grandma for money?" The thought of becoming a drug dealer at fifteen was not something I wanted to add to my resumé.

"Never mind, Brooke. I'll just have to beg your father for more money. Nothing can ever be easy." She picked up the remote.

"No, it's okay." I thought about Judd. He ran around with some shady people who I knew smoked weed. Maybe they did other drugs too. "I'll do it."

"Okay. We'll keep it between you and me. I want to sell them for thirty dollars a pill." She un-muted the TV and moved onto the next topic as if we'd just had a normal mother-daughter conversation. "So, are you excited to get back to cheerleading next week?"

* * *

Judd was more than happy to oblige in helping me pool together a clientele list for Oxycontins. "Me and you, we're gonna run this town. I have lots of people looking for them. Where are you getting them from?"

"My mom."

"What? Really?" Judd nodded his head. "Yeaaaa buddy. Well, don't get all red about it. It's cool. Chalky's mom smokes weed with him."

"I'm not keeping any of the money," I added.

"Oh? Well, all right. You can make bank selling those though. Your mom needs the money?"

"Yeah. Hard times."

"Don't sound so down, I got you Brooke. We'll get this."

As summer came to an end I continued going to cheerleading practice but struggled to catch up on all the new routines I missed. Work was from nine in the morning until six at night, and then I would go home, shower, and meet Judd to start our evening gig. By the end of the month I had given Mom well over two thousand dollars.

"Damn, you sure you're not keeping any of this?" Judd flipped through a wad of twenties after making a drop-off.

"Yeah, I'm sure. You know, this would be a lot easier if we drove. Then we wouldn't have to meet people in weird places, waiting on our bikes."

"Yeah, it's all right. They don't care as long as they get their stuff."

"Who's left?" I had one more summer reading book to get through before school started the following week. It was a long day and I just wanted to go home.

"James." Judd looked at his phone. "Should be here in ten minutes."

The name was not familiar. "Is he new?"

"Yeah, sort of. I've seen him around. He wanted forty of them though. He's giving us a little over a grand. Nicey nice."

The sun had just set when a black Honda rounded the corner and pulled up in front of us. The back window rolled down and a hand stuck out, motioning me over.

"Go get em'. Do your thing." Judd motioned toward the car but didn't move from his spot on the curb.

I grabbed the baggie of pills and stuffed them in my back pocket like Judd had taught me. "Don't give them the pills until they give you the money," he had instructed.

"Sup?" A gruff voice met me.

I strained my eyes to see into the dark car. A few pairs of eyes stared out at me.

"Not much. Got forty Oxys." I pulled the bag out of my pocket to show them. "You got the twelve hundred?"

A gun was in my face before I knew what was happening. "This gun says they're free. Give it here!" he shouted. He reached outside the window and grabbed the pill bag.

I was on the ground as Judd pushed me aside. The wind was knocked out of me and I heard tires screeching away while Judd leaned halfway in the car punching the guy in the face.

"Judd! NO!" I screamed.

He let go of the door and rolled onto the ground as the car's tires screamed around the corner and disappeared into the distance. I ran to him.

"Oh my God, Judd! Are you okay? Are you okay?"

"Stop screaming, I'm okay. I'm okay. Are YOU okay? Who are they to point a gun in your face? Oh, this isn't over. Oh *man* this isn't over."

My hands trembled as we rushed over to our bikes and hopped on. "Brooke, go home. I know where that guy lives."

"No, Judd. No, I'm going with you."

"Go HOME Brooke." Judd pointed.

"NO! I'm coming with you."

He sped off and I followed behind him. The temperature dipped as we pedaled with rampant intensity. I silently thanked Coach for the hours of running and jump rope; otherwise I wouldn't have been able to keep up with Judd whose adrenaline was taking over.

We must have pedaled for over ten miles before we laid our bikes down in some bushes outside a trailer home.

"His car isn't here. That guy thinks he's just gonna get away with that? Watch this."

Judd strutted to the front door and I trailed him, watching out for the black car. Several hard thuds on the door coaxed an overweight woman in a bathrobe to appear. At first she looked like she was going to call the police, then she spotted me. "What's this about? Do you know what time it is?"

"Do you know what your son just did? He stuck a gun in my girl's face."

His girl?

The woman's mouth opened and she brought her hand to her face. "What? *My* James?"

"Yeah, *your* James." Judd squeezed his hands to control himself.

"I don't understand."

"He wanted some Oxys, drugs. I guess he didn't want to pay for them. You tell him we'll be looking for him. He stuck a gun in my girl's face and fled. I'll be looking for him, tell him that."

"Oh, oh my." The look on the woman's face told me she had no idea her son was a junkie. I felt bad for her.

"Oh honey," she said, turning to me. "I'm so sorry."

I stared at her.

"I'll make it right. Here, I'll make it right." She fumbled the pocketbook sitting in the foyer.

"No, no it's all right," I said.

Tears ran down the mother's face as she pried open her wallet.

"Really, it's okay. Tell him to never call us again." I took Judd's hand and led him away from the house.

"Why'd you do that?" Judd pushed out his chest and scanned the neighborhood for the black car. "I'm gonna—"

"Do nothing," I said, finishing his sentence. "You're going to do nothing because we're better than that. Come on."

When we reached my house the adrenaline had worn off and we had to practically drag our bikes up the driveway. I pushed the front door open and Mom was standing in the living room. "What happened?" She hissed. It was after midnight. "I've been sitting here waiting."

Judd told her what happened as I hid my face behind him. I was disappointed that I wasn't able to hold onto the pills as the car sped away. When Judd finished Mom just looked at me.

"You let him *get away with my pills*? You got *nothing*? Not one cent?"

She threw her hands up and walked into the kitchen. "Jesus, Brooke. What the hell am I supposed to do now? I don't get another refill for another two weeks. I needed that money."

Judd raised an eyebrow at her reaction. Mom didn't mention the gun that had been pointed in my face. "I'm out," he whispered, backing away. The confusion on his face made me feel embarrassed.

I nodded.

He snuck out the front door and I watched him cruise down the driveway.

"It won't happen again, Mom. I'm sorry."

She tapped her foot and looked at the empty pill bottle in front of her. "It better not, Brooke. If you want to make sure you guys have food to eat, it better not."

Chapter Ten

Paul and I started walking to his house everyday after school to hang out. It was also convenient that he lived so close to where I worked. We could spend time together for an hour before I started my shift and I could spend time with Paul without having to tell my parents.

"So what time does your little brother's bus come?" I poured a glass of orange juice and sat down on the oversized sofa in the living room. Paul's mom had recently accepted a job as an ultrasound technician and needed Paul to get his little brother off the bus every afternoon.

"Around four. You don't have to go to work until five, right?" He plopped down next to me, hooking our elbows together. The familiar scent of his skin sent a pulse through my veins as I let his arm melt into mine.

"Maybe," I smiled.

He set my juice down and grabbed my sides, tickling me until I begged him to stop. Satisfied that he had won the tickle war he pulled me closer to him, wrapping his arms around my waist.

"Go out with me." His eyes softened when he was serious. I knew the question had been burning in the back of his head ever since I turned him down at the fair. Curled up on his couch, I watched him fidget with a pillow as he waited for an answer. Outside the living room window leaves started to drift to the ground.

"Brooke?" He looked so vulnerable.

I cradled his face in my hands and coaxed him closer. I kissed him, lingering on his bottom lip, and pulled away before he could return the favor. "Okay." I nodded. "I'll go out with you."

To mask the overwhelming smile that spread across his face he hid his face in my hair.

"One condition," I said, holding up a finger. "I don't want to lose you as a friend. If we ever break up, promise me we'll still be friends."

He nodded immediately. "We won't have to worry about that, because I'm never letting you go."

"Smooth," I said and rolled my eyes. "But promise me."

He drew an imaginary X over his heart and lowered his eyes to mine. "Promise."

"Just one more thing."

"Ugh, what now?"

"Go get your brother. We're late."

Paul jumped up off the couch and I grabbed my coat as we bolted out the front door. The bus had just come to a stop as we reached the corner. Red signs flashed as the double doors opened to let the kids off, and Joseph hopped off the bus shrugging his SpongeBob book bag onto his shoulders. "Hi Paulie!"

"I need to go to work, I'll call you later?" I pressed a quick kiss to his cheek and floated towards the center of town.

"Ew, gross." Joseph wrinkled his nose. "I'm telling Mom."

"No you're not. Go on, get inside." Paul winked at me and put his hand on Joseph's shoulder and led him toward the house.

Joseph *did* tell Gina that he had seen me kiss Paul when he got off the bus. After work that night, Paul called to ask me to come to dinner at their house so I could meet his dad.

"Sorry," Paul apologized. "My mom's all excited that I have a girlfriend and I think she just wants to get to know you. And my dad has never met you."

"It's fine. I'd love to come over."

Instead of asking for permission to have dinner at Paul's, I called off work the next evening. I planned to have Gina drive me home around the time I would usually get home from work.

"Maybe Brooke will play with me since you don't," Joseph teased, poking his head into Paul's room for the hundredth time that night.

"Moooooooooom. Get Joe out please!"

Joseph disappeared and raced across the hall to his bedroom, yelling as he ran. "I'm not even *in there* Mom, I'm right here in my *own room.*"

I could hear Gina's footsteps waltz down the hallway. "Joe, leave them alone." She pressed the bedroom door open and peered in on us lounging on the bed watching TV. "And this door stays *open* you two. That means more than a crack." She winked at me but her eyes were serious.

"Come on, Ma." Paul buried his face into his pillow.

"Dinner in five." She turned on her heel and headed back towards the kitchen.

"Your mom's cooking smells amazing."

"I bet it does, your stomach has been growling for the past two hours."

I nudged him and he nudged me back. Paul flipped on top of me and moved his lips across mine as I laughed into his kiss.

"Oooooh." Joseph's voice carried through the room.

Paul looked behind him. "Joe I thought I told you to—"

"Kids! Dinner, come eat."

As if on cue, Lou walked through the front door and set his briefcase down in the foyer. "Where's my beautiful wife?" He scanned the kitchen and watched her set some plates down. "Ah, there she is! There's my girl." Before doing anything else, he crossed the room and smothered her in several kisses. "How are you, darling?"

"Dad, really?" Paul sat down and pulled the chair out next to him, motioning for me to sit down next to him. I did and watched the romantic comedy unfold before me.

There was pasta with vodka sauce, sausage, and salad. Warm bread, baked fresh hours before, was nestled in the middle of the table and Gina filled Lou's wine glass for the second time. I introduced myself between bites of macaroni and bread. Lou seemed impressed that I had a job and was enrolled in all honors classes.

"That's really great, really something. Good for you." His grin was ear to ear as he ran his fingers through his salt and pepper hair. Gina admired him and blotted the red lipstick she put on seconds before Lou had walked through the door.

Joseph talked about the art project he made at school that day and everyone listened, laughed, and helped themselves to seconds.

Paul sipped his water and glimpsed at me for signs that I was going to run screaming from the table.

Fixated, I observed in awe and silence. His parents' genuine concern, their knowledgeable advice and humor caught me by surprise. The dinner table was warm and inviting. Something sparked deep inside the cavities of my chest. A profound and dragging realization crossed my mind as I finished seconds of macaroni and thirds of the salad.

My family was *not* normal.

The kissing, loving, and caring families I saw on TV or read about in novels were not just playing charades. They were right in front of me, laughing with each other and loving every second of finding out what each other's day was like. They ate pasta, made fart jokes, and hated their jobs just like everyone else. They were real.

The sudden cognizance about my defective family was hard to swallow. Somewhere in the depths of my gut I knew something wasn't right, but I could never put my finger on it. No one ever pointed out that my home life was not normal. Now, no one had to. I was witnessing it with my own eyes. I was hearing it, watching it, tasting it, and loving it.

Joseph reached across the table to grab the Parmesan cheese and on impulse I grabbed at the glass of milk he spilled over. My mind flashed to what happened when a glass was spilled at my house, and the daydream I had immersed myself in about Paul's family quickly dissipated. I couldn't watch Joseph get hurt. Paul didn't move from his spot at the table, making no attempt to shield Joseph from his dad. I immediately went into protective mode.

"Joseph, come with me. We'll go in your room." The pitch of my voice rose in panic. I couldn't watch Lou hit him or shove him into a wall. I didn't want to hear the glass smash across the kitchen floor with threats to have it cleaned up 'or else'. I grabbed Joseph by the hand. "Let's go!"

Everyone at the table was staring at me.

Gina, eyes wide, ascended from her seat and grabbed the closest napkin. Lou put his hand out in a welcoming and cautious gesture of kindness. "It's okay, Brooke. Really, it's all right sweetheart. It's just a little spilled milk."

I waited for the rage to start, the yelling and the chair throwing. Lou grabbed a few more napkins and mopped up the white puddle underneath Joseph's chair. "There we go, all better. You want some more milk little man?"

Joseph nodded with an eager smile.

"All right, here ya go. Leave the milk *in* the glass this time, okay?"

Gina let out a nervous chuckle at Lou's joke as she watched me make my way back to my seat. She was trying not to, but her eyes were screaming for answers to questions she didn't want to ask.

Sweat masked my face from the adrenaline that had no outlet and I started to push the food around on my plate.

Gina noticed. "Paul, you and Brooke look finished. Why don't you two go hang out for a while before I have to take her home?"

Paul nodded and took my hand as we made our way down the hallway. "Wait," I said. I turned around and headed back towards the dinner table.

"I'm sorry," I said. "I'm sorry that I—you know, I just thought—"

I was so used to apologizing. I felt that I had to but I wasn't even sure why.

"No, honey. It's okay. Everything's fine." The corners of her mouth turned upward. "Go be with Paul, everyone's fine here."

I moved towards the living room to catch up with Paul. "Can we go outside for a minute?" My heart raced underneath my hoodie and I needed to breathe a minute. "I just need some fresh air."

"Yeah, sure. Let's go."

We walked in silence for two blocks as I tried to process what had happened. There was the overturned glass, the spilled milk, but his father didn't yell, hit, or throw anything. The reaction that I had anticipated never came, and it left me standing at my chair in flight mode without a reason. I turned my head away from Paul and he must have noticed.

"Brooke, it was just a glass of milk, you know? No reason to get upset."

I nodded, but he didn't understand. How could I *not* get upset? Everything I had ever known was a lie. Dads didn't react like wild beasts in every house. Not all moms ask immoral questions or make illegitimate requests for their own benefit. It was a world I didn't know or understand.

I recalled when I tried to run away with my sister to my Grandma's house. Even then, I didn't have a real reason for fleeing.

I knew something was wrong, but until that very moment at Paul's house I could never understand why.

Suddenly it was clear.

Families didn't have to be perfect, but the fear and manipulation that fueled my household was unconventional. Homes *could* be safe places after all. I was in disbelief.

"Did you hear a thing I just said?" Paul stopped and stepped out in front of me. I was so wrapped up in my own thoughts I didn't realize he had been talking.

"Yes," I lied.

"Then what'd I say?"

I looked down. "I know the milk was an accident. Sorry I overreacted."

"The milk?" Paul looked lost. "I was asking you if you thought we could see each other tomorrow after school. What's going on?"

My face was on fire. "Nothing."

"Nothing?" Paul crossed his arms over his chest. He was so handsome, so normal. I didn't deserve him.

"Kids, I need to get Brooke home." Gina was standing in the doorway, yelling down the block.

"We need to go." I grabbed Paul's hand and steered him towards his loving, safe, milk-spilling house.

* * *

About a month later I called Gina from the school nurse. When I told her I felt sick, she didn't skip a beat to tell me she'd be at the school in ten minutes to pick me up. I felt bad calling her at work, but I couldn't stay in school. I barely made it through the first ten minutes of homeroom before I asked for a pass to the nurse.

Dad took full advantage of Mom being in New York, since she had a consultation for her next back surgery. Gina didn't ask questions as she signed me out, but she glanced at me over and over as we made our way into the parking lot to get into her minivan.

"I can tell you don't feel good, honey. You look like Paul wearing those sweatpants and sweatshirt like that." She tried to get me to smile, but I pulled the hood closer around my head.

"Yeah." I shifted my weight. It hurt to move.

"I'm surprised they let me just sign you out like that. I thought only parents could do that."

My turn to smile. "I put your name down as an emergency contact before I handed the sheet in to my homeroom teacher."

She nodded, eyebrows raised. "Oh. Yeah well, that will do it."

We rounded the corner of her block and I concentrated on the click-click-click of her turn signal.

I left my book bag in the car and inched my way to the front door. Gina followed me inside and when I got to the top of the stairs I turned around and caught her staring at me.

"Brooke, you're moving very..." she trailed off. "Maybe we should call your mom?"

I closed my eyes. Talking was taking all the strength out of me. "No. Please. I know Paulie is going to a friend's house after school today. Is it okay if I just sleep here for a while?" Familiar pain rose in my stomach. I had to lay down.

Gina bit her lip. I took comfort in how much Paul looked like her. "Sure, sure. Go ahead and sleep. Close the door if you want so you don't hear me out here. I'll just be cooking, so call if you need me."

It was around nine in the morning when I finally settled under Paul's covers and drifted to sleep. I fluttered in and out of a deep slumber over the next several hours. Around five in the evening, I woke up when the bedroom door creaked open.

"Nah honey," I heard Lou say. "She's still sleeping." The door closed behind him and I fell back into a deep sleep until eight, when I felt a warm body lay next to me.

Paul.

He stroked my face and placed a hand on my forehead in the dark. "She's still sleeping?" Gina whispered. "Maybe we should wake her up to eat something?" She sounded concerned.

Paul shifted his weight to the edge of the bed and I heard him retreat from the bedroom. "She's okay Ma, just let her sleep." I faded to blackness again.

Intense banging echoed down the hallway and I sat straight up in bed, suddenly wide-awake.

At the end of the hall, Gina hissed through her teeth. "Who *is* that? Paul, get the door. It's ten o'clock at night."

I heard the front door open and some confused conversation between Gina and Lou. Then a familiar voice filled the room. "Where's Brooke? She was supposed to be home an hour ago."

Dad.

I sprang out of bed, still half asleep. I grabbed a pair of pajama bottoms from Paul's top drawer and pulled them on over my sweatpants. My hands shook as I combed them through my hair to pull the mess into a somewhat polished ponytail and I took a huge gulp of air before I opened the bedroom door.

When I looked down the hallway Gina and Lou were looking at each other uneasily. They didn't know how to respond to Dad's tone of voice. I approached the foyer area and held my breath.

"Hi Dad."

Paul looked up, surprised to see me. Dad tightened his lips and looked at what I was wearing. He craned his neck and struggled to maintain his composure. "Brooke, we need to go. *Now*. Get your stuff."

"I'm, uh…" My tongue stuck to the roof of my mouth. "I'm staying here…tonight."

Dad's eyebrows clashed together. "You're *what?*"

"They said I could stay the night." My voice wavered as I nodded towards Gina and Lou, who were now looking at each other to see which one had given me the permission. "I have to be at school early tomorrow for a project. Gina said she would drive me in the morning."

Dad molded his hands into fists and tilted his head. Before he could speak Gina piped in.

"Yeah sure. I did. I said that. She's got a project. No big deal, I pass there in the morning and she…" Her eyes darted around the room as she made up the storyline. "She will sleep… on the couch! No problem. We gave her pajamas." She crossed her arms in front of her chest, content with her explanation as she nudged Lou to agree and smile.

Dad erupted into a fury of carefully subdued curse words before directing his bickering directly at me. "No way are you sleeping at your boyfriend's house. Get your stuff and get out in the car before I drag you out. *Now*." He backed towards the door and I searched my brain for a rebuttal but couldn't find one. I turned in defeat, heading to Paul's room to grab my things.

"David, do you want a cup of tea? Or coffee?" Gina's voice told me my dad's demeanor scared her. She was trying to stall. She didn't want me getting into the car with him while he was angry.

"No." He rubbed his five o'clock shadow and crossed his arms in front of his chest. "Brooke!" he yelled down the hall. "Hurry it up!"

I shimmied off the pajama bottoms and wrote a note on Paul's dresser saying sorry and asking him to bring my book bag into school the next day since it was still in his mom's van.

Gina and Lou were expressionless as I shuffled past them. I looked at Paul in fleeting glances as Dad walked out the door in front of me.

I looked back, once, in an attempt to apologize. Their eyes told me I didn't have to. I squeezed Paul's hand and readied myself for the long night ahead as I trudged out the front door.

Chapter Eleven

"Everything you hear about cheerleaders is true." I slammed my tray down next to Cristin and looked around the cafeteria to make sure no one else had heard me. "They're so petty. I mean, it's not like I tried out thinking I was going to take over some girl's spot to be a flyer. It's not my fault I weigh twenty pounds less than the other girl." I munched on the skin of an apple, and then slid my tray out in front of me. "I can't even eat I'm so annoyed!"

"Whoa, don't take it out on the apple." Cristin snatched it from my hand and replaced it with a piece of her chocolate chip cookie. "This'll help you gain a little weight. Then you won't have to worry about those girls lifting you up into the air anymore. Problem solved."

I wrinkled my nose at her.

"Okay, I know. They're horrible," she assured me. "How many games are left before the season's over?"

"Two."

"Ah ha, see? You'll be fine. Just punch them in the face next time they drop you *on purpose*, I don't like that."

"*You* don't? I'm the one they keep dropping."

During the last practice, Coach insisted I try a stunt called a Liberty. Instead of having both feet securely placed in my bases' hands, I had to raise one leg and support everything on just the one foot. The flyer position I 'took over' left the disgruntled ex-flyer as one of my bases. Obviously still upset over Coach's choice, she fumbled me as I nailed a Liberty on my first try. If it weren't for

Coach standing right in front of me, I would have added a dramatic face plant as my finishing stunt.

"I'll punch them in the face." Paul took a seat next to me as Judd slipped in next to him.

"I'll pamper their wounds when you're finished," Judd offered. He winked at me. "You know, take care of them, do massages and whatever. You break em' and I'll nurse them back to health with my sweet lovin'."

Judd and I hadn't talked much since Paul and I officially became a couple. Cristin said he was bitter he missed his chance. I never even knew he wanted one.

"Brooke, they're just jealous you look bangin' in your little cheering outfit," Sonia said, pointing to the emblem spread across my chest. "Why you gotta wear that thing all the time anyway?"

"For team spirit," I said, tilting my head to the side and forcing a wide-toothed grin.

"Who said Brooke's bangin'? I'll punch them too." Paul ripped into his chicken patty and darted glances at me.

Sonia rolled her eyes. "No one, Romeo. Take it easy."

The bell rang and the cafeteria turned into a swarm of chatter as everyone gravitated towards the double doors. Walking next to Paul, I grazed his hand with mine. "Coming to my locker?"

"Nah." He searched through the sea of people. "Gotta meet Chalky. See ya."

I tried not to let his mood bother me but my heart sank a little as he pushed through the double doors and went in the opposite direction of my next class. We had been dating several months and we had been arguing over the fact that his buddies were hounding him to share stories of our sex life—but we didn't have one. When I told him I wanted to wait, his solution to protect his ego was to tell his buddies that we were having sex anyway. "Just to get them off my back," he said. "I don't get why we have to wait though, but whatever."

"I'll walk you to your class, loner." Judd appeared and grabbed my book bag. "What do you have in there, bricks?" He pretended the bag was too heavy and fell to the floor. "It's...too heavy. I can't go on. Just...go Brooke. Remember me."

"I'll remember you," said a cafeteria aide, nudging Judd with her foot. "Up, Judd. Or you can stay behind with me to visit the principal."

Judd bounced up off the floor. "Ah look at that, I suddenly have superhuman strength. Thanks Bertha!" He winked at the cafeteria aide and led me to my next class.

* * *

Paul and I walked to his house in silence after school. When we got there, he went straight to his room and shut the door behind him. I stood in the hallway, waiting for him to remember that I was out there.

Annoyed, I knocked on the door. "Paul? What's wrong?"

Silence.

"Can I come in?"

His bed creaked and I heard the TV come on. I opened the door and his back was to me. His hood was up over his head and he had wrapped the blankets around his body. If he were any more closed off I would have needed a can opener.

"What's up?" I sat down next to him as he looked past me and flipped through channels. His face was serious, and he pulled his hood down lower in response.

"You've been acting weird all day. What's wrong?"

He looked at me and spoke in a sarcastic tone. "You're in my way. Cartoons are on."

"I don't understand."

"Nothing to understand."

"Do you want me to leave?"

"If you want to leave, then leave."

"Is this about the sex?"

"What sex? I'm certainly not having any."

"Paul, that's not fair."

"No, it's not."

I turned away from him. I didn't understand why it was so important to him that he could tell people we were having sex. The choice of topics among guys in the locker room were limited to sex or drugs. I assumed his stories were getting harder to make up since he didn't have any real experiences to share with everyone.

"Well I gotta get to work," I said.

"See ya."

Secretly I hoped he would get up or tell me to come back. His gaze stayed on the TV and he continued to flick through channels as I closed the door behind me.

"What's wrong, Brooke?" My boss circled my desk and gave me a face. "You've been here two hours and haven't made one appointment? You usually have five by now. Are you feeling okay?"

I jumped at the opportunity to possibly go home early. "Oh, no. Not really. I'm feeling kind of sick." I rubbed my stomach for visual confirmation.

"All right. Give it another half hour. If you don't book anything, call it a day."

Making sure I was a safe distance from the office, I sprinted in the direction of Paul's house. He refused to answer any texts I sent him during work, and I wanted to talk. Gina answered the door, looking confused. "Hey, honey. You know Paul's not here right?"

My heart sank. "Oh yeah. I know," I lied. "I got out of work early and thought if I stopped by and called him he would want to hang out."

Gina nodded and opened the door. "All right, but he only left to go to Mack's house about an hour ago. Give him a call."

I held my breath as I dialed Paul's number. After the fourth ring he picked up. I was met with an irritated tone. "What?"

"Hey, it's me."

Silence.

"I got out of work early, so I stopped by to see if you wanted to hang out."

"You're at my *house*?"

"Well, yeah I figured—"

"Why would you go there? Didn't you get the hint when I didn't answer your texts?"

His honesty hurt. "You were purposely ignoring me?"

"Look, I don't have time for this. Bye."

I held the phone against my face for another minute, unwilling to believe that he had just hung up on me. I re-dialed his number and it went to voicemail after a few rings. When I tried again, it went straight to voicemail. He had turned off his phone.

I sat on his bed trying to decide what to do when Gina came to the door. "He's not coming back?"

I didn't want to hear the disappointment in my own voice so I just nodded. Gina saw right through it.

"Okay, well we're going to eat. Come join us."

Lou was already helping himself to seconds of salad when I sat down. As I tried to figure out what to do with Paul, Gina's voice interrupted my thoughts. "So, how are things at home?"

The question caught me off guard.

"Oh. Good?"

"Oh." Gina nodded. "Everything, you know, going okay?"

I moved my fork around. "Yep. Everything's good." My face never cooperated with my lies, and I hated the heat that started to flow over my cheeks.

"Good. That's good." Gina gulped her wine. "You and your dad get along?"

My mouth opened but Lou interrupted. "All right, well, looks like we're done here. Joseph, you want to help clean up?" He pushed himself away from the table and Gina nodded following suit.

The front door opened and Paul bounded up the stairs. He didn't notice I was sitting there at first but when he did threw his hands up. "You! What are you still doing here?"

"Paul!" Gina glared at him.

"What? I didn't invite her. She just shows up and thinks she can have dinner with my family and not tell me? This isn't her family."

He looked at me. "This isn't your family. Go be with your own. No one wants you here." He stormed off towards his room and slammed the door, vibrating the house.

Lou slid his chair back and flicked his napkin onto his plate. "I'll talk to him."

Gina picked up plates from the table. "I'm sorry, honey. I don't know what his problem is. Lou will talk to him."

Some yelling floated down the hallway, and then it got quiet. After a few minutes, Lou appeared and ran his fingers through his hair. "All right hun, uh, why don't you go ahead and bring Brooke home."

He shook his head at me. "Sorry, he just doesn't want to talk right now."

Gina backed the minivan out of the driveway and headed towards my house. The tension between Paul and me was crushing. I had no idea what I did to make him so angry.

"Don't worry about him," Gina said. I always felt like she could read my mind. "I'll talk to him when I get home. He has no business talking to you like that."

I nodded and said nothing. We passed the main part of town and I focused on anything that was outside the window.

"So how are things at home, really?"

It was the second time she had asked me, and I still didn't know how to answer her. I wanted to trust her. Over the past few months we had become fairly close. Paul said it was because she always wanted a daughter. I thought it was because she picked up on something that she couldn't quite put her finger on and wanted to know more about me. Either way, I enjoyed the long talks we got to have whenever she would drive me home, which was starting to become an every night thing.

"Sometimes I feel like I don't belong in my family."

Gina nodded but said nothing. She was an excellent listener.

"I don't know." I shrugged. "You know my mom is pregnant, and I have a lot of things going on. Sometimes it's just a lot."

"You're a strong person." Gina turned into my development. "You take on a lot of responsibility for your age from what you and Paulie tell me. Strong people sometimes have to make hard decisions because they can't rely on anyone else. But God only gives you what you can handle, nothing more, nothing less."

"Yeah." I sighed as we came to a stop in my driveway.

"I'll always listen. You know that?" I nodded and she brushed my cheek. "See you tomorrow, sweetheart."

* * *

Adam got his license and started driving to school in the mornings. I felt distant from him ever since we moved to Pennsylvania. He found a group of friends that dressed in skull clothing and painted their nails black. They listened to screaming rock music. We started to have less and less in common and I barely saw him. When he got his license I figured we could spend time together if he drove me around, so I lied about not having rides to and from places just so I could have some quality time with him.

I thought about what Gina said as Adam drove me over to Paul's house one weekend. Maybe if I wasn't strong enough to face what was going on at our house alone, I would feel better knowing I had an ally. Who better to support me than my own brother?

"I don't understand why Dad has to scream so much. Most of the time I just block him out." Adam fiddled with the radio and paid little attention to the conversation I was trying to start. "Is it me or is he really loud?"

"Yeah, he's loud."

"I hate when he screams. Don't you?"

"I guess so."

"You guess?" I sighed and tried to go in another direction. "I hate when he hits you guys."

"Yeah I bet. He never hits you." His tone was flat.

"Yeah...he treats us different."

"Just you, Brooke."

I was sure there was animosity in his tone that time.

"What is that supposed to mean?"

"It means you're the favorite. You always get what you want, when you want it."

"I do not."

Adam whistled. "Someone's in denial. Tell me, when's the last time you said 'Daddy, I really want the kind of sneakers Cristin has' or 'Daddy, I want to go on the field trip that costs fifty dollars' and he told you no?" Adam shook his head. "We all know you're the favorite. I'm surprised you don't."

He was right.

Anything I wanted, I always got it. I never realized how often he told Adam, Thomas, and Kat 'no', but now that he pointed it out, it was often.

It was different with me. There were special bedtimes, special Christmas gifts, and other things they never got. Adam pointed out that I had a little more control over Dad than I thought I did. Anything I wanted, to keep his secret, was mine. All I had to do was ask.

"I guess I didn't notice that before," I said.

Adam pulled into Paul's driveway and unlocked the car doors. "Well, now you know."

I gripped the door handle and looked into Adam's sea-blue eyes. He looked worn, like me, but his eyes didn't have the spark that mine did. There were burning questions behind my eyes, ever since dinner at Paul's. It pushed me to start questioning and probing. I started re-evaluating my family, and I tried piecing together the new information like a scrambled jigsaw puzzle.

"Yeah. I do know now. Thanks, Adam."

He looked confused as I hopped out of the car.

Paul was propped up on his bed with the TV on when I walked into his room. He looked at me and his eyes told me he was sorry. I didn't call or text for two days after he had yelled at me, and I think my silence scared him. He held out his arms without saying anything, and I more than eagerly fell into them.

"I'm sorry." He kissed my forehead. "The guys have been giving me a lot of pressure lately. I'm the only virgin and they keep asking for details."

I ran my fingers over his arms. "I know. I just don't feel comfortable with them knowing details like that about us. It's private, between us, ya know? It's not that I don't want to."

He nodded and pulled my face closer to his. After a few minutes of kissing his hands caressed my sides and flowed down to linger over my zipper. I held my breath as his fingertips slid under the top of my jeans and I pushed his hand away. "Your mom—"

"Won't be home for another hour," he finished.

"Do you have…?"

"Yes."

Using one arm he slid me underneath him and put his other hand through my hair. His lips were searching, needing, all over my face and down my neck. I pulled at his shirt and it dropped to the floor.

He lifted me upward and slid his hand underneath my shirt. His chest pressed firmly against mine, as he coaxed our bodies to fuse together. My skin danced with every detailed movement he made and I moaned, softly, making him rise against my leg in response. We both wanted it. When I felt him inside me, I eased into his rhythm and sank deeper.

We sprawled across the bed afterwards, smiling, and holding each other's hand. He brushed a piece of hair from my face and molded my lips into his. "I love you, Brooke."

I closed my eyes. I didn't tell him previously, but I had wanted to hear him say those three words, sincerely, before I gave myself to him. The timing was perfect.

"Hey, let's get our clothes on. My mom'll be home soon." He reached for my shirt and threw it towards me, facing away as he slid his pants on.

"Hey. Wait a minute."

I pulled my shirt on. "Yeah?"

He looked down at himself. Then at me. "Something's not right."

"What do you mean?"

"I don't know. I mean, I guess everyone is different but—" He continued to look down and check things out.

"What's wrong?" I started to panic. *Did he know?*

"I mean, the guys just told me how cool it was to pop a girl's cherry. And since we're both virgins, I thought it would be like what happened with them."

"It's not?"

"There's no blood."

"Huh?"

"I don't have any blood on me. There's no blood." He pointed into his boxers.

I realized he was talking about me not being a virgin. What could I say?

"Yeah, um. I mean I don't think that happens to every girl. Just some of them."

"Really?" Paul pulled his shirt on to hide the disappointment in his face.

"Yeah, I'm a girl. I would know." It wasn't a total lie.

"Oh. Well, okay. Are you feeling all right?"

I sighed at the change of subject. Paul had given me the perfect opportunity to explain my dad, the house I grew up in, and all about my childhood. The moment of truth presented itself, but I didn't want to remember my first time like that.

My *real* first time.

Instead I vowed to tell someone soon, anyone, it didn't matter. I wasn't sure to what extent my life was different from everyone else's, but the only way I would find out was to talk to someone about it. I nodded my head and pulled Paul closer.

"Never better," I said, kissing his lips.

Chapter Twelve

"Did it hurt? Were you scared? Did you make weird noises? No one was home, right?" Cristin asked, continuing her game of twenty-one questions after I made the mistake of telling her that Paul and I had sex.

I wanted to dodge the inevitability of people talking about my sex life, so I waited until school was over to tell my best friend. I munched on a tortilla chip and twirled around on the chair in her bedroom. It was tradition to have a sleepover on the first night of summer vacation when the school year ended. I had waited over a month to tell Cristin, but she would never know the difference.

"Jeez, you would think this concept is new to you," I teased. "You would think you *never* had sex before."

Cristin rolled her eyes. "Well of course *I* have had sex before, I just never thought *you* would."

"We waited ten months."

"I know." She shook her head. "Poor kid."

We both laughed.

"Why'd you wait that long anyway?" she asked.

I shrugged. "I don't know. I wanted to make sure he wasn't going to get what he wanted and bail. I knew if he stuck around this long, it wasn't just for the sex."

Cristin twirled a piece of her hair like she often did when she considered something. "True. Good point. I should try that sometime. So anyway, when is your mom due? I saw her at the grocery store last week and she looked like she was about to burst."

"Any day now. Hopefully not before I get back from my aunt's though, I want to be there."

"You're going for a week?"

"Yeah. Just to get away. She paid for the airline ticket and *then* asked my parents if I could go to Florida. She said she needed help with my cousins, so they didn't really have a choice but to say yes." I tapped my foot thinking about the warm weather and ocean. "I'm excited."

"To scope out the cute guys there?"

"To see my cousins."

Cristin slid off the bed and cocked one hip to the side to study the library of movies she had on her shelves. "Wanna watch something? I'm not tired yet."

"Sure. Pick whatever."

I crumpled the chip bag and set it on the floor next to her bedroom door so we'd remember to bring it down to the kitchen. Cristin's mom had inquired about my mom's pregnancy earlier.

"So there are quite a few years between the baby and Kat, huh? It's almost like he'll be an only child. Everyone else will be all grown up by the time he's your age." She smiled as if what she said was pleasant news, but she brought up a point I hadn't thought of.

This baby was going to be on his own, living in the house by himself while I was off at college and starting my life. There would be no one there to protect him. We would all be older and moved out by then. He would have to face Dad alone. The thought gave me a sense of urgency, that maybe I should start to gauge people's reactions about what was happening in my house. The thought turned my stomach, but I needed to know if the relationship I had with my dad was any different from the one Cristin had with her dad.

"You okay? You eat too many chips or something?" Cristin slipped a DVD in and grabbed the remote before joining me on the bed. She propped up some pillows and crossed her ankles.

"Yeah, maybe. I'm okay." I clenched my hand in a fist and silently rehearsed what I needed to say one more time. "Cristin, can I ask you something?"

"Sure. Shoot." The number four was jammed on the remote and she pressed the input button with hatred to get the TV to switch over.

I couldn't look at her when I said it. "Have you ever had a dream that your dad comes into your room?"

She looked at me. "Hmm, my dad coming into my room?"

The length of time that passed while she considered the question was agonizing. *What if she asks me why? What if she doesn't believe me? Her dad is so nice, there's no way she could understand.*

"I had a dream my dad showed up to school with a My Little Pony lunchbox once. Horrifying. Does that count?"

Her response confirmed what I was dreading.

For anyone who wasn't experiencing what I was, they didn't even consider the question I posed to have any deeper meaning than it did. The last thing on her mind was that something sexual or physical needed to be explained. Instead, she took the question as innocently as I had given it to her.

If Cristin would have asked me if I ever had a dream that my father was in my room, my first question would have been 'To do what?' Our minds were in completely different places. For Cristin's sake, I was glad they were.

A similar feeling to the one I had when Adam didn't understand what I was saying presented itself. Every person I told, when they didn't take the bait I was taunting them with, gave me one more reason to keep looking for answers. Maybe I needed to say something different, or try again to find someone who knew exactly what I was asking and meant without even needing to say it out loud. There had to be someone.

I gave her a crooked smile. "Could have been worse. He could have shown up with a Barney lunch box."

She fumbled around with the remote and clicked the lamp off that was next to her. "Ah, very true."

***

My plane touched down in Florida and I cruised through the airport toward the baggage claim signs. I spotted Aunt Nikki waiting several feet away and quickened my pace.

"Ohh beautiful how was your flight?" She pulled me close and then held me back at arm's length. "You're stunning, and so tall! I haven't seen you in almost two years."

"I know!" I beamed at her. Aunt Nikki was Mom's youngest sister. There wasn't much of an age difference between us. She knew all the latest music and style trends. I could guarantee a shopping spree was in my near future.

"Uncle Jake has the car waiting so let's grab your things and hurry hurry hurry."

I shut the car door and Uncle Jake turned to look at me. "Wow, look how big you are. Everyone grows up so fast. Sorry I couldn't get out to give you a hug, they were giving me a hard time about sitting here with the car."

Once on the highway we chatted about school and work until we pulled into their development.

"The boys still have one more week of daycare." Aunt Nikki turned and winked at me. "I figured it would give us time during the day to catch up and do some girl things."

I nodded and winked back at her. I knew when she told my mom and dad she needed me to visit to help her with the kids it was a ploy. She was always a more than capable mother.

After my cousins went to bed that night, Aunt Nikki and I caught up on the current events of our lives out on her expansive deck.

"You're sixteen, aren't you?" Aunt Nikki said, taking the recliner next to me while passing me a glass of white wine.

"Fifteen. What's this?"

"Expensive. Just drink it."

We both laughed.

I had been here before; the peaceful charade of chatting and laughing through superficial topics as my life was in turmoil.

She had on pressed khakis and a tailored blouse. She wore minimal makeup and you would never guess that she was Irish with her sun-bronzed skin. Her tennis rackets leaned against the house on the other side of the porch. I imagined her with her trainer that morning, gushing about her favorite niece that was coming to visit later that day. The house was immaculate, dinner was perfect, and the wine was dangerously smooth.

We sipped and made comments about the gorgeous weather and my aunt's ten-pound weight gain. It trailed off into talk of boys and honors classes, with the conversation ending where it always did.

"So your mom is due any day now, huh?"

"Probably next week. Hopefully. I don't want to miss it."

"I know you don't." She swirled her glass. "It was definitely a surprise to the family that she was pregnant again. We all told her we didn't think it was a good idea."

I was only aware of a few times that Mom had asked my aunts and uncles for money. Since she broke her back, we had lived off of Dad's income exclusively. Money was the main reason why the family didn't approve of the pregnancy, but so was her deteriorating health.

"She smokes like a Banshee and has a broken back. I'll never understand her." Aunt Nikki cracked her neck. "We all told her, you know, that we would pay for her to take care of it. When she first found out she was pregnant. Health wise, I didn't think she could manage another pregnancy and baby."

Mom never told me that my aunts and uncles offered to pay for an abortion, but it didn't surprise me. Uncle Bruce was shocked when he found out. He called my dad a number of names before telling my mom she was making a big mistake. No one seemed happy about the pregnancy except me.

"She's stubborn." I wet my lips with wine. "You know I'll be there to help her though, everything will be okay."

Aunt Nikki turned towards me and put down her empty wine glass. She held up both hands. "Ah, Brooke you're so…" She smoothed her hair and her eyes glimmered with barely-there tears. "You're so mature. And together. I envy you." She sighed. "How are things with your dad?"

I sucked in a breath.

Great. Fine. Wonderful. It's okay.

As I tried to figure out which lie to use, I realized I paused one second too long.

"Brooke?"

I twisted my hands around my wine glass. "They're…okay."

Whenever Dad got brought up in any conversation I would offer the answers that everyone wanted to hear. I looked at Aunt Nikki. This time, I didn't want to try and mask it.

I forced her to recognize the change in my demeanor. My eyes pleaded with her to probe further, to ask me more questions. I wanted her to serve more wine so I could tell her the truth. I couldn't say what I needed to out loud on my own. I needed her to ask. I needed someone to notice the changes in my face and run with my hints.

The questions never came though.

Aunt Nikki slid the back door open and grabbed the bottle of wine. She topped off my glass and sat down with the bottle between her legs. "We'll go shopping tomorrow." The bottle tipped into her mouth and—without looking at me again—she slid down into her recliner. "When in doubt, go shopping."

Aunt Nikki had to buy me a new suitcase so I could lug all the new clothes back to Pennsylvania when the week ended. She pushed a strand of blonde hair behind her ear as she made me promise to make sure I visit at least once a year, to call her because she would forget, and that she loved me.

On the plane I had a chance to regroup. Dad never got brought up again, even though I tried one more time while we were making dinner the night before I left. I was beginning to think that I would never be strong enough to admit to anything, and that even if I put out an S.O.S with fireworks, whoever I was trying to tell just wouldn't understand.

I constructed a Plan B. After high school I would find a college as far away from Pennsylvania as I could. I would tell Kat what was going on right before I left so she could move out, and I wouldn't let myself get attached to the new baby enough to care. I was starting to feel broken down and for the first time the thought of leaving everything behind and never coming back put a smile on my face.

They wanted to induce Mom's labor a few days after I got home since they were concerned that if they let her go into natural labor it would be harder to manage because of her back. Mom and Dad left around seven that night to go to the hospital, and Grandma came up from Long Island to help Mom with the baby after she got home.

Around eleven that night we still didn't hear anything from the hospital, but a lot of family kept calling to ask. Grandma and I decided to put everyone in bed, and since I knew she could sleep through a tornado, I offered to keep the phone by my pillow for when they called.

At three in the morning the phone screamed next to me and I jumped up. "Hello? Dad? Is the baby here?"

"Put Grandma on, Brooke."

"Okay. Did Mom have the baby?"

"Brooke." His voice was barely above a whisper. "Wake up Grandma and put her on."

I fled down the stairs and shook Grandma awake, handing her the phone. She covered her eyes against the living room light I had flicked on and before she could speak she fell quiet. She pressed the phone to her ear and tears started falling.

It wasn't until Dad came home two hours later that I realized the seriousness of what had happened to Mom. Grandma wouldn't tell me anything even though she hung up with my dad and started calling all my aunts and uncles, telling them they needed to get to Pennsylvania as soon as possible.

When Dad walked through the door, his eyes were red and he led Adam and me into the kitchen. "Mom had somewhat of a heart attack. She lost a lot of blood. A lot. She's on a respirator 'cause she can't breathe on her own." Several family members had shown up and everyone crowded in the kitchen.

"Everything was going perfect until the last three minutes. Mom kept saying she felt like she was going to pass out, so the nurse put an oxygen mask on her. She kept trying to pull it off." He wiped a tear from the scruff on his cheek. "Then, the baby came out. He wasn't breathing. The nurses tried to revive him, and then suddenly Molly just got limp in my arms." He held up his arms to show where she had been laying. "She turned blue. The doctor just stood there a minute, like he didn't know what to do. They asked me to leave. A few minutes later a nurse came out and told me that if she had any family that I should tell them to come to the hospital. They're convinced she isn't going to make it."

"Did the baby die?" I was the first to ask a question.

Dad nodded. "For ten minutes he did. They were able to get him back and he's on a respirator too. They worked on Mom for over fifteen minutes before they got her back."

Moms don't die.

Mine couldn't. She broke her back and had shingles. She popped pills to keep functioning and popped pills to keep numb. She had leg surgery and foot surgery. She always made it seem like she *could* die because of whatever sickness or injury she had at the time, but she never did. The one time she's sure she'll be back, and something goes horribly wrong?

As family members filed through the house Dad had to re-tell his story several times. It wasn't until the third or fourth time I heard it that everything started to sink in. Mom was leaving us. She was going to die. I leaned on my grandma, traumatized, unable to cry. Grandma looked down at me, for the first time looking old.

"Okay," Dad said. "Let's organize into groups to head up to the hospital."

After three cars of people were claimed and a friend of the family offered to stay behind to cook and watch after the kids, I pushed my way to the front of the crowd.

"Dad? Can I go to the hospital?"

He shifted the glasses on his face. "Well, I um, I'd really rather you didn't."

I locked eyes with Grandma and pleaded with her. She shook her head.

"David," she started, "I think Adam and Brooke are old enough to make this decision, and I think, considering the circumstances, that if they feel they need to go... then they should."

Grandma was afraid that if Mom died I would need to say goodbye. Dad was afraid that if Mom were on her deathbed, I would make it a point to tell her everything. Absolutely everything.

They were both right.

He shifted his weight and looked down at his watch. My aunts and uncles nodded in agreement with Grandma and left him little choice. "Well, if you want to go."

Dad insisted I ride with him, Adam and Grandma. "Dad, I don't want to ask, but..."

"You should."

"What are the chances Mom's going to die?"

"Right now, about eighty-five percent is what the doctor said."

Dad hustled us down long hallways to a door marked *Waiting Room*. He waited until everyone was inside and looked at the packed room of family. "Who wants to go first?"

I wanted to scream out that I did, but I was scared. Since only two people were allowed in at a time with my dad, Grandma and Grandpa claimed the first visit. I settled into a leather chair instead. One unimpressive light buzzed overhead and nobody bothered to put on more lights. The soda machine hummed in one corner and I turned my nose up at the smell of latex that floated through the room. I hated that everyone sat in silence, heads hung low. It reminded me of a funeral home and we weren't even there yet.

The door opened and Grandma needed help getting to a chair to sit down because she was crying so hard. My stomach twisted to see her like that; I had never seen her cry before. Adam remained motionless in one corner of the room and my stomach flipped every time the door opened and someone else came in from seeing her. Adam and I were next to go in.

"Now, before I take you in," Dad said, "I want you to know that Mom doesn't look like herself. She's very swollen because of all the medication."

I'm not a child, and I can handle this. Stop talking to me like I don't understand.

We pushed through the ICU doors and I tried to calm my heart. She was in the second room on the right. After shutting the door, Dad led us around a curtain.

I wish I hadn't gone inside. She was lying on the bed motionless. It wasn't my mom at all. Tubes emerged from her neck, mouth, nose, and hands—anywhere they could stick her. Life sustaining fluids ballooned her eyes and face beyond recognition. Her eyes sloshed off to the sides, seemingly heavy and devoid of life. There was a thick blue tube between her teeth and the pump next to her bed pushed air in and out of her lungs.

I couldn't see through my tears to make it over to her bedside, so Adam led me to her. I reached out for her hand, careful not to touch any IVs.

"Ohhhh," I cried, and I couldn't talk. An orchestra of monitors drowned out my sobs as I tried to make sense of the beeping and zigzagging lines.

A doctor pushed past the curtain and whispered to my dad for a minute before asking if Adam and I had any questions.

"Why won't she wake up?" I asked, wiping my nose on my sleeve.

He looked at my dad. "We have to keep her sedated, sweetheart. It means asleep. We have to keep her asleep with medicine that way she can rest and heal. She would be in too much pain if she were awake."

Aunt Nikki arrived when Adam and I made our way into the waiting room. "I got on the first flight I could." She hugged me briefly before being whisked away into the ICU. The afternoon went on like that. Family coming in and out, crying, falling asleep in the stiff leather seats in the waiting room, and then doing it all over again.

"Dad, can I see the baby?" I asked.

He nodded and we walked down to the NICU where he was staying. I had never seen a baby so fragile looking, and he had just as many tubes sticking out of his skin as Mom did. 'BOY NOLAN' was printed on the side of his bassinet. A nurse appeared and asked my dad if he knew the name yet. He rubbed his chin and turned to walk out of the room. "I don't care. Brooke, you name it."

I looked at him as he walked out the door, not sure I had heard him right. When I looked at the nurse she was smiling at me, pen poised, waiting to write down a name. Mom and I had talked about a few names here and there but nothing really jumped out at us.

"Ethan," I said. "His name will be Ethan."

Sometime after six someone mentioned something about a shower and food and it seemed like a good idea, so a few of us packed into cars and made our way back to the house. Uncle Bruce started up the grill and I passed out on the couch. I didn't realize I slept so late and when I woke up dinner was over and everyone was hustling to get back to the hospital. Mentally exhausted, I stayed behind with Aunt Nikki.

The crying and running around didn't stop for weeks. My aunts and uncles took turns feeding the kids, keeping us entertained, and visiting the hospital. Aunt Jean came home with news that the respirator had come out.

Not even two days later Uncle Jake walked into the waiting room to address everyone. He was smiling. "Well, she's awake. She must be feeling better because she's cursing at the doctor and asking for a cigarette."

I wanted to see her right away so I was led back into her room. Mom's eyes were slits of dark space, barely open, but she was awake. I needed to see her awake with my own eyes. My instinct was to cry or scream from the relief but I couldn't. I found myself slumped over the rail of her bed, pressing my face into her shoulder just breathing her in.

She slurred incomprehensible ramblings between curse words, and kept crying out in pain over tubes that were coming from her groin area. When they started to wean her off the drugs she finally realized who I was and broke down crying. She was propped up on a pillow and was able to get her arms around me for the first time.

I fell back into a chair that was sitting next to her bed and sighed. A doctor came in, briefly, and mentioned something about a lung surgery to clear up an infection she developed from being laid up for so long. They scheduled it for two weeks later when they felt she would be strong enough to withstand the anesthesia. The doctor shook his head at my mom. "I don't know how you're alive, never mind awake and talking. What a miracle."

Dad looked at me while he held Mom's hand.

He winked.

I felt defeated. There were ample opportunities to talk to one of my aunts during those grim weeks of watching my mom fight for her life and I didn't; it wouldn't have been fair to Mom. She was the one suffering and trying to get better. My family was in turmoil, an emotional mess, and the last thing I wanted to do was ask them to deal with another crisis. I felt like the timing would never be right.

I pushed those thoughts to the back of my head as Mom reached out and motioned for me to take her hand. Her hand encased mine and I brought her hand up to my lips. "Welcome back, Mom."

Chapter Thirteen

I thought it was a miracle that baby Ethan was born in the beginning of summer. Mom eventually came home with visiting nurses that stopped by once or twice a week. Dad returned to his normal work schedule and most of the family that had been staying with us was long gone. The majority of Ethan's care became my responsibility.

The first night Ethan was home I got up every two hours to feed and change him. Dad wanted little to do with him, Mom couldn't, and my other siblings didn't want the responsibility. In a little over a month I was a diaper guru and bottle warmer extraordinaire. It was impossible to situate him on my non-existent hips while I cooked dinner, but I could undress, scrub, and clothe him before he realized he hit the water for bath time.

I was exhausted. Paul took the back burner and the only time I saw him was when he came over to my house, which wasn't often. I missed him, even when we started fighting over what he did with his free time, which consisted of experimenting with alcohol and weed.

Cristin would come over to hold Ethan and play with him and, more than once, I would find myself asleep with him on my chest in the living room or on my bedroom floor while I folded laundry.

I cradled him on my lap as I typed up book reports for my English Honors class that upcoming year. He accompanied me in the bathroom, while I cleaned the house, and when I played with Kat and Thomas. I bathed him, dressed him, burped him, and rocked him when he had an upset stomach.

I fell in love with him.

I became so engrossed in watching Ethan breathe and grow that it took me about two months to realize I couldn't remember the last time I had my period. Dad left for work that night and Ethan had just taken his last bottle. When everyone else was asleep, I sat at the desk in the kitchen and turned the computer on, placing the baby monitor next to me.

It roared to life and I waited the ten minutes it usually took to boot up. A few clicks later I opened up Google. I wasn't sure what I was looking for so I typed in 'LATE PERIOD.'

Several websites popped up. The top three hits flashed titles of pregnancy-related late periods and menstrual cycles. I opened the first link and scanned the article.

"Yes, your missed period might be because you're pregnant! A simple pregnancy test can usually help you determine if you have missed your period because you are pregnant."

Clicking the x in the corner of the screen I shook my head and looked for information elsewhere. Another article caught my attention. I read on:

"Pregnancy due dates can be determined by knowing the first day of your last period with a simple online due date calculator. Prenatal care is extremely important in the first trimester."

That article disappeared just as fast and I scrambled to type in 'PREGNANCY CALCULATOR.' I couldn't think straight but I remembered my last period being in June, right before I went to Florida.

"All right. Figure June eighteenth, just to be safe," I whispered out loud. I scrolled through the date selections and turned away from the screen when the results popped up:

Congratulations!
Your baby is due on or around: MARCH 24th
You are currently: 7 ½ weeks pregnant
Symptoms at this time: Constipation, light-headedness, some nausea...

As if on cue, I leapt from the computer chair and ran to the bathroom. After a few minutes, I wiped my mouth and splashed cold water on my face. This couldn't be happening. Paul and I hadn't had sex in months, way before I could have gotten pregnant.

Weary, I headed back into the kitchen to grab the baby monitor that had started to glow a soft green. Ethan was awake. I didn't have time to deal with anything.

I fought sleep that night thinking about the possibility that I might be pregnant. My hand stretched across my stomach and I begged for my period to just be late and to show its ugly face the next day. When it didn't, I put it off for three more days before the nausea and exhaustion were indication enough. I knew I was carrying Dad's baby.

Eyes sore from crying, I cradled my stomach as I tortured myself on what to do next. Who was ever going to believe this? I couldn't just ask someone to drive me to the pharmacy to get a pregnancy test.

Who was going to take care of Ethan? How could I hide this? I don't know anything about abortions or having a baby, I only take care of them when other people won't. Agonizing over what to do, I decided to call a friend first thing in the morning to drive me to a parenting center a few towns away. I needed to talk to a professional about what options I would have.

Drenched in sweat, a pain in my stomach shook me from my sleep that night. I grabbed my clock and turned it around; 2:47 a.m. Thinking it was a cramp and that my period was finally starting I turned over, relieved that I wouldn't need to visit the parenting center. Another jolt of pain shot down my back and around the front of my stomach.

"Ughhh," I moaned, trudging towards the bathroom, suddenly nauseous. When I didn't get sick, I sat and rocked myself on the toilet waiting for each wave of pain to pass. I stifled my voice as much as I could, trying not to cry out. The room started to sway. "Stay with it, Brooke. No one's here to pick you up off the floor if you pass out." I coached myself out loud, pinching the space between my eyes.

A rush of relief in my stomach was met with intense fear as I noticed all the blood. I knew it could only mean one thing. I remained motionless for a few more minutes, then started to sob uncontrollably as I shed my clothes and turned the shower on full blast. I placed myself on the bottom of the tub and watched the red sea of water stream out from underneath me and disappear down the drain.

My body rocked and swayed, and I found comfort in the pellets of water kissing my body. Still facing stomach cramps, I eventually stepped out of the shower and toweled off. I swallowed three ibuprofen and crept back to my bedroom. The clock was still facing me as I lay down, and it read 5:16 a.m. I had been in the bathroom for over two hours, and I was positive I had miscarried. I clicked on the heating pad I used for period cramps and drifted into sleep.

"Was that you taking a shower earlier?" Mom noticed my damp hair as I made my way into the kitchen around ten that morning. "You're not feeling good? Adam had to feed Ethan because you weren't awake."

I nodded, not bothering to look up. "I'm sick, Mom. I had to shower." I poured a glass of water and headed back upstairs. The world could have ended in that moment and I didn't care; I wasn't planning on leaving my bed.

So I didn't.

I didn't leave it the next day either, or the day after that.

"You don't have the flu." Mom pressed her lips to my forehead. "I haven't heard you throw up or anything. You've been in bed for three days."

I stared through her. I didn't even have the energy to humor her. There was no energy to lie, talk, or even care.

On the sixth day, when everyone was getting ready to go to an end of summer barbeque, I had lined up twenty-one pills on my bedroom floor. Composed of a concoction of Vicodin, Percocet, Ibuprofen, Oxycontin and Valium that I borrowed from Mom's medicine cabinet, I color-coded them before putting them all in a drinking glass.

The reality was that I had become so numb that I couldn't keep up with the charade anymore, the double life. I was David's second wife, his slave, his plaything—and not by choice. I failed to alert anyone I knew as to what was happening, and I didn't have the strength or words to explain to anyone what was going on. Terrified, I knew now that what was happening between Dad and me was not normal. It seemed like there was no way to stop it.

I had failed my brothers and sister. The honor roll student, mother's helper, cheerleader, perfect child was giving up. I opened my journal to the next clean page, ripped out a piece of paper and scrawled my last entry.

Your secret has died with me.

I set the paper down next to me. Defeated, I opened my mouth and listened as the pills slid toward the front of the glass. Harsh knocking on my bedroom door jolted me and I hid the cup behind the leg of my bed.

"What?" I yelled.

"Brooke." It was Kat. "Phone call."

I didn't care. "Take a message." I waited to hear footsteps walking away.

"It's Paul. He called three times already. He won't let me hang up."

I stuffed the note under my pillow and opened the bedroom door, grabbing the phone. "Okay. Now go away please." I sat cross-legged on the floor. "Hello?"

"I had a horrible dream about you last night. I never dream." His voice was panicked. "Look, I know you are going through a lot right now with your mom and the baby. And I haven't been there for you like I should have. I'm really sorry. All day I've had a stomachache thinking about you and what it would mean if I lost you. I've kinda been a jerk and I want to make it up to you, okay? Come over tomorrow night? Just you and me. No baby, no parents. My mom and dad are going to dinner and Joseph is going to a friend's house. Does that sound okay? I really want to see you."

I nodded into the phone as tears gushed down the sides of my face. Realizing he couldn't see me, I told him I thought it would be nice and hung up. I leaned forward and covered my face with my hands.

In a moment of weakness the only logical choice was to end my life. Where would that leave my siblings though? No one would protect them like I could. He would probably prey on Kat next, no doubt. What about Ethan? I shook my head. It would never happen, I would never let it.

I walked the cup into the bathroom and opened the lid of the toilet. I smiled as the colors swirled around and disappeared.

Things were going to change.

Chapter Fourteen

Paul and I spent a few hours catching up and laying around. I forgot how much I missed looking into his eyes and letting him make fun of me for my braces or tickling me until I couldn't breathe. We were both overly sarcastic with each other and everything with him just felt so easy. It was late when Gina told me she'd drive me home. "Stop calling me Mrs. Moretti. It's Gina, call me Gina."

Gina had figured out the longest possible route to get me home and we drove it often. I stretched out in the front seat and listened while she talked about her childhood on Staten Island and how she moved to the Poconos to give Paul and Joseph a better life. My parents had done the same thing, moving us from Long Island, but the perks of being isolated from everyone we knew had only recently became apparent to me.

I loved the way Gina dressed, like a business woman straight off the streets of New York City, but with the charm of a housewife. I never knew her to frown, or be sad, or show any emotion besides the bubbly character that she was. As per her request, I accompanied her to almost every hair and nail appointment she made. I was starting to think it was less because she needed my opinion and more because she wanted a stand-in daughter to do girly things with her.

Either way, she absorbed everything and anything I ever said with complete acceptance and I valued her opinion and her company more than anything. There was never any doubt in her mind when I told her of my dreams to be a writer one day or to go to medical school. She reminded me of my grandma in that way. "You're smart, beautiful, and talented. You absolutely can do anything," she'd say.

Gina was also the first person to actually take note of the way I addressed my dad and the things going on in my family. She had a sixth sense, realizing when something was bothering me, but she would only call me out on it when we had our long car rides together. She was discreet like that.

"I told my mom that I wanted to talk to a counselor, like you said. She told me we couldn't afford it." I slowly started filling Gina in on things going on in my house. Small things. The yelling, the tension, and sometimes the electric getting turned off.

She started to do some observations of her own when she brought me home. She told me there were people whose job was to listen to children when they needed someone to talk to. They had confidentiality rules that the law held them to, so no matter what I said they would never tell my parents or anyone else if I didn't want them to. If we had insurance, sometimes it would even be free. The idea sounded too good to be true.

"So I told my mom about how insurance can cover the costs so we wouldn't have to pay, and she said there would still be a small co-pay when we would visit. She couldn't afford that either."

"I thought she might say something like that." Gina sighed and shook her head. "So I started looking around. Did you know most counties have free counseling services for people who have domestic or sexual violence issues in their house?"

I stiffened. "Uh, no, but what's domestic violence?" I was pretty sure I knew what sexual violence was. I wasn't too sure of the other word.

"I think maybe some of the things your dad does is domestic violence. It's when someone abuses the people they should love. Abuse can mean so many things, like threatening someone, hitting them, or controlling them by making them feel worthless." She tapped the steering wheel with her fingers.

"How do you know about all that?"

"I had a girlfriend in college who was in a very abusive relationship. She told me all kinds of things. She got the help she needed though and never had to see the guy again." I nodded and Gina continued. "Maybe we can call the place and make you an appointment. They're the experts, and you can figure things out with them."

"Are they free?" I already used most of my money every month to help Mom with her bills and I was trying to save for a car.

"Yes and they're confidential too. Just like any other counselor."

"I don't know how I would get there. Could you take me?"

I wasn't just asking her to drive me to the counseling center. I was asking her if I could trust her, if I could open up to her just a little bit more, by agreeing to go to a place that specialized in domestic and sexual violence. Whatever would be thrown at me when I went, I needed to know that she would be there for me. I couldn't do this alone, and I didn't want to.

Gina smiled. "Of course, of course I'll take you. Let me know when you're ready and I'll make the call."

We pulled up to the Women In Crisis building three weeks later. I figured it would be easier to explain where I was going if school had started. Gina could pick me up a half hour before school got out and I would be able to make it back in time for work.

The center was just an old Victorian home with a white sign on the lawn. A tire swing hung from the branches of one tree out front and the sidewalk sloped leading up to the doorway. Gina told me she would wait in the car for me, so I pushed open the heavy door to the waiting room and was greeted by the receptionist.

"Hi there, can I help you?" She smiled and looked behind me, likely looking for a parent.

"I'm Brooke. I have a 2:30 appointment."

The receptionist ran her finger over a thick schedule book and tapped the page. "Yep, here you are. I'll let her know you're here. Go ahead and take a seat."

I picked the closest chair to the entrance and gazed at all the toys and coloring books that littered the cramped waiting room. It looked like a lot of children went there.

"Brooke?" I was greeted by a wide smile and a soft tone. She was a hefty woman in a flower printed dress. Her skin contrasted the pale colors she was wearing and she reached out her hand. "I'm Midge. Want to follow me?"

I nodded and followed her up a steep staircase. "These steps ain't meant for us bigger women." She snickered at herself. "They need to make the stairs bigger or I need to make myself smaller."

We passed two other doors, one that had a sign on it: *Quiet Please, Sharing Is In Session*! I tried to calm my nerves by telling myself that if I didn't like it there, I never had to come back.

"Pick any seat you want. Except the black one, I sit there because my knees won't let me sit in the bean bags. But they are the most comfortable seats in the room."

I chose a chair not too close but not too far away from the black chair she mentioned she would be in.

"Whew, all right then. I'm Midge." Sweat glistened off her forehead, and she patted it with a tissue. "I'm so glad you're here, Brooke. It's not every day we get a brave girl like you to come in here by yourself. You know what kind of counseling center this is?"

"I think so."

Midge shook her head. "We work with all kinds of people here. Children, adults, teenagers." She pointed at me. "A lot of people come here looking for answers because something in their heart is telling them they've been wronged or that they deserve better." She leaned forward in her chair. "That sound about right, sweetheart?"

I nodded, smiling at the southern slang in her voice. Her demeanor and lingo almost made me doubt her professionalism, but the degrees and certifications hanging on the walls surrounding us told me otherwise.

"What brings you here all alone?" she asked.

"Well, I knew what insurance my parents had, so I looked up counselors in the area. There were a few but they had co-pays my mom didn't want to pay. But I needed to talk to someone. So my boyfriend's mom found this place."

"You looked up counselors based on your parents' insurance?"

"Yeah."

"How old are you again?" A smile spread across her face, like she was laughing inside.

"Fifteen."

"Mmmhmm. All right well before we get too deep, just a few things I need to tell you first so you know what to expect. We can meet for an hour today and any other day you want to come back and talk to me. There's never any charge, and everything we say in this room stays in this room under the law. You understand?"

I nodded. It was good to know.

"Now, there are a few exceptions." She held up her hand. "By law, I have to report the three following situations. If you tell me you're going to hurt yourself." She flipped up her index finger. "If you tell me you're going to hurt someone else, and if I suspect or you tell me about any child abuse. Reason being is you's only fifteen, you still a minor." She wiggled all three exceptions. "That's the only three times I can ever tell anyone about what we talk about in here. Understand?"

"Yeah." My heart dropped when she told me about having to report child abuse. I didn't know how I could talk to her without her needing to report something. I suddenly felt like I made the wrong choice. What if someone found out I was there? What if Gina told?

"Now look, I want you to know this is a safe place." She opened her arms and looked around the room. "There ain't one thing you can tell me that I haven't heard already and I've heard *a lot* of things. But no need to rush, I feel like we gon' be good friends you and me. I don't want to push you to tell me anything you ain't ready to tell. Sound good?"

I sighed and relaxed a little. Her accent made me feel like I was in a movie somewhere in the south, chatting with a friend over a glass of sweet tea.

"So, Brooke, tell me about yourself. Anything and everything you want to tell me, go ahead. If you got a question, go ahead and ask it." She rested her arms into the crest of her stomach and let me have the floor.

"I want to know what domestic and sexual violence is. How do you know if you're being abused? Like, what would it look like?" I tried to make my question hypothetical.

Midge nodded and pulled something out of a folder on her desk. "That's a great place to start. A great question."

She handed me a paper with a pie chart. In the center were the words *Power and Control* and each pie piece represented a different category of physical abuse.

"This is the best way to explain it, so you can see how domestic violence is a whole bunch of things put together and not everyone's situation is the same." She pointed to each section of the chart to explain them.

"This one is called emotional abuse. Not everyone is abused by getting hit or slapped around, no child. Some people get put down by being called names, or the abuser makes them feel like they crazy and that the abuse ain't happening."

She slid her finger across the pie chart. "This here is economic abuse. Abusers like to keep all the money and control. They dictate when and where a person can work or don't let their family have jobs at all because it lets them have outside relationships. Domestic violence can mean isolation or threats, too. The abuser will control who the other person sees or where they go or where they live. They make threats to hurt you. Or they'd say no one would believe you."

She moved her hand over to the last section of the pie chart. I leaned over in my chair in anticipation, hanging on every word.

"This here is sexual abuse. That's anytime someone make you do something with any private parts of your body that you don't want. An abuser can make people do things to *their* private parts too. It's all sexual abuse. Big thing to know is that if you don't want to do it and they make you, it's sexual abuse."

I shook as I tried to absorb everything. Midge explained my life story fairly accurately, according to a pie chart, and everything started to come together. The move to Pennsylvania, Dad's control of the money and food in the house, making it seem like nothing happened between us to the point that I felt like I was going crazy...It was all there. My trembling fingers reached out to take the chart from Midge.

"Okay." *How could I word my next question without outing myself?* I thought carefully before speaking. "What happens...if someone didn't know that this stuff was wrong? What happens if they didn't know they could say no? What if they thought this happened to everyone so they never knew they didn't have to do it?"

Midge narrowed her eyes and brought her body closer to mine. Her voice was smooth and reassuring. "Child, let me make one thing very clear. In the state of Pennsylvania—no child, not one— can ever consent to *anything* sexual if they under the age of sixteen and there's a four year or more age difference between the two people. Never. You understand?"

My brain bobbled around as she continued. "It don't matter if you didn't know, it don't matter if you never said no. What matters is they was breaking the law, that it's not your fault. You ain't the adult, child, you done no wrong."

I blinked away tears and focused on the paper-sized window on the far wall of the room. I nodded at Midge and we sat in silence for eternity. I think she could sense that we had an understanding. I was allowed to hide behind my hypothetical scenarios, as long as I would come back to see her.

She changed the subject as my bottom lip trembled with anxiety. "Tell me more about you. Tell me about your family and where you're from." The hour flew by and Midge had to hold up her hand to tell me we had to end our session for the day.

"Already?" I looked at the clock.

"Now look at you, already coming out of your shell. Let's go downstairs and schedule another appointment and you can come back here and tell me more about Long Island and your school and your big family." She meant it. Her eyes told me she wanted to see me again, even if all we did was talk about friends and teenage things. I asked her if I could keep the power wheel.

"I'd prefer if you did."

I scheduled my next appointment and rushed outside. As I flung the door open, Gina didn't even have to ask how it went. "I'm coming back next week. I made the appointment. You sure you can still take me? Maybe I can give you some gas money."

Gina held up her hand and told me to buckle up. "Nonsense. I'll take you as long as you need to."

I slept with the power wheel under my pillow. It served as a constant reminder, and I would check it every so often to make sure that what Midge had said was still there in black and white. A rush of empowering chatter danced throughout my head over the next couple of weeks. Rage flooded my veins when I would hear Dad downstairs beating on Thomas or Adam. Mom would beg for more money for food. The signs were all there, every piece of the pie chart slowly molding into my reality right before my eyes.

Midge and I met at the same time, once a week, until the end of tenth grade. I gave her Gina's cell phone number so if there was ever a cancellation or issue Midge could call and I didn't have to give her my house number.

Midge was right about one thing—we became good friends. I told her all about Paul and my job, my siblings and the role I had with them, and school. She knew what I wanted to be when I grew up, and she was impressed with the passion I had for writing.

What I liked best about Midge is that she never asked me to talk about my mom or dad unless I brought it up. For weeks we would talk about superficial things like football games and grades. Sometimes I would tell her about how my dad yelled or the way he shoved my brothers around, but the second I thought she was getting too interested, I reverted back to talking about my boyfriend and anatomy homework. She didn't mind, though. She'd rest her arms on her soft stomach, nodding and probing me, but she never pushed me.

So I kept going back for more.

Chapter Fifteen

I remember the night Dad found the power wheel under my pillow. I don't know why he was in my room or what he was looking for, but he found it.

He gripped the edges of the paper so hard that they crumbled in his hand. I probably could have cooked an egg on his face from the steam that appeared to surround him. There was little time to come up with an excuse, and even less time to react when he started to trash my room. Trembling, I stood my ground and watched my dresser get overturned, my vanity crash to pieces, and my belongings thrown in every direction.

When he finished, and after he tore the power wheel into specks the size of snowflakes, he charged at me. My body braced itself and I closed my eyes, but the impact never came. A rush of wind past my face and the smell of his aftershave following told me he was targeting someone else, anyone else. At this stage of the game, he finally understood how to get me where it hurt.

He couldn't touch me. I felt no pain for him. But when he laid a finger on one of my siblings, my insides bubbled with pain and fear. I desperately tried to recall who was home that he could hurt. Mom was at the pharmacy filling a prescription. My heart in my throat, I turned to run after him.

"Dad, NO!" My legs were useless, they wouldn't move fast enough. By the time I reached the bottom of the stairs and turned the corner, tears burned my eyes when I caught sight of Ethan.

Just learning to walk, stumbling across the living room with a Lego block in his hand, he smiled when he saw me. His doll-like arms stretched towards me and his baby blue eyes were so focused on my presence that he never saw Dad closing in behind him.

"Leave him alone!" I screamed, and charged at Ethan. I scooped him up against my chest like a football just as Dad's steel-toed boot made contact with my stomach. I doubled over, the baby in my arms, and lost consciousness before I knew if Ethan was okay.

Soft hands pulled at my face. Bits of sound became clearer and I focused on Dad's voice, telling me it was my fault and that I shouldn't have got in the way.

Ethan was crying above me when I finally opened my eyes. He didn't look hurt, but I struggled to get up. Snot ran down his face as he cried out "Da! Da!", pointing at Dad from across the room. I used my sleeve to wipe his face and I cradled him against me, making my way towards my room.

I strained to listen for Kat and Thomas. They were home, but were undoubtedly hiding from the moment they heard the commotion coming from my room, just like I taught them.

If I ran away after high school like I had planned, Ethan would have to fend for himself. There would be no one else to protect him or diffuse Dad's anger. He wouldn't be able to hide, and he wouldn't be old enough to communicate if something happened to him. I shook my head as I sat Ethan on my disheveled bed with a book so I could pick up the remnants of the tornado that had ripped through my room.

By the time my siblings and I would be old enough to move out, Ethan would be the only target. He'd be the only one left who Dad could still hurt, and in turn, hurt me.

I remembered back to when we lived on Long Island. Adam and I usually wore Dad's old t-shirts to bed because we didn't have pajamas of our own. One night we stumbled upon a stash of magazines with naked women in them at the bottom of one of Dad's drawers. We giggled and pointed at our unusual find until we decided that Dad just *had* to see what we found. I must have been around six years old at the time.

Adam held the magazine as we entered the garage just off of the kitchen. Dad was tinkering with something and looked up as we came out. "Daddy, look what we found! This magazine is so funny." Adam pushed the magazine under his nose.

A wheelbarrow is what stopped Dad from grabbing Adam, as we both screamed and ran from him. His voice bellowed behind us and as we turned the corner to the living room, Adam pushed me behind the grand piano to hide.

I'll never forget the look in his eyes as he accepted that he had given me the only hiding spot in the room. Lowering himself to the floor, he sat in a cross-legged position and put a finger to his lips to motion for me to be quiet.

I watched in horror as Dad turned the corner, realizing what Adam had done. He had sacrificed himself. He had put himself dead center of his path.

All for me.

Dad kicked him like a linebacker and I covered my mouth as Adam's body soared through the air, ending with his limp body crashing into the front door behind him.

Dad never found me.

I wanted to believe, for years, that Adam didn't remember that night because of how hard he hit his head. The truth was, I think Adam's spirit was broken in that moment. It was the first and last time he ever put himself in Dad's path. Unbeknownst to me, Adam had taken one blow and immediately passed the martyr torch to the next in line. It wasn't ignorance, the years of ignoring and denying what happened in our home, it was a deliberate surrender.

Ethan flipped through pages, pointing and calling out baby gibberish. My hand moved through the silky blonde straws of his hair and my lips sunk into his cheek.

For years, I thought that ignoring and denying what happened in our home was protecting my brothers and sister. I knew, now, that it was only enabling him. The longer I kept his secrets, the longer he could continue to do whatever he pleased. As Ethan nodded off to sleep in my arms, I touched his nose with my index finger.

"You, little man, are my saving grace."

***

Paul went to the bus stop to get Joseph, and I watched him cross the front lawn before I picked up the phone in his kitchen. My hands trembled as I dialed the number for Social Services and I fetched a piece of paper from my pocket. I knew I would forget something, so I wrote down what I needed to say in a paragraph. An operator picked up and I smoothed the paper out in front of me.

When I finished rattling off what I needed to say, she asked for my name and to explain how I knew what I knew.

"I can't tell you my name. But you have to believe me. Listen to my voice, I'm a child and I'm terrified. Please, you need to help." I hung up and returned the phone to the dock in the kitchen.

Joseph bounced through the door. "Hey Brooke, wanna watch SpongeBob with me?"

"No," Paul replied for me. "She doesn't. Watch it yourself." Paul walked past me and stormed off to his bedroom.

"What's wrong?" I asked, following close behind.

"Why do you *always* ask that? Do you have a guilty conscience?"

"N-No, you just seem…"

"Seem what? I don't have time for this. I'm going to Judd's."

"I just got here." My voice rose when I didn't want it to. "I thought we were going to hang out today?"

"Why, because it's convenient for you? Are you sure you don't have to go meet with your counselor or go spend hours talking in the kitchen with my mom?"

"What is your problem?"

"You. You are my problem." He chucked his book bag onto the bed and shoved a pair of jeans inside. "I'm only fifteen. I don't need to be worried about you like I am all the time. All I do is wonder if you're okay, and I don't even know why!" His hands shot up into the air. "You don't tell me anything and when I finally do get to spend time with you, you look like you're going to cry or all you want to do is talk in whispers with my mom."

"Are you sure this is all about me?" I pressed. "Nothing else *bothering* you?"

His eyes narrowed. "What's that supposed to mean?"

"You know, it's funny that you're upset with me for talking to other people about *my* life. Maybe I don't like *you* telling half the school that we have sex all the time, mainly because we don't, but also because it's none of their business. I know about you sneaking off with your guys to smoke weed and drink, so don't think I'm stupid. I'm your girlfriend, and maybe you should—"

"No, you're not."

I stared at him. "I'm not what?"

"My girlfriend."

He threw his book bag over his shoulder and rushed out the bedroom door.

"What?" I said, following him.

"Go away."

"What? No, I won't go away."

I followed him into the driveway just as a car pulled up and honked. A guy I didn't recognize stuck his hand out the window and motioned for Paul to get in.

"Paul, wait." Panic rose in my chest.

"Brooke, I'm done. I don't want to do this anymore." He turned towards the car.

"Wait, Paul. Don't." I reached out and grabbed his elbow. "Can we talk?"

"No, we can't. And if you don't stop following me, I'll never talk to you again. I need time."

"How much time?" I couldn't control the pitch in my voice.

"It's not up to you! Weeks, months, years, whatever it takes. I'm not doing this anymore. Have fun playing mommy or housewife, whatever it is you do. See ya later."

The car sped off and I could hear the music thumping until they drove past where I worked. I stood in the driveway with my hand on the bridge of my nose. Everything happened so fast, I wasn't sure how to feel.

As I stood there thinking about the phone call I just made, Paul walking out of my life, Ethan at home alone... It was too much. My body sank to the ground and I wrapped my arms around my knees, trying to figure out what I had done that made God hate me so much.

* * *

Paul ignored every phone call I made over the next few days. He never came to my locker, and when I finally saw him in the hallway I asked him to meet me after third period. "Please," I said. "I just need to see you for a minute." He nodded in agreement, walking in the opposite direction before first period started.

I couldn't concentrate on the Spanish vocabulary I was supposed to be writing down in my notebook. I hardly noticed when a student walked in halfway through the period and Mr. Caruzo had to say my name twice before I noticed he was motioning to me. "Brooke, you're needed in the front office."

The front office was narrow and blue and I slumped into a seat as I waited. I checked the clock and as I looked up Adam came walking through the doors. My heart skipped. "Adam? What are you doing here?"

"I don't know. I was just about to get on the bus for a field trip though. They said they'd only hold it for ten minutes. I don't wanna miss it."

Principal Hemlorn poked his head through one office door. "Adam, Brooke? Can you guys follow me?" Light reflected off his bald head and his smile was warm.

We followed him a few feet before stopping in front of a door. "I have someone here who wants to talk to you guys. Might take a little time, half hour maybe." He checked his watch. "Just see the receptionist when you're done, she'll give you a pass."

"Principal Hemlorn I have a field trip." Adam pointed toward the door. "Can this wait? I already paid and everything."

He licked his lips. "I suppose that's fine. I'll let them know you already got on the bus. Brooke, you go ahead in."

Them? What is going on...

Adam turned to catch the bus and the principal put his hand on my shoulder. "It's all right, go ahead inside Brooke."

The light was dim and my eyes had to adjust, but when they did, I was staring at two police officers and a lady in a business suit.

"Mrs. Shafer, this is Brooke Nolan. Her brother already left on a field trip, so you might have to catch up with him later."

"Thank you Mr. Hemlorn. Brooke, would you like to take a seat?"

The door closed behind me. "My name is Elise, sweetheart. I'm from Children and Youth Services. Is it okay if we talk for a few minutes?"

I stared at the bulky police officers standing in the corner of the room. Their arms were crossed in front of their chests. I could hear their uniforms squeak from all the items they had in their belts. "What did I do?"

"Oh, nothing dear. It's okay, you're not in trouble. Don't mind these guys." She waved to the officers behind her. "They're just here as a witness to what you and I talk about, they won't bother us any. You can call me Elise, all right?"

I took a seat as I noticed the expensive suit Elise had on. She had a pink collared shirt on underneath and she whisked her bangs away from her face. She couldn't have been older than thirty, but there was something old about her face.

"I'm from Children and Youth Services. Do you know what that is?"

I shook my head and traced the outlines of her face. She wore a lot of makeup, but I decided she was pretty. She looked concerned.

"We protect children from bad situations. Sometimes children need someone to stand up for them when they're being hurt, or when something bad happens to them, so that's my job."

She had huge green eyes and I twisted my hands in my lap. Social Services sure did respond to anonymous phone calls in a timely manner.

"I'm here because my office got a few phone calls about your family. About some things that go on in your house."

A few phone calls? I only called once.

"So, I was hoping we could talk? I have a few questions."

I remained silent. My body started to tremble as the reality of what was happening set in.

"Now we don't know who made these phone calls, but we do know that one came from the middle school about your brother. Thomas, right? A teacher there saw some bruises on him and called last week. Then we got another call saying there was no food in your house, about the children there being hit and yelled at, and some other things."

I nodded, knowing that I had made that phone call.

"So tell me, Brooke, what are your parents like? Do any of these things sound true?"

Elise wanted me to trust her, I knew, but I was terrified. The police officers stared at me, waiting for a response. I knew that calling Social Services would lead to this. I just didn't realize it would be so soon.

"Brooke, I want you to know that anything we talk about here today stays between us. You don't have to be afraid to tell me about what goes on in your home. You won't get in trouble, okay?"

"We sometimes don't have food," I started. My hands twisted around my shirt. "My dad yells, a lot, and he hits my brothers." Elise picked up her pen and started writing. "We're all afraid of him. I don't like him."

Elise nodded. "You're doing great honey, keep going. What kinds of things does he yell about? Where does he hit your brothers?"

"On their backs, their stomachs, sometimes their face. Sometimes he uses a belt. Or he'll throw things. He yells about everything. When we're too loud, if we leave a cabinet door open. If we don't do whatever he wants."

Elise put down her pen and looked at me. "What kinds of things does he want, Brooke?" Her voice was comforting, reassuring. I couldn't shake the stares from the police officers though; their eyes bore into me and I felt like I was on display.

"Brooke, we got a call that your dad was touching you inappropriately. Do you know what that means?"

I shook my head. Everything was happening so fast.

"Has your dad ever touched your private parts? Has he ever made you do something to him that you didn't want to do?"

Tears forced themselves to the surface but I blinked them away. My white flag couldn't go up that easily. I didn't even know what would happen if I told on him right then and there. Something just seemed off, and my gut was battling with my head.

"Maybe. I mean, I don't know." My gaze fell into my lap.

"Did you ever tell anyone that these things were happening to you?"

My stomach churned. *What did I do? If I tell her what's happening they'll take us away for sure, and we'll all be split up.* I didn't have enough time to think about what would happen when Social Services finally showed up. There was no game plan, no escape. I needed an escape.

"I told my boyfriend's mom I had a dream my dad touched me," I said. It sounded like a safe way to watch her reaction.

"You had a dream?"

"Yeah." I shifted my weight.

"So you never told anyone your father touched you?"

I paused. "No." It wasn't a lie, technically I didn't.

"And he never touched you? Never hurt you?"

"No." I looked away. Even *I* knew when my face got too red for anyone to believe I was telling the truth.

Elise wrapped up the questioning and thanked me before telling me she was going to talk to my brother at the middle school. I nodded and backed up towards the door. The bell rang as I raced down the hallway, my heart nearly bouncing out of my chest.

When I saw Paul, tears were streaming down my cheeks and I wrapped my arms around his neck. "Brooke, I know us breaking up is hard for you, but—"

"It's not that." I leaned into his ear and told him about what happened in the front office. He pulled away, slowly, staring at me. "Is it true?"

"Paul, I just need you right now."

He shifted his weight and looked down the hallway. "I'm sorry, I gotta go."

I watched him turn his back on me for the second time and walk away. My body trembled all over as I searched for the nearest EXIT sign and pushed through the double doors, running towards the football field.

***

Two days later, Mom walked into my bedroom with an envelope in her hand. It was a letter from Children and Youth, explaining that they had investigated an accusation that Dad had been sexually abusing me and that I, specifically, gave indication that the dreams I was having may be substantiated. They wanted to come out to the house to talk to my mom and dad and launch a full investigation.

My gut had saved my life. Not only did Children and Youth promise me that what I told them would be confidential, and they lied, but they sent a letter home claiming that I was the only one who would talk to them out of all my siblings. I became the only target.

Mom sat on the bed next to me. "Is this true, Brooke? Tell me if this is true. I'll change the locks tonight and he won't ever come back."

My eyes widened. *She believed me?*

"I mean, I don't know how we're going to survive. I don't know how we'll get money to pay our bills or eat, but I'll change the locks. I will. Is this true?"

A promise of freedom with an extra-heavy side of guilt, coming right up.

I shook my head. "I don't know what to say, Mom. It's not true."

Mom wiped a tear from her cheek. "Oh, all right. Well…" She stood up, smiling. "As long as it isn't true, I guess there isn't anything for me to worry about, right?"

She showed the letter to Dad. After reading the letter, he wanted to talk to Mom and me in his bedroom. "This is very serious, Brooke." He waved the letter in my face. "If this were true we would lose the house. I would lose my job, and you kids would wind up in foster care. Do you want that?"

"It's true, he's right. We would lose everything," Mom chimed in.

Mom never asked what would make me say such things. Neither did Dad. They never asked if I had a grudge or if I watched too much TV or if someone had put me up to it. They didn't care what the reason was, they just wanted to make sure that I kept telling Social Services that it wasn't true.

And I did.

The case was unfounded and closed within two weeks. Elise asked me, for the last time, if I wanted to tell her anything, anything at all. I shook my head, watching her car leave the driveway after her last visit. If anything, I was thankful for the break I got. Dad seemed afraid and the investigation was too fresh for him to try anything, so he stayed away from me for over two months.

I tried to talk to Paul numerous times but he never returned my calls, and chatting online always ended in him calling me pathetic or a long line of names before he would block me or sign off.

I didn't understand what I did to make him so angry, and he refused to give me the closure I needed. We both got our licenses and with the money I had saved up from working I got myself a used car, asking my mom to co-sign for the remainder of the balance. Dad was furious Mom co-signed for me, but since I had the money Mom didn't see the issue.

Then I got a phone call from Aunt Jean asking me to come visit them on Long Island. She said it was important and she wanted me to sneak away without telling anyone.

"Tell your mom you're staying at a friend's house and come visit. I don't like you lying, but it's really important I see you." It was the first time I drove outside of Kunkletown and I was a nervous wreck driving over the bridges to get to New York.

I pulled up in front of Aunt Jean's house and wondered what she had to tell me that was so important.

The front door opened before I could even knock.

Chapter Sixteen

My cousins met me at the door and I was hugged a million times before I took off my coat. Aunt Jean handed me a cup of hot cocoa and Uncle Bruce took me into his arms for a bear hug.

"Tell me about your license and school. Junior Prom is coming up soon, right? Do you have a dress? I can't believe you're sixteen already, my goodness." Aunt Jean rattled on as Uncle Bruce picked up his newspaper.

After I tucked my coat into the hallway closet I pulled up a chair next to Uncle Bruce. It felt soothing to be around family. I missed living on Long Island. New York had so much character and culture. It was impossible to ever be bored, and a mouth-watering slice of pizza was always available at any corner.

"Hey guys, why don't you go put on that movie we rented for you?" Aunt Jean said, coaxing my cousins into the back room.

"What movie? I'll watch with them." I picked up my cup of cocoa.

"Actually Brooke, we'd like to talk to you." Uncle Bruce folded his paper. He patted the seat to invite me to sit back down. "Take a seat."

I settled down in-between them. Their faces looked meek and I could foresee bad news coming my way. The tension was uncomfortable.

"Brooke, your mom called us a few weeks ago and told us about the letter she got in the mail. You know the one?" Uncle Bruce said.

I shook my head and took a long sip of cocoa.

"Right. Well, we uh, your aunt and I talked about it some. And we need to let you know that, sometimes…"

He held up his hands like he was holding an imaginary basketball, staring at it intently, struggling to find the right words. "Sometimes, people need to know about the bubble that surrounds a family. This bubble protects everyone, and it keeps everyone safe. It's like a safety zone." Aunt Jean nodded in agreement as Uncle Bruce continued. "Our family has a very strong bubble." He reached out for Aunt Jean's hand. We want you to know that you are a part of our family and we know you are a very smart, strong, and beautiful young woman." His face started to turn several shades of crimson. "We are worried about you, and we want you to know that the bubble we have in our family will protect you too." He pointed at me. "Anything you are going through or anything you say, we will protect you." Uncle Bruce turned his face away.

Was he crying?

"Brooke, sweetheart," Aunt Jean said, stepping in. "We need you to know that this is a safe place. Uncle Bruce and I can protect you, your mom, and your siblings. All of you. In fact, we talked about it, and if we needed to we would move you and your mom back here to stay with us. We already set up the bedrooms. There is room for everyone."

Uncle Bruce nodded. "We'll take you in, all of you, so you can stay together if that's what worries you. But Aunt Jean and I are worried about *you*. And this?" he said, holding up the imaginary bubble again. "Baby girl, no one can hurt you anymore. Not while I got this thing wrapped around you."

Aunt Jean's knuckles turned red as she squeezed into Uncle Bruce's hand. "Brooke honey, is anything going on in your house with your dad? Has he hurt you?"

I lowered my head, my hand covering my eyes. They had just told me exactly what I needed to hear. They were going to keep me safe, and keep all of us together. It was all I needed to know.

"Yeah, he's touched me. And—" I started.

Aunt Jean let out a sob as she reached across the table. "Oh, baby. Oh Brooke I'm so sorry."

Covering my face in shame, I couldn't bring myself to speak again. Uncle Bruce stood up from the table and slammed his fist through the wall in the kitchen, his face a bright burgundy, tears sliding down both cheeks.

"I need to talk to Gina," I said, finally catching my breath.

Aunt Jean got up from the table. "I'll call her. She'll be expecting me, I told her you were coming here to talk. She'll know what to do from here."

"You did? How did you—?"

Suddenly the mysterious phone calls to Social Services that Elise had told me about were clear. It wasn't a teacher who had called over and over again. It was Gina. While she never straight out asked me, she poked and prodded like she knew all along. Maybe she knew it would take sitting down with family, having them tell me they would catch the pieces as they fell, that would finally get me to talk. I closed my eyes in silent thanks.

As I sat at the table with my hands over my eyes I felt a hand over mine. Uncle Bruce looked at me, his eyes hurting for me. "I got you now, okay? No one's gonna hurt you anymore." He patted my hand and I believed him.

Aunt Jean told me that I should eat dinner with them and then head back to Pennsylvania and go straight to Gina's house. Gina wanted to sit down with me before heading over to the police station since they were going to have a lot of questions. Aunt Jean and Uncle Bruce would meet me there in the morning and we would all go to the police station together.

Instead of eating, I asked to take a shower. I scrubbed and washed every inch of my body three times, and when I thought I was finished, I washed again. After a few spoonfuls of soup I asked to take a shower one more time before I left. My body wouldn't stop shaking.

Three times I got lost making my way back to Pennsylvania. My mind was in too many different places and I couldn't concentrate on which way to go. When I finally pulled into Gina's driveway, it was a little after ten at night. I hadn't been to Paul's house since we broke up, but it was a needed comfort when I walked in the door and smelled the faint aroma of gravy coming from the kitchen.

"Brooke, I told Paulie what was going on. I wanted him to have time to process everything before you got here. I'm sorry if that was wrong…"

I shook my head and hugged her. "No, it's fine. I don't know how I would say it anyway. Thank you."

The front door opened and Paul walked in, his face sunken from crying. He kicked off his sneakers as he made his way over to me and before the tears started falling down my face he had me wrapped in his arms, his face buried in my hair.

Gina stood off to the side for a minute before interrupting. "All right Brooke, I want you to try to sleep. I have a warm blanket here." She opened a quilt and threw it over the couch.

"Ma, she's sleeping with me tonight."

Gina looked at Paul. "Paul, honey I don't think that's a good idea."

"Mom, please. She's trembling. Nothing's gonna happen. She needs me."

He was right, I did need him, and I was glad Paul suggested I stay in his room.

Gina sighed. "All right, please don't make me regret it."

She kissed Paul on the forehead and me on the cheek. "Night kids."

Gina gave me a pair of pajamas and after washing my face I snuggled in next to Paul and put my head on his chest. I listened to his heartbeat and traced his fingers with mine in the dark. "Paul?" I whispered. "I'm sorry your mom had to tell you."

He sighed. "It's all right, we don't need to talk about it. You're here now." He tilted my chin to bring my lips to meet his. I melted into his arms and tried to focus on his hands moving around my stomach and down my hips.

"Paul, not now." I pushed his hand to the side and put my head down on his chest. *Why would he try anything right now?* "We aren't even together."

"So?" I could feel him shake his head in the dark. He shifted his weight and slid me off his chest and onto the mattress. I could tell he was staring at the ceiling. "You know, Brooke, it's a shame. You're never going to find a guy as good as me." He rolled over with his back to me, and within a few minutes I could hear him breathing rhythmically in his sleep.

My body stiffened and I didn't doubt that Paul was right. No one would want to be with me knowing what had happened to me.

The TV blared on at nine thirty the next morning. I searched for Paul with my hand and when I found nothing, I opened my eyes to see him sitting in his beanbag chair watching cartoons.

"Hey," I said, half asleep. "Why don't you come lie here for a while? It's not every day we get to sleep in the same bed."

He clicked through channels. "Just because you're here doesn't mean I'm going to change my whole routine. This is what I always do Saturday mornings."

I shook my head and sighed, sinking back down into the pillows. His mood swings were exhausting. The TV clicked off a few minutes later. "I'm going to my cousins. Later."

With no energy to chase after him, I fell back asleep. When I woke up again it was almost dinnertime and my Aunt Jean and Uncle Bruce were in the kitchen of Gina's house.

"Morning sleepyhead," Uncle Bruce said, kissing my forehead.

"You hungry?" Gina poured a bowl of soup before I could answer.

"Why am I so tired?" I rubbed my eyes and sunk into a chair at the kitchen table. My head throbbed and I felt like I wanted to sleep for days.

"This is very emotional for you honey, it's going to take a lot out of you. Here, eat up."

Lou came home about an hour later and embraced me. "You're a strong, brave girl. We're all here for you." He crossed the kitchen and kissed Gina and shook hands with my aunt and uncle.

The plan was to wait until Dad went to work that night, sometime around seven. Aunt Jean and Lou would go to my mom's to tell her what happened, while Uncle Bruce and Gina took me to the police station to file a report.

"All right, Brooke. We need to write down dates, where things happened, and what happened." Gina looked up at me. "This won't be easy, so let's start from the beginning, okay?"

"Why do we have to do this?"

"The police need to know that we have all this information, so they know what to investigate. They will ask the same questions, so I want you to feel confident that you have everything you need to say."

I nodded. Gina wrote as I talked. Lou, Aunt Jean and Uncle Bruce sat at the table too, listening. I told them about New York, about him coming into my room as young as I could remember. I told them about moving to Pennsylvania and how it happened more frequently because we didn't have family around. I explained how he would bring me into his bedroom and then pretend the next day that nothing had happened.

"Okay Brooke, good, good. Now, try and remember. When did he first rape you?"

The word made me flinch. My uncle looked away and Lou cringed. I was embarrassed enough, listing everything he had done to molest me, and I couldn't bring myself to talk to them about the rapes.

I hung my head in response.

"Brooke, you're doing a great job. We need to know the dates. It's important." Gina put her hand on my shoulder. "It's okay."

"We thought he touched her," Aunt Jean said, sounding frantic. "The report from Children and Youth only mentioned touching, not rape."

I covered my face with my hands as I tried to rub the shame off my skin.

"Brooke, I picked you up," said a soft voice.

I looked up at Gina.

"I picked you up from school the day after, remember? That's one date."

I couldn't believe she remembered. Gina's eyes looked moist. I wondered how long she knew and didn't say anything to me. She just waited for me to feel safe enough to tell her. It must have been killing her inside that I never did.

"Is it true, Brooke?" Aunt Jean pressed through tears.

Uncle Bruce nodded. "It's okay, Brooke. The bubble, remember?"

I shook my head and lowered my forehead to my hands. The four adults in front of me were about to be crushed and I didn't want to watch.

"He did," I said, my voice screeching. "He raped me."

I could feel the vibration from my Aunt Jean falling to the floor in hysterics and I turned my whole body away from everyone, covering my face and trying to fade into the background.

Lou and Gina had their arms around me. "Don't you dare be ashamed." Gina's voice was strong through her tears. "This is not your fault. Come here. Oh, let me hold you. It's okay, it's okay."

I sobbed as my body shook.

"I'm gonna get sick," I said. Once in the bathroom, I could hear Uncle Bruce trying to comfort my aunt as she sobbed and cried out. A genuine nightmare was unfolding before them.

When I sat back down at the table, tissues were getting passed around and everyone's bloodshot eyes were worn. "Feel better?" Gina nodded in my direction.

I closed my eyes. Years of suppressing, ignoring, and denying had just escaped. Beneath my trembling skin, I felt something deep within my bones that I had never felt before.

Serenity.

Chapter Seventeen

There were so many incidents, but I couldn't tell them that. I didn't think they would be able to handle it. I wasn't sure *I* could. So I chose the ones I knew the most about; the one time Gina had picked me up from school the next day, which also gave me a witness. I recalled the time my mom was in the hospital, since I had tried to fight back and escape. Gina said it would be enough and didn't press me to try and remember the dates of any more.

I didn't want to anyway. It wasn't like a birthday or vacation memory I was trying to recall, and I had tried to push many of them to the back of my mind, never to be thought about again.

After eight o'clock, Gina drove me to the police station with Uncle Bruce in the front seat. I watched the trees float by from the back seat and tried not to doze off again. My body was coping with a large amount of adrenaline and anxiety. I was having a hard time keeping my eyes open at that point.

The radio hummed a Dixie Chicks song. Gina looked up in the rearview mirror and smirked. "You know this song?"

The tune sounded familiar. When the chorus started, Gina turned the volume knob so I could listen. A smile spread across my face as Gina belted out the tunes.

It was about a man named Earl who was abusive to his wife, so the wife and her best friend poisoned him with black-eyed peas when the law wouldn't hold him accountable for the abuse. The melody was uplifting and catchy, lightheartedly poking fun at the murder of her abusive husband.

The irony of the song playing on our way to the police station was suddenly funny. Gina shook her head. "Oh, oh gosh. That's wrong. Okay, I'm done. But seriously, we don't use the name David anymore. Not Dad, not Father, not David. Earl is all he's worth. From now on, we call him Earl."

The thought was actually a comfort. Since everything was about to come out, I didn't want to call him Dad. He didn't deserve that title. I didn't want to call him anything really, but calling him Earl would give me a reprieve when I spoke about him at least, even if it was just with Gina.

Gina had called ahead to explain the situation so we didn't have to do that when we first got into the precinct. It definitely helped ease the transition with the police officer, and he ushered me into a back room to make my statement. Gina called after me, telling me that she would be right there waiting when I was finished.

An orange haired guy in his mid-forties pulled up a chair next to me and cleared his throat. "My name is Officer Stubaker. You're here to make a report about your father?"

I nodded.

"All right, can you tell me what happened?"

Gina and my family had really tip toed around asking me to explain the situation. The bluntness of this police officer was a little uncomfortable. "Um, you mean with Ear— uh, my dad?"

He tapped his pencil. "Yes. That's why you're here, isn't it?"

I sighed and looked into my lap.

"You uh, you told your family that something happened to you. I just need to know what it is you told them so I can write it down for our records too."

I could tell he was trying to make the situation as comfortable as possible, but I didn't know what to say. I never so much as cursed in front of an adult. Now I was sitting in front of a stranger, and he wanted me to explain such a personal circumstance.

"From the beginning?" I asked.

He nodded.

"Okay. Uh, when I lived in New York, my dad used to come into my room at night and touch me. When I would bathe with my sister he would use his hands to clean us instead of a rag. After we moved to Pennsylvania he..." I trailed off. I just did not have the vocabulary to make this comfortable. "He uh, raped me. Twice where I know the dates."

An overhead fluorescent threatened to go out above us, and there wasn't even a poster in the room I could pretend to stare at.

"Did you ever tell anyone about this? I mean, before tonight?" he probed.

"Social Services came to my school once. They asked me about it but I told them it was all a dream."

"Why's that?"

"I was afraid they would take my brothers and sister away from me."

His green eyes softened and he rubbed his fingers through his prickly looking beard. "Right, right. Hey so, do you like to write?"

My face must have brightened because he shook his head. "This might be easier if I have you write down what happened. Does that sound better to you?"

"Yes, please." I nodded and smiled a little.

"All right, just be sure to be as detailed as possible. Don't be embarrassed, just write what happened word for word."

He grabbed three pieces of paper and set a pen down next to me. "I'll come back and check on you in a little bit, all right?" He ran his fingers through his hair and cleared his throat as he shut the door.

After twenty-five minutes I was finally finished. I folded the papers in half to keep anyone else from seeing them and waited for Officer Stubaker to come back.

"All finished?" he asked, handing me a glass of water.

"Yep." I handed him the papers.

He stared at them. "I'll need to open these and read them, then have you initial them in front of me. That all right?"

My face flamed. "Oh, sure."

He read for several minutes and I chipped away at the nail polish on my fingernails to pass the time. When he finished, he showed me where to sign and led me back out to Gina and Uncle Bruce.

Office Stubaker suggested that my aunt and uncle take my mom and the kids to New York until they could talk to Dad about my testimony. "Technically she can't just pack up the kids and leave the state, but it isn't illegal to take an impromptu vacation." He winked. "Maybe everyone suddenly doesn't have cell phone service too, you know? Just for a few days."

Uncle Bruce nodded his head, understanding the subliminal advice.

"You all right kiddo? You did a great job." Gina turned and smiled at me as we headed out of the parking lot.

"Yeah, I think so. I had to write down what happened. It was hard for me to talk about it. I didn't know what words I was allowed to say in front of him because he's a police officer."

"Oh, honey. I'm sure he's heard it before, but I'm glad you could write it down if that's what made you comfortable."

"Where are we going now?"

"Your Mom's. Aunt Jean and Lou are there now letting her know what's going on."

I cringed. I remembered back to when she got the letter in the mail from Social Services. She didn't have much to say, except for how hard it would be for the accusations to be true because of money. Now that other people were involved, I imagined her reaction would be much different.

As if on cue, when I walked through the front door Mom came towards me with open arms and tears streaming down her face. "Ohhhh Brooke! I am so sorry. Oh my God, oh my God."

When I pulled away from her I was surprised to see Thomas coming at me with tears in his eyes. "Brooke, are you okay? I'm sorry." I held his head to my chest and Kat was suddenly at my side, squeezing me and crying just as hard. Adam was at a friend's house, but Mom had a call out for him to come home.

"Okay, everyone listen here." Uncle Bruce took the reins. "I need everyone to go upstairs, pack a bag with at least a weeks worth of clothes. We want to be out of here in half an hour. Go."

Uncle Bruce explained to Mom that the police officer suggested the safest thing for her to do would be to stay with family until they could start their investigation. "What about school?" Mom asked. "Do they know you live in New York?"

"Just call the school in the morning, tell them you have a family emergency. Don't tell them where you're staying though. Also, leave a note on the bulletin board that you had to take the dog to the vet so David doesn't wonder why she's gone when he gets home in the morning. We'll take her with us too. Tomorrow is Monday so he'll think the kids are in school and you're at the vet. It will buy us a few hours until the police move in."

Gina nodded. "Make sure you go to the bank first thing in the morning since you have a joint account. Take everything out. If you don't, he will. You have kids to take care of."

Mom nodded and went off to pack a bag.

"You were so brave tonight." Gina wrapped me in her arms and stroked my hair. "You're in good hands now, you're safe. Lou and I are going to go home now, we should talk to Paul."

I nodded. "Tell him I'm sorry."

"I will not." Gina shook her head. "There is nothing in this world you need to be sorry for."

We didn't get to New York until three in the morning. We were all exhausted and crashed on the beds they had set up. I didn't wake up until after two in the afternoon the next day and I moved through the motions of going downstairs to face everyone. After eating some crackers I headed upstairs to take a shower again. I felt like I couldn't get clean enough.

The calls to our cell phones started around four p.m. and every time 'DAD' flashed across my screen I jumped a little. I eventually turned off my phone. A week went by and the police stayed in touch with my mom.

I overheard Mom telling my aunt that Earl had called her friend Ellen, someone she frequently visited to have tea. Ellen truly did not know where we were when he asked. Out of ideas of where we could be, Earl huffed into the phone, "Well, Brooke must have said…"

"Brooke must have said what?" Ellen had asked. Earl ignored her question and hung up the phone.

I started to get a flurry of text messages from people at school and work. Judd's attempts to get me to talk to him were hard to ignore, but I couldn't respond to anyone.

Brooke u ok? Ur dad came into work 2day. Wanted to see where u were, where u at?

Are you ok? Haven't heard from you. No one was at your house. We still working on that computer project?

BROOKE CALL ME. YOU HAVENT BEEN AT SCHOOL FOR TWO WEEKS.

I miss u. Its Judd. Im borrowing Chalkys fone. Text this # plz. R u alive?

Since the police suggested we not answer any phone calls or texts, we weren't allowed to let anyone know where we were. Instead I had to listen to voicemails of Cristin and Judd pleading with me to call them. They had no idea what was going on.

The only one who *did* know was Paul, but I never heard from him. I hoped, every time I heard my phone go off, that it would be him. Instead I got an explanation to his absence via a text from Cristin:

Paul's dating soccer chick Lea, since when?!? Seriously CALL ME.

I shook my head and turned off my phone. My aunt must have noticed me moping around and I told her all about Paul, his mood swings, and how he dumped me to date one of the easiest girls in school.

"Did you guys…you know?" She raised an eyebrow.

"Twice. He wanted to more but I didn't, really. A lot was going on."

Aunt Jean nodded. "You know what though Brooke, he wouldn't be a man if he didn't experience what a fake girl was like, you know? Let him have sex with other people and when he comes crawling back to you, make him fight for it a little." She winked and ruffled my hair. "You're too pretty to be hung up on one guy anyway."

It made me feel a little better, but I still wished he would text to see if I was okay. He was the only one who had any idea I was even alive and I wanted his support too.

A few more days went by before the police told my mom that Earl was no longer allowed back at the house and we could come back. We had filed for a Protection From Abuse order to keep him out until they could gather more evidence. The PFA meant that if he came anywhere near the house, school, or work that we could call the police and he would be arrested.

As we headed back to Pennsylvania I tried to come up with reasons to tell everyone why I had suddenly disappeared. I turned my phone on and was bombarded with six text messages from Judd. I closed my eyes and smiled, anticipating being able to see my friends again soon.

Chapter Eighteen

"I bet you're excited to get back to school, huh?" Mom chipped away at small talk as we crossed the George Washington Bridge. The sun was just setting as the city disappeared in my side view mirror.

"Yeah. Not excited to catch up on all the work I missed. Especially chemistry." I groaned just thinking about it.

"Chemistry? I didn't know they offered classes like that in high school."

"Yeah."

We were all headed back to start a life we didn't know how to live. With Earl out of the picture everyone was going to have to adjust, make sacrifices, and learn how to grow as a family. I imagined us all sitting at the dinner table laughing, passing around food, and talking about each other's days.

"It's going to be hard to go back into that house though," I said nonchalantly, and flipped my phone open to see if Judd had texted me back.

"What do you mean? Dad won't be there."

"I know. But the memories are." I shuddered picturing Earl in every room of the house. It was going to be a hard adjustment to convince myself that he wasn't coming back.

"Yeah?"

"I don't know," I started. "Don't you think it would be nice if we sold the house and started somewhere new?"

"Are you kidding me? I love that house, it's my dream house. I just lost everything and now you want to talk about me selling the only thing I have left?"

Her defensiveness alarmed me. "No, Mom. You didn't lose everything. You still have your kids. And it'll be hard for us to heal in a place where all we think about is him still being there. That's all." I meant to sound optimistic, like moving into a new house would be a fresh start for everyone, even Mom.

"He won't be there Brooke, he's gone. Who cares that he lived there? We can live there just as happy." She lit a cigarette and puffed on the end of it.

"Who *cares?*" My voice was the one rising now. "Did you really just say that to me? I care! How about I care that in every room of that house all I'll get to think about is how I was brutally raped or how I had to stand between him and one of my brothers so he didn't kill them."

"No one asked you to do that!"

"They didn't have to," I bellowed back. "That's just what you do when you love someone!"

"OH! So *now* I don't love my own kids? This is my fault then?"

I threw my hands into the air, exasperated. Arguing with her was like talking to a wall.

"It's always my fault, huh?" she continued. "I'm the one to blame for this? All right. All right."

She threw her cigarette butt out the window and turned the wipers on to fight the rain that started to pour from the sky.

"I don't see how you can choose a house over your kids, Mom. You love the house, so what. It's a stupid house. You can always replace that. You can't fake happiness. I'll never feel safe there. Ever."

"Then you can leave because I'm not selling my house. Not for you, not for anyone."

"FINE!"

The argument had overwhelmed me. I couldn't believe that she wouldn't even be open to the idea of moving. It was a suggestion, not a demand. She didn't want to hear about how I felt, or how uncomfortable it would be to live there pretending nothing happened.

I understood she loved the house. It was massive compared to the one we lived in on Long Island. Who would even *want* to live in a house where your own children were victimized? To me it would be difficult to start over when the house would be a constant reminder.

That weekend Aunt Nikki flew in and stayed the weekend at the house. Mom asked me to watch the kids while her and Aunt Nikki ran some errands. A few hours later, they stuffed themselves through the front door with bags of things. "Ohhh what's that, Mom?" Kat asked, eyeing the comforter set.

Mom and Aunt Nikki dragged the bags upstairs and by the time they were done Kat and I had new comforters, sheets, and pillows. The curtains were changed and a throw rug covered the floor. A wall clock and posters were secured to the walls and a lamp was fixed into one corner of the room.

Without a doubt, Aunt Nikki had paid for everything. Mom must have told her about our argument. She stood next to me after Mom walked out and patted me on the shoulder. "Brand new everything. Okay, hun? No reason to worry. We bought all new locks for the doors too. He's not coming back. Hope you like your room, your *new* room." She squeezed my hand.

It was going to take more than a few new sheets and a throw rug to mask the memories in that room. Mom just didn't get it. I walked past her bedroom and peered inside. She still had all the same bedroom things. *How could she sleep in there knowing what happened?*

I tried to look forward to going back to school but I still didn't know how I would face everyone. I was approved for a parking pass earlier that year and was thankful I didn't have to ride the bus. I parked my car as far away from the entrance as possible and watched everyone file into the school.

Paul got out of a red Saturn halfway across the parking lot. Emerging from the driver's side was a beefy, blonde girl named Lea. She was pretty, but her personality was vile. She chewed tobacco and made it a point to sleep with everyone on the soccer team. If sex was what Paul wanted, he was certainly going to get it from her. I dabbed on some chap stick and took a deep breath.

"BROOKE! Oh my gosh!" Cristin flung her arms around my neck and circled around me, staring in disbelief. "Are you okay? What happened to—"

My feet left the ground as Judd tackled me, scooping me into his death grip.

"Judd…Brooke can't breathe!" I tapped his shoulder and laughed at his warm welcome.

"There is nothing funny about you disappearing. Nothing." He set me down and his eyes burned into mine.

"Judd, I'm sorry, I—"

"Brooke Ghostly Nolan, can it be true?" Sonia flashed me a quick smile before wrapping her arms around me. "We were so worried. You okay?"

I managed to shake my head. I didn't know who to talk to first.

"Get to class! Let's go, two minutes 'til the bell!" A hall monitor swept through the corridor.

Judd grabbed my hand. "I'll walk you to class."

"But your class is on the other side of—"

"I don't care. Come on."

He steered me through the hallway and I listened to him tell me how worried he was and how he couldn't believe I wouldn't return one message.

"I mean, is it true what your dad did?"

I abruptly stopped walking and flung him by the arm to face him. "Who told you my dad did anything?"

Judd's eyes widened. "Listen, if it's just a rumor it's okay. People were just worried."

"Judd, TALK!" My grip tightened on his upper arm.

"Wow! Okay muscles." He moved my hand down. "Some of the cheerleader girls were saying stuff. Some of their moms work in the front office, and they said they got some paper saying that if he showed up to the school they had to call the police."

Oh my God.

"They only told a few people. I mean I don't know who knows anything. You still haven't told me what's going on!"

A silvery voice from behind me made my heart skip. "Well, I see you've settled in easy enough."

Paul was standing inches from my face when I turned around. I followed his gaze to my hand, which was still resting on Judd's arm in my attempt to make him talk. He nodded, assuming the gesture was a sign of affection. "Right. See you later then." He turned and started down the hallway.

"Wait, Paul!" I let go of Judd's arm.

"Judd I'm sorry, we'll talk at lunch okay?" I called over my shoulder. Paul quickened his pace. "Paul! Will you wait?"

"Why? You obviously didn't." He blew through a group of girls.

"I'm sorry! Can you just wait?" I called after him. "Paul. Wait!" I reached out for his arm and he stopped, pulling his arm away.

"Don't touch me. Don't ever touch me again."

"Paul, please. What did I do to make you so—"

"You're disgusting. I bet everything that everyone is saying is true, and I had to hear about it through half the cheerleaders. I had no idea. I mean, I thought things happened when you were little not…" He ran his fingers through his hair and shifted his eyes. "I wouldn't touch you with a ten-foot pole. Don't ever talk to me again."

I watched, open mouthed, as he disappeared into the sea of people around us.

In homeroom I buried my face in my arms and tried to control the tears that were brimming around my eyes. I didn't call out when the teacher called my name for roll, and I didn't look up when she asked us to take out our books. Paul's voice echoed in my head all morning. *You're disgusting. I wouldn't touch you with a ten-foot pole. You're disgusting. You're disgusting.*

My stomach was uneasy as I tried to avoid contact with everyone all day. I skipped lunch and found a quiet spot under the bleachers in the gym. I moved through the motions just to keep up an appearance.

During fourth period my chemistry teacher put on an episode of Law and Order to show the forensic side of our chemistry lesson. The storyline was of a girl who got raped in Central Park. Halfway through, I got up, suddenly nauseous. I bolted for the classroom door and made it ten feet before Mr. Salorski's voice was behind me. "Brooke? Brooke, just a minute."

I turned around, unsure if I was going to lose what little breakfast I ate that day in the middle of the hallway.

"Look uh, I heard some things, you know. And I didn't want to single you out, but maybe I should have since I know what you're going through is probably very sensitive."

Please, God. Why?

"I'm okay with you spending the rest of the period in the guidance office if you want. You don't even have to come back to class. I'll send Cristin to the office with your stuff after this period."

I nodded and forced a 'thank you' before turning on my heel. I heard the classroom door click behind me and I raced past the bathrooms. I moved through the stairwell, down the old east hallway and out through the parking lot double doors. I didn't stop when I heard a hall monitor call after me, radioing for someone, and as I raced towards my car.

I needed to talk to someone. I had to get out of there. I reached my car and turned the ignition, ignoring the flailing arms of two hall monitors who had followed me outside.

"Gina, I hope you're home," I said to myself, watching the high school disappear into a blur behind me.

***

It took a week or two before I was able to snap out of it enough to get caught up on some schoolwork. Just when I started to get into a routine of going to all my classes again, more court dates rolled through.

Heather was my designated victim advocate. She was in charge of making sure I understood what was going on during the court proceedings and looked after my best interests. I listened to her rattle off information about our PFA, but I was having a hard time concentrating. Basically it was a piece of paper that said Earl couldn't come near anyone in the family, otherwise we could call the police and he would be arrested on the spot. I secretly hoped he would violate the order just so I didn't have to worry about him running around while they conducted the investigation, which seemed to be taking forever.

We stepped off the elevator and Heather stopped in front of the first door on the right. "Okay, you ready to go inside? Any questions?"

I shook my head. All I had to do was listen to what the judge said and maybe answer some questions. It seemed pretty straightforward.

Heather pulled open the door and whisked her hand motioning for me to go ahead. We sat on a bench behind a strawberry blond guy dressed in an expensive looking suit. He half smiled at me when he saw me sit down. "That's your lawyer, he works for the District Attorney's office," Heather whispered.

The door creaked open and I opened my mouth when Earl walked in. I reached out for Heather's hand so fast I startled her. "What's he doing here?" I hissed. A large jolly man with a very round face bobbled in behind him.

"He's here for the hearing too," Heather said. "It's all right. There are guards." She pointed toward the judge's seat and a uniformed guard eyed Earl as he sat down. I relaxed a little.

When the judge walked in everyone stood up, and I was surprised to see it was a woman. The TV always showed male judges. We sat down and I listened to my lawyer, trying to follow what he was saying. After a few minutes, the judge looked at me.

"Brooke Nolan, please take the stand." She turned over a piece of paper in front of her.

The stand?

I thought I would have to answer a question or two from my seat. I looked at Heather and she nodded. The judge pointed. "Up here, if you please, Brooke."

In a daze I sat down and was sworn in. "It states here on the report you filed with police that you had been molested by your father in the state of New York, is this true?"

I nodded.

"Is this true, Miss Nolan?" Her voice was icy. "Please speak up."

"Oh. Yeah, that's true."

"Yeah?" The judge raised an eyebrow. "Very well. Can you also tell me what happened between you and Mr. Nolan after moving to Pennsylvania?"

I looked at the paper in her hand. *She had the police report right in front of her, couldn't she just read what I wrote?* Embarrassed again, I fumbled trying to say the words: *rape, penis, vagina.*

"Do you remember what you wrote, Miss Nolan?" The judge narrowed her eyes at me.

A wave of regret washed over me the second I looked up and my eyes met with Earl's. *How am I supposed to do this? This judge is the definition of sophistication. I have to sit in this wide, open court full of people I don't even know and say that I was raped? Who is this jolly fat man behind Earl? Who is the man sitting beside the judge? Why is the officer staring at me?*

I looked up, blinking hard. "I was um. It's hard to…"

"Miss Nolan I need to know if anything happened between you and Mr. Nolan after your family moved here to Pennsylvania." She tapped a long fingernail.

"I think it was, um, I was…it was rape."

"You *think* you were raped?"

"No. I mean, yes. Yes, I was raped." My voice trembled above a whisper.

The judge sighed. "Brooke, it says here you claim you were raped twice by Mr. Nolan after moving to Pennsylvania, is that true?"

Jeez, much better. Yes or no questions please!

I nodded. The judge stared.

"Yeah. I mean, yes. Yes ma'am."

"All right." She shuffled through papers and rubbed the bridge of her nose. "That's all Miss Nolan, you may step down."

My pace quickened as I approached Heather and for a second I was terrified Earl would stand up and try and grab me. "Do you want to go out, get some fresh air?" Heather said, studying my face. I nodded.

I dangled my feet in a chair outside the courthouse and sucked in several deep breaths. Seeing Earl sitting right in front of me as I struggled to tell the court what happened was beyond the realm of terrifying. His eyes dug into me even when I didn't look up, I could feel them.

Heather escorted me into her office and sat down, my mom trailing behind us. "The judge has ruled in your favor. You have a PFA order that doesn't allow David to come within two hundred feet of anyone in your family. He can't call you, text you, or otherwise have any contact with any members of your family. If he does, just contact the police and they'll be there as soon as they can."

"I mean, this won't stop him from trying to come into the house or anything." I felt nervous at the idea. "It's only a piece of paper."

"It *is* only a piece of paper. But if he's stupid enough to violate it, it means he goes to jail sooner than later. Just keep on the lookout if you really feel he'll try to get near you."

* * *

It didn't help that the local fair started that week. Judd begged me to go and I was a hopeless wreck looking over my shoulder every two seconds. "It's all right Brooke, I got you." He pulled me closer to him. My cell phone rang and I pulled it out of my pocket. '*MOM*' flashed across the screen.

"Hey."

"Are you at the fair?"

"Yeah, why?"

"Leave. Leave now!"

"Mom…why? What's going on?"

"One of the neighbors just called me. Dad's walking around the fair, he's by the arena. Leave now."

I hung up and grabbed Judd by the arm. "We need to go." The alarm in my voice didn't give him a chance to question me.

"All right." He grabbed my hand and pushed me through the crowd, cruising through the sea of people like a security guard at a rock concert. We didn't stop until we got to his truck and he let me inside and locked the doors.

My heart was thrashing against my chest. "I'm sorry Judd. I'm sorry." I put my hand up to my mouth and tears formed around my eyes. It seemed like I was always on the verge of a breakdown.

"Hey no, no. It's okay. We can go to my house." He grabbed the back of my jeans by the belt and pulled me closer. I put my head on his shoulder and let the motion of his truck rock me to sleep as we drove into the countryside.

Chapter Nineteen

The nightmares started almost immediately after Earl was gone. Several of them would wake me from my sleep screaming, and others I would wake up sobbing uncontrollably. Sometimes I could remember them, other times I pushed them from my mind and took a steaming shower at three in the morning to relax. The body twitches were the worst. My arms and legs would fight to keep me awake to avoid the nightmares. My limbs would spastically jolt until I would become so exhausted sleep would find me.

Midge told me she was sorry my mom couldn't understand the trauma I was revisiting every time I stepped into the house. "She changed those sheets… and expects you to sleep soundly like nothing happened?"

The chair I chose most often was seated right next to Midge, and I shook my head confirming her statement.

"I'm sorry child. You found something that triggers you and unfortunately you can't help what other people do. No ma'am. The only thing you can change is yo'self."

"The only way I'd feel safe is if I wasn't there. But I'm only sixteen. I mean I work, but I don't know what I would do, where I would go."

"Do you have a friend you can stay with? Family maybe?"

I shook my head. I didn't know anyone's parents that would let me stay long term like that. Gina would, but Paul and I weren't even on speaking terms, never mind attempting to become roommates.

Midge got up from her leather chair and headed to a small bookcase adjacent to her desk. "I want to give you some information. I know you like readin' so you go ahead and read it." She placed a white packet in my hand. "It's about emancipation. You know what that is?"

Midge had taught me so many things about myself and other people. I didn't know how I could ever repay her. She told me that the day I walked into her office and told her I had finally told a family member about the abuse was payment enough. "I thought you was going to take that one to the grave, I did," she had said.

"Emancipation of a minor is when you become your own parent. Your mom won't be responsible for you no more, but you would need to prove you can support yourself, have a place to stay and take care of things like your school."

"All right, so why don't I just do that?"

"It's a long process sometimes. You have to file a petition with the family court, and your mom might try'n fight it. The judge does whatever's in the best interest of the child. It's not easy to get. Sometimes when a child's been abused it makes it easier, but not always. Depends on your judge an' what they think."

"I can't stay there anymore, Midge. You know, I walked into the bathroom the other day and saw the toothpaste sitting on the counter..." My gaze trailed off somewhere behind Midge as I remembered the panic attack that ensued. "I thought I was going to die. My heart nearly came through my chest just from looking at a tube of toothpaste. Why?"

"Child, listen to me." Midge clasped her hands over mine. "This is a long road you're headed down. You did a mighty brave thing for you and your siblings. Mighty brave. But now you need to focus on you. You gonna find out what triggers you, what upsets you, and it's gonna bring back memories. Sometimes good, but mostly bad. Ain't nothing you can do about that. What you can do, is figure out why it's happenin' and make sure you have those coping skills to beat it. You hear me? Now, don't focus on the fact the toothpaste made you have the anxiety, think *deeper*." She pointed to my heart. "Why do you think it made you as upset as it did?"

The toothpaste was always in the bathroom, and nothing had ever changed about it. It was an upright, white canister that dispensed two different kinds of toothpaste. It never changed.

"It never changed." I looked up at Midge, smiling. "The toothpaste never changed. Earl always bought the same kind. When I saw it, it made me think of him."

Midge nodded and winked at me. "There ya go, you found your trigger. Now you jus' gotta work on coping with it."

I read over the packet several times over the next few days. Ethan lay on my bed pulling at my hair with a toy brush as I highlighted some important parts. The thought of leaving him was my biggest hurdle, but Midge was right. I had to start focusing on myself and healing if I was ever going to be any kind of functional adult.

The suitcase I dragged up from the basement smelled musty. Mom followed me up the stairs, half panicking and half in tears. "Brooke you can't just leave. We changed that whole room around for you, your aunt spent a lot of money. What would she think?"

"I'm sorry Mom, it's not enough." If I was going to leave, I would have to do it fast and with minimal talking to avoid conflict.

"You're only sixteen! Where are you going to live, huh?" She watched me put a pair of jeans into the suitcase. "I'll just call the police. I'll tell them you ran away and they'll bring you back to me."

The packet Midge gave me was in Mom's hands. I had anticipated a remark like that from her, so I regurgitated what I had practiced in my head. "You can't, Mom. I'm emancipated. Since I was abused the court considers me emancipated, which means I am my own dependent now. I have a job, a car, and a place to go. I don't need your permission. Call Heather if you want, she'll tell you."

It was a risky lie. The packet showed that emancipation procedures could take months or years to decide upon. I didn't have that kind of time.

The nightmares were becoming increasingly vivid, and the tension surrounding my mom and me walked a fine line between uncomfortable and hostile. She felt I owed her something for taking the bread winner out of the house, and I felt she had no right to blame me for the financial mess she found herself in since I told. She could no longer afford the house with only her Social Security Disability checks to rely on and she refused to downgrade to a smaller home.

She stared at the white packet in her hands and shook it at me. "How could you do this to me? You're just going to leave, run away from your problems? How will that solve anything? What about us?"

My mom and siblings refused to go to the Women In Crisis center I had told them about. Mom was shocked to find I had been going there for over a year. I never told her Gina brought me. The services were free, and the healing couldn't just be on my end alone. Everyone was going to be dealing with a lot of anguish. It was unfair for Mom to ask me to support her and my siblings when I needed time to heal myself.

"I'm sorry, Mom." I reached over and kissed her cheek. "I need to do this for me."

Long weeks of sleepless nights leading up to me committing to the decision to leave, I decided that sleeping in my car would be more favorable than having to live in a house I could only see myself being tortured in.

A local gym hired me to work a few hours a week, which gave me a place to spend time and shower when I needed to. I had plenty of friends' houses I could bounce between when the temperatures would dip too low for me to sleep in my car and, since I got free breakfast and lunch through school, I only had to worry about dinner. Most of the time I was working at the telemarketing job in the evenings anyway and would get a hoagie or stromboli from the pizza shop next door. I still felt guilty, though, and gave Mom almost all of my paycheck each week, while still saving for my own place too.

Cristin was thrilled I was going to sleep at her house a few school nights every week, and assumed my new carefree schedule was Mom's attempt to win me over.

"My dad did that when my parents divorced. I could ask him for anything and he felt so guilty about not living at home I would always get what I wanted," Cristin said.

"Do you want seconds, dear?" Cristin's mom asked.

My plate was smothered in chicken, penne pasta and spinach. I shook my head with a mouth full of food. "No thank you, Mrs. Vanderport."

"*Miss* Vanderport. *Miss, Miss.* Not a *Mrs.* anymore." She twirled through the kitchen in an ocean blue mini dress and popped out her hip. "What do you think, girls? Think I could meet Mr. Right in this?"

"Ugh, Mom. Go away." Cristin waved her hand at her mom. "Where are you guys going anyway?"

"Not sure." She mumbled through the bobby pins sticking out of her mouth. "I'll be home late though, don't wait up. Bed early, you girls have school tomorrow."

Cristin's phone rang within minutes of her mom leaving. "Talk to me," she said, cradling the phone against her shoulder. "Mmm yep. Dustin's picking us up, so we'll be there around ten. All right? Yep. Bye."

"Who was that?"

"Party tonight. You know the guy I've been seeing, pizza parlor guy?"

I shook my head, smiling. "Sorry, can't keep up."

"Anyway, he's having some people over in the backroom of the pizza place after they close. The managers gave him a key."

"That a good idea?"

"Oh yeah, we do it all the time." Cristin shoved a piece of biscuit into her mouth. "Let's get ready. Dustin will be here in an hour to get us."

I only recognized two people when we walked into the backroom of the pizza parlor. About twenty or so faces turned in our direction when we pushed through the double doors. Cristin threw her arms around a girl I didn't know and they disappeared into another back room. I made my way around the kitchen making small talk with one person who looked vaguely familiar from my home economics class.

Cristin disappeared and reappeared all night, and I started to worry about where she went sometime after one in the morning. Making my way towards the back door I was engulfed in a plume of smoke.

The kitchen was on fire and Cristin was nowhere in sight. A sea of people blocked my way as I struggled to push through them, following the smoke. There was a bright EXIT sign above a back door and I flung it open just in time to catch Cristin explode in laughter, surrounded by a group of people.

Embarrassed that I had mistaken the smoke for a fire, I inhaled and watched the joints get passed around. When it got to Cristin, she wasn't coherent enough to keep it between her lips. She squealed when we saw me, though, and pushed a much older guy aside to give me a hug. Her breath reeked of alcohol.

"Cristin, you're drinking *and* lighting up?"

"Yaaaa man, come on, I'll get you some."

I held a hand up as a joint was passed to me. "That's okay. We need to get home."

A dark haired guy who was standing near Cristin earlier protested. "Ah come on, we just got here. Need to chill a little, ya know?"

I ignored him and led Cristin by the hand to find our ride home. Dustin was standing at one of the kitchen counters with two other guys in track jackets. He downed a shot of Jack Daniels as I tugged on his sleeve.

"Dustin, come on, we gotta go. Her mom'll be home soon."

Eyes half-closed he pointed at Cristin. "Heyyy you sloppy mess. You need'a go home?" He wiped a dribble of Jack that missed his mouth. "Mmk. Lesss go."

I squeezed Cristin's hand when we got outside and Dustin reached into his pocket for the keys. "We can't get in the car with him. He's wasted, look at him."

Cristin strained her eyes. "Ohh nah, he's okay. He does this allllll the time." She waved her hands above her head in the shape of a rainbow. "No problem."

"I'm *not* getting in the car with him." I stopped in front of her and crossed my arms. *Was she serious about letting this guy drive us home?*

"Ah, come on Brooke. He's good. Look. He's good."

Dustin dropped his keys on the pavement in front of him and cursed.

Cristin stared. "All right, maybe ask him if you can drive."

"Me drive? I don't even know this guy." Dustin reached into his pockets to try to find the keys that were already in his hands. I shook my head. "Hey, Dustin. Let me drive, okay?"

He squinted at me and brushed the blond hair from his face. "Ah no, it's cool. I got it."

Talking to either of them was getting me nowhere. I wasn't about to play mind games for the next two hours.

"Give me the keys." I held out my hand. "You're *not* fine, and you're *not* driving. I haven't had anything to drink." Cristin giggled beside me. "Or smoke. Don't be stupid."

Dustin smirked when I called him stupid and ruffled my hair. "All right little warrior, go for it. Don't wreck my car man, I love this car."

Within two miles Dustin was passed out cold in the backseat. "See Cristin?" I peered through the mirror. "He's out cold. What would have happened if he was driving?"

Cristin huffed as she turned around. "Oh wowww. He never does that, I swear it. He's like the best drunk driver I know."

"You've done this before?" My voice rose.

"See Brooke, that's why you're better than me. That's why you're gonna have a great life and be so successful." She completely ignored what I had just said.

"What do you mean?"

"You always think." She tapped a finger against her temple. "You know what to do all the time. You're like, the bestest friend ever." She looked out the window. "Oh hey, look. That tree looks like a cow."

"You're drunk. And you're smart too Cristin, you just make…" I fought for the right words, "Bad choices sometimes," I said, pulling into the driveway. Her mom's car wasn't there yet so I still had time to get everyone inside.

"No, not like you. I don't even really know what happened with your dad. I saw something in the paper but, I'm not sure. I mean, you must be really brave to stand up to your dad. I couldn't do that. I had an abortion last year, did you know? No one really knows. My mom would have killed me."

My eyes widened. "Cristin, I had no idea. I'm sorry."

"No, no it's okay. You're so brave. You don't follow the crowd, like *some* people." She pointed to Dustin snoring in the back and giggled. "Plus it makes you totally hot, guys love that you have a mind of your own. Jason wouldn't stop staring at you all night."

"Jason?"

"Yeaaah. The guy with the dark hair. Tan skin. He's yummy. He stared at you all night. Stared. I saw him. How did you not notice? I ate a pickle before. Oh, Brooke?"

"Yeah?"

"Imma throw up now. Can you help?"

I threw my door open and raced around the front of the car.

Chapter Twenty

Cristin was tired of watching me mope around over Paul and thought meeting someone new would be a good idea. "Jason's a total sweetheart. He used to smoke weed, but not anymore, I know you don't like that. I told him to meet you at your locker after gym."

I moaned. "You didn't." Cristin *would* finagle a blind date in high school somehow.

"What's the big deal? You met him already."

"No I didn't."

"Yeah, you did. He was tan-boy staring at you all night at the party Dustin took us to. Remember?"

"Vaguely." I shut my locker.

"He drives a really old pickup truck. I'll show you after school in the parking lot. He's a real country boy. Just wait. He'll be here."

Jason never showed up.

He didn't show up anytime that week either. It turns out he wasn't too interested in the random meet-and-greet our high school hallways had to offer either. I was on my way to Cristin's from work one night when I noticed his 78' Ford truck taking up two spaces at the Shop'N'Stop gas station. He waved nervously when he saw my Cavalier at the stoplight. Too embarrassed to just drive away after I had been spotted, I cruised into a parking spot beside him.

"What does this thing get, ten miles to the gallon?" I asked, trying to project my voice over the roar of the engine.

"Eight, actually." He jumped down from the raised truck, brushing his hands on the leg of his Carharts. He leaned against a rusted fender and cocked his head to the side. The smell of oil blasted my nostrils when he moved closer, and I cringed at the rips and holes in his clothes. I knew I hated clothes shopping, but he took that hostility to a whole new level. When he smiled, though, I forgot all about the quirky smells and the cosmetic indifference of his appearance.

"You're Brooke, right? I'm heading to a buddy's house. Wanna go?"

The rest, Cristin would say, was history.

The truth was that Jason didn't speak to me for weeks after hanging out that night. I made no attempt to reach out to him either. It wasn't until I was with Sophia at the local auto shop, getting new windshield wipers, that she spotted Jason working behind the counter and called me out on the obvious. "Hey, isn't that the guy Cristin tried to hook you up with a few weeks ago?"

I craned my neck. "Yeah."

He was in his work uniform, helping a guy with tired hands pull a part out of a box. He appeared enthusiastic about the conversation, flashing a handsome smile every time the guy said something.

"You like him." Sophia pointed at me.

"I do not. I don't even know him."

"You should have seen your goofy face two seconds ago. You think he's totally hot. Let's go tell him."

I grabbed her wrist. "No, don't. Come on, let's go."

"You're seventeen and have had one boyfriend. *One*. Prom is at the end of this year. You know, Senior Prom? So either you go tell him he's hot or I'll do it for you."

I compromised. "I'll leave my number on his truck. He's busy. I don't want to interrupt him at work." He thanked the customer as he left and made a goofy face at one of the guys he worked with. It was the same face he would use over the next several months to get me to laugh until I couldn't breathe.

"Fine." Sophia rolled her eyes. "Chicken. I'm gonna watch you write the note."

Jason texted me sometime after eleven that night. I felt like a creeper explaining to him why I left my number on his truck. He didn't seem to mind though, and we thought it would be a good idea to hang out again.

He kissed me when he left after our second date. He ran his hand over my cheek and through my hair as he pulled me closer. When he backed away he touched our foreheads together, wrapping an arm around my waist. He smiled and I could feel the nervousness rattling in his fingertips. We were inseparable after that.

Jason's parents had recently divorced and on the day I saw him at the gas station he was headed to sleep at his buddy's house. Technically he was living out of a motel outside of the school district's boundaries. He slept at a friend's house during the week to avoid the fifty-five minute commute and tried to pretend that his life was somewhat normal by surrounding himself with friends. I respected and understood that. The responsibilities and burdens that we both shared were more than any teen should have needed to tolerate, but it drew us closer.

Right around the time his mom found a small house in a beat-up part of town is when Jason realized I was mainly living out of my car. Two days later, and after meeting his mom only once, I was moved into one of only two bedrooms that the house offered.

Jason's older brother took the only other bedroom, and his mom slept on the futon in the living room. I felt like I was putting her out and was uncomfortable with it, but she insisted that the futon was sturdier for her back. "And besides," she had said, "there is no way I am going to let you live in your car".

Going to court became difficult when I had to explain to Jason where I was going all the time. Paul's reaction, when he found out, scared me into thinking that I should hold off on telling Jason what was really going on. All I told him was that I was going to court because of my dad. I let his imagination fill in the rest of the blanks, and for a long time he never pressed me for any explanations beyond that. I dreaded the day he would want to have a deeper conversation about it. I wanted to tread lightly because I found myself falling hopelessly in love with Jason, even though I wasn't ready to admit that to myself yet because of Paul. I didn't want to scare Jason away.

Earl was finally officially arrested, and he made bail the very next day. Eight months had passed since the time I filed the police report and they conducted their investigation. The judge ordered forty thousand dollars bail, but he only had to come up with ten percent, or four grand in his case, so he was free to go until the preliminary hearing.

Heather called and explained about the preliminary hearing. "Now the purpose of this hearing is just to establish *if* a crime was committed, based on the facts, and *if* it was the defendant that probably committed the crime. A preliminary hearing doesn't mean he's guilty or not guilty, it's just there to establish if we can move on to the next step. Understand?"

I nodded into the phone, the weight of the anatomy textbook in my lap grounding me. "Do I have to do anything?" I asked.

"We have the burden of proving a crime was committed. That means you'll have to testify in front of a judge again and explain what happened. It won't be at the courthouse though. Preliminary hearings happen at the magisterial district court. It's a smaller court closer to where you live. We'll also introduce the things we found in the home as evidence."

"What did they find?" Mom didn't tell me anything about evidence.

"You really want to know?"

"Yeah. Please."

"They found a Barbie in one of his toolboxes. One of your old Barbie dolls. She had a hair tie in her hair that belonged to you. The Barbie was naked."

I closed my eyes.

"They also found a lot of pornographic material. Magazines, videos, that kind of thing." Heather paused one second too long.

"What was wrong with having the porn?"

Heather sighed. "There was a picture of you between the pages, an older one. You were maybe eight or nine. It was taped to one of the faces of the women."

Heather told me Earl would be at court, but it would be unlikely that he would take the stand since the burden of proving anything was on my lawyer. Bail could be modified if the judge thought he might become a flight risk. I hung up the phone and tried to concentrate on the anatomy terms in front of me. It was going to be a long week.

Since the preliminary hearing was held in the magisterial district court, Mom and I crammed into the eight by eight sized waiting room. There was a tiny window on the front door and a dim overhead light. Heather hurried inside and pointed towards another door on the other end of the room. "In there, quickly. David is here. We'll wait in the courtroom."

Heather ushered us into a cramped space and I started to look around. We were surrounded by boxes of files, mops, and cleaning supplies. "Heather, are we in a closet?"

"Might as well be." She rolled her eyes. "These magisterial courts jump from place to place depending on the rent. This is definitely one of the smaller ones. We'll wait in here until your lawyer and the judge get here. This way you don't have to see him."

It made me feel better that she tried to not use his name around me. She never would call him *Dad*. Adam and Thomas still did though, whenever they would ask for an update on what was going on. I heard Thomas in the kitchen one day when I was over visiting. "Mom, is Dad ever coming back?" The heaviness in his voice could crush a car.

"Let's go." Heather whisked us into the musty courtroom and I saw Earl watch me come out of the room in my peripheral vision. We stood only eight feet from the judge and less than five feet from Earl and his lawyer. I silently hoped that I would not have to go up next to the judge to tell him what happened, and that I could stay standing next to Heather. I would be so close, too close, to Earl. I hated that he and his lawyer got to stand next to the only exit in the room. I was trapped.

"All rise for the Honorable Judge Constance."

It was harder to concentrate with a guy judge sitting in front of me. I felt like every time my lawyer made a remark about rape or abuse, the judge glanced my way. Once again I had to tell the judge, in my own excruciating words, what happened.

With my hands clasped together, I sped over the information at lightning speed to prevent my face from getting too enflamed. The judge was satisfied with my overall general description and didn't ask me to give further details on any of the rapes or abuse. Heather had said to keep my explanations simple since this was not the place where it was determined if he was guilty or not guilty.

Earl was lead from the courtroom after both sides provided their evidence. Even though I had to go before a judge to get the Protection From Abuse order, it was no easier to stand in front new people to explain my situation all over again.

By the time I arrived back home, exhaustion had kicked in and I didn't care that I had an exam the next day. I dropped my things at the bedroom door and crawled under the covers next to Jason.

"So how'd your court thing go?" He pulled a blanket around us and stroked my hair as my cheeks molded into his bare chest.

"Okay I guess. Just have to wait now."

Jason nodded. "You seem tired."

"Exhausted."

He yawned in response. "Me too. I think we're the only seventeen year olds that work as much as we do."

"Wouldn't be surprised."

The bed groaned as Jason leaned to his left and grabbed something off the dresser. He moved his hand under the blanket and placed a cell phone sized box in my hand. I scrunched my face and looked up at him. His pearly teeth greeted me. When I sat up and opened the Littman Jewelers box, a diamond encrusted pendant necklace reflected off the light in my eyes.

"I mean, if I didn't work so much I couldn't afford to get my baby a six-month anniversary gift, so I'm okay with it." His grin was so wide I could see his gum line. He brushed the hair away from my neck to clasp the back of the necklace.

"There's three diamonds. One for the past," he said, lips moving over my neck. "One for the present. And one for the future." Warm, shallow breathing caressed my ear.

His lips were pressed firmly against mine as we lay back on the bed. My cheeks in his hands, he pulled away long enough to say I love you and then resumed drizzling my face in kisses.

I pulled at the pendant and looked it over in my hand. "This is so beautiful. Thank you. That was so sweet." Secretly, I was impressed he made such a big deal out of our six-month anniversary.

Earlier that week when I was with Midge, I had given her an attitude during our session. I still missed Paul so much, and I felt guilty being in a relationship when I was still thinking about someone else.

"I haven't even told Jason I love him back yet, because I don't think you can love two people at once. I do love him. But I miss Paul."

"Why do you miss him?" asked Midge.

I sneered at her. "What do you mean *why*?" The answer seemed obvious to me. He was my first boyfriend and I loved him.

"Tell me about the things Paul did that make you miss him."

I considered what she was asking me. Every time I opened my mouth, no words came out. Any response I could come up with was irrelevant. What I missed was the closeness I felt to him and his family when I shared my day with them. The memories of how

Paul and I kissed and laughed were missed too, but it wasn't the reason my heart was hurting. His family filled a void when I needed it the most. I missed that.

Grasping the pendant in my hand, silent tears slid down my face. By the time Jason realized I was crying he was leaning over me, wiping them away with his finger. "Baby, what's wrong?"

"I need to tell you something. But I don't know how to tell you."

He brought his face closer to mine. His voice was barely above a whisper, and it was soothing. "Tell me."

"I don't know how."

"Just try."

"Doesn't it seem weird that I'm the only one who has to go to court all the time? Adam, Thomas, and Kat don't."

"I've thought about that." His arms encased my body. "I thought it was because of your parents' divorce."

"I miss so much school. Isn't it weird that I have to miss that much school for court? For a divorce?"

He was silent for a minute. "Brooke, I know you want to tell me something. It's okay. I'm here to listen. You don't have to cry."

"My dad…David…" I realized that Jason probably didn't even know my dad's name since we'd never talked about it. I shifted and turned toward him, face to face. I had to see his reaction when I told him. I needed to know what he felt the second I said something.

"He raped me. I have to go to court because of the things he did to me."

Jason's expression was agonizing. His grip tightened on my sides as he blinked. "I'm sorry, Brooke. Baby, I'm so sorry." He picked up my face. "Why are you crying? Did you think that what you said would change how I felt about you?"

"It's not up to me if things change." I remembered Paul's face in the hallway and the hurtful comments he made before turning his back on me for the millionth time. "It's up to you if you want things to change."

I held my breath as Jason thought for a minute. He always needed a minute to gather his thoughts, almost as if he considered every viable solution and circumstance before he would speak.

"That isn't going to change anything at all." His gaze shifted from somewhere off in the distance to my face. "It wasn't your fault. What kind of person would I be to leave because of something so…so…" He lifted a hand to exemplify his loss of words. "…Stupid. Something like that would *never* change how I feel about you, because that's something that *happened* to you. It's not who you are. I love *you*, Brooke. I'll always love you."

"Are you sure?" I asked, smiling through tears.

Jason's reaction had been so completely opposite of Paul's, I thought for a second he was being sarcastic. His eyes told me differently. They were hurt for me, confused, and trying to figure out why I felt responsible.

"I'm going marry you one day, Brooke. I'm sure of that. And I'm sure that there is nothing about your past that would make me love you less."

Exhausted from crying and the emotional rollercoaster of the preliminary hearing, I settled into Jason's arms. Relief rushed through my veins and drowsiness crept in.

"I have to tell you one more thing," I whispered.

"Anything."

"I love you, Jason."

Chapter Twenty-One

"Brooke Nolan, could you please stand up?"

Hearing my name evaporated the daydream I was in as I looked around Mr. Heinz's history class. There were two weeks left until graduation. The parade of court hearings I was summoned to was overwhelming and I was having a hard time making it to class, never mind actually paying attention to what was going on.

"Up, up. On your feet." His white moustache bounced all over his lips as he used an index finger to visually make me rise from my seat.

"Now that you're standing, could you please inform the class what is so important that you consistently feel the need to skip my class?"

Chuckles from the back of the room initiated a flood of heat to my face.

"I don't believe the answer is in your textbook, Miss Nolan, no need to look down. Look at me. That's better. Now, if it's not too much to ask, as soon as we get your response we can continue today's lesson. Unless you planned on not being here for that either."

Judd gripped the sides of his desk and I knew it would be a matter of seconds before he erupted in Mr. Heinz's face if I didn't respond. "I'm sorry if asking a classmate for the notes I missed was disrupting your lesson. I'll wait until after class next time."

"No no, don't sit down. I appreciate the apology but you still haven't told the class exactly what it is you're skipping my class for."

"I have notes."

"You have notes? So now as long as you have a note from Mommy or Daddy it's okay to skip school?"

"It's none of your business."

Mumbled laughter and whooping noises rose from the crowd behind me. Exhaustion had a way of making me care less about what other people thought, and his persistence crawled under my skin in a way that normally wouldn't have bothered me before.

"*Excuse* me?" he asked, crossing the room. "This class *is* my business young lady. Your *grades* are my business, so you can pick up your things and head to the principal's office." A finger jabbed in my face.

My book bag was over my shoulder before he finished his sentence. Judd started packing up his things too, in an act of solidarity and support.

"And *you* can add some more wax to that gleaming bald head of yours and go to hell, Mr. Heinz."

Judd raced down the hallway after me and as we turned the corner we could still hear the chaotic laughter echoing from the classroom.

"That was *amazing*," Judd said. "Did you see his face? You know you're getting at least a week of In-School Suspension for that, right? No one will be able to take that guy seriously for the rest of the year now. Ah man, I wish I recorded that."

"I won't get any In-School, I *am* going to the principal's office."

After talking with the principal about what happened, he had a sit-down with Mr. Heinz. A day later he apologized for outing me in class. "I uh, didn't realize your situation. I'll be a little more discreet next time."

Heather called as I was leaving school later that week and I fumbled through papers and books, listening to her ringtone chime away in my bag. She got right to the point when I picked up. "Hey Brooke, got a minute?"

"Yeah, go ahead."

"You okay? You sound…"

"Rough week at school. It's okay."

"I bet. Hang in there. Anyway, you know the defense has asked for a continuance for a fourth time with the next hearing. They're really trying to drag it out since they probably don't have much to go off of as far as any kind of defense is concerned."

"What do they keep continuing for? How long can they keep doing that?"

"Who knows? They say they need time to gather more evidence for the defense. And it can go on as long as the judge allows it. But we had a hearing this morning, you know you didn't have to be there, and the judge decided that they won't move ahead until you undergo a psychiatric evaluation and a physical. The defense requested it."

"*I'm* the one that needs a psychiatric evaluation?"

"I know. We have thirty days to complete it, so I have a few calls out. We'll try and get this done as soon as possible okay?"

"What's the physical for?"

"They want to check for STDs."

"What? What for? Heather, did he have STDs? Did he give me something?"

"Calm down, sweetie. We don't know. All we know is that they want to have you tested."

An uncomfortable silence traveled through the lines before anyone spoke.

"Did you find out your ranking yet?" Heather changed the subject. She never liked to hang up until we talked about something other than the trial. She always tried to distract me from the weight of our conversations.

"Yeah, I did actually. I'm ranked thirty-two out of four hundred fifteen students. Nowhere close to valedictorian anyway."

"That's great Brooke, Penn State would be crazy not to take you." Her enthusiasm was genuine.

"They did."

"They did? Oh honey, congratulations! Did you tell your mom yet?"

"Not yet."

I hung up with Heather, realizing that I hadn't told Jason I was accepted to Penn State either. College meant I would be leaving town, but he knew how much it meant to me. Now that I got my acceptance letter, it was something we would need to talk about.

Jason threw his uniform on the floor and flopped onto the bed, staring at the ceiling. "I can't believe the people who own this house are making us move out. It's not our fault Jersey schools suck and they wanna move their kids to Pennsylvania instead."

"How much time are they giving us?"

"Barely thirty days, which I don't think is legal. We'll have time to graduate and go on vacation with my mom to Canada, but we'll only have about a week after we get back to move."

"To where?"

"I don't know, Brooke." He covered his face with his hand. "I can't work more than I already do. My brother is moving in with his girlfriend and my mom has a friend she can stay with, but she won't go unless she knows I have a place to stay too."

"Do you?"

"I'm not going anywhere without you. Come here."

My head was on his chest and I could feel the frustration building up inside of him. It seemed like an ideal time to bring up my acceptance letter. I had an idea.

"Well, maybe we can move. Together."

"Where?"

"Two hours from here?"

Jason let out a long breath before replying. "What are you not telling me?"

I sighed and sat up. "I got accepted to Penn State."

He moved his hand from his face and the pools of chocolate in his eyes softened. "Are you leaving me?"

"I don't want to."

"Then why are you getting upset?"

"Come with me."

"I can't live with you at college."

"We'll get an apartment. I don't want to live in the dorms anyway."

"We haven't even slept together yet and you want to get an apartment two hours from here, not knowing anybody, so you can go to school?" The idea sounded ridiculous when he said it out loud.

"Yes?"

He had moved from the bed to the wall length dresser and was staring at his reflection while he tapped his fingers. He had four inches of height on me, which gave me the perfect place to rest my head against his chest when I wanted to and I could kiss him without going up on tiptoes. His leather-like hands brushed over his crew cut and rubbed the stubble that covered his neck.

The corner of his mouth turned up as he looked at me. "All right, baby. I'm in."

"Yeah?" I uncrossed my legs and wrapped my arms around his waist, bringing my face up to his.

"Yeah, are you crazy? I'm not letting you go. So stop crying."

***

Heather's phone call about getting a physical to check for STDs crept into my mind every waking second, so I made an appointment at Planned Parenthood so Jason and I could get tested sooner. I told him it was the responsible thing to do if we were going to plan on being sexually active, which was true, but I had to know.

Both of us got a clean bill of health a week before high school ended, and we made fun of each other over our inexperience and ignorance about the pamphlets they gave us when we left. Instead of rushing, we held hands under tangled sheets and whispered in excited voices about living together in an apartment all of our own.

The graduation ceremony was moved indoors as the sky threatened to rain all morning. Paper fans littered the stands as we filed to the front of the gymnasium to claim our fake and temporary diplomas. They mailed the real ones a few weeks later, just after I got a call from Heather telling me that my psych evaluation was flawless, and enough evidence was finally submitted to bind the case over to criminal court.

"They'll have a formal arraignment now. David will have to enter his plea. He could plead guilty and there would be no trial, but I wouldn't count on it. They pushed too hard during the preliminary hearing."

Earl entered a not guilty plea and a trial date was set for three months later. I realized I would be in the middle of my freshman year of college when it started, but I tried to focus on our upcoming vacation, work, and packing to move instead.

Our vacation to Canada marked the first time Jason was ever out of the country. We stopped along tourist spots and landmarks, snapping pictures and saving candy wrappers that were written out in their native French language. Moments before arriving at the campgrounds where we would be staying, Jason's mom pulled off on the shoulder and pointed to a sign as we exited the car.

"It's called Bridal Veil Falls. You can walk behind it, you know. It feels like you're part of the waterfall," Laura said, holding hands with her boyfriend Sam.

"How long have you guys been dating?" I asked.

"About five months now, right?" Sam said, motioning to Laura while she nodded. "Yeah, about that."

"How did you find this place Sam? It's breathtaking."

"Since it's on an Indian Reserve, you can only get here if you have the proper I.D., which I do. I wanted to bring you guys here. It's one of the most peaceful places I know."

"Brooke, follow me." Jason descended the boulder-encrusted path leading to the waterfall.

The serenity that warmed my bones the further we drove from Pennsylvania was welcomed. I needed to get away, even if only for a short time. By the time we planted foot on Manitoulin Island, I was coaxed into an absolute dreamland state of mind. Jason pointed. "Let's get behind the waterfall."

"Have you ever seen something like this?" I yelled, as blankets of water cascaded over the ledge in front of us. Specks danced on my face and I beamed at Jason.

"It's beautiful. Just like you."

A marquise cut diamond was perched on my ring finger before I realized why Jason was getting down on one knee. "Is this for real?" I asked.

"I want to know if you'll be mine forever. It was my mom's ring and I'll get you your own, when we have the money. It's my promise to you, Brooke. I want to marry you one day. Will you wear it?"

His body pressed against mine, I steadied my feet on the rocks and kissed him in response.

"I can't believe this. Does your mom know?"

His eyes smiled. "Turn around."

Laura and Sam had followed us down to the water's edge and were snapping pictures of us. Laura noticed we looked up and shook her left hand at me. "Hello lovebirds, smile here!"

"Oh my gosh. I'm the *only* one who didn't know?"

"You know now. And stop covering your face, she's trying to take pictures."

Jason nudged me as he sat down at the table that night for dinner. "You don't need to make sure it's there every two minutes. It won't fall off ya know." He passed a beer to me from the cooler and clinked the necks of the bottles. "To us."

Jason had consumed six beers before I realized he was an emotional drunk, and I hustled him to bed with his arm around my neck.

"Baby, I love you, you know. You're the greatest—" He hiccupped. "The greatest woman of them all. You, right here." He patted the bed next to him and I struggled to keep a straight face while I pulled his sneakers off.

"I know, Jason. Hey, come here. Are you crying?"

"I would have stopped it you know."

"Stopped what? I think you should lay down."

"I would have stopped him, that jerk. I'm so sorry he did that to you, Brooke. I wasn't there. I wasn't there and I couldn't stop him."

I suddenly realized his intentions and my heart sank as I soothed his wet face with kisses. "It's not your fault, baby. There was nothing you could have done."

"Why? Why though? I could have stopped him." His helplessness ripped my heart in half. Drunk-Jason had no doubt that if we were together, he would have been able to save me.

The truth was, *I* wasn't ready to save me. I had kept it a secret for so long, that when it finally did come out, the people closest to me felt like they missed something and blamed themselves. It told me I did an exceptional job of concealing my secret, but a lot of people I loved felt responsible.

"No, baby. It's okay. I wasn't ready to let people know yet. Even if we were together, you wouldn't have known."

"I would have known. And he'd be dead. That's for sure."

"Okay, all right, let's lay down." My hand feathered through his hair until he was breathing softly beside me.

The next morning was rough for Jason as we packed up the car and headed for the Canadian border. I turned on my cell phone only after we got into upstate New York to make sure I didn't get any roaming charges. I had two voicemails from my mom.

"Hey, I'm still on my way back from Canada but I saw I had two voicemails. What's up?"

"I don't have the six hundred dollars you owe me for this month. I need it."

"Ethan okay? He's screaming in the background."

"He's fine. I need the money."

"I had to buy my textbooks for college. I got them online but they were still over three hundred dollars."

"I don't care how much they were, my name is on your car and if you don't make a payment it's *my* credit that gets screwed. When will you have the money?"

"I know, Mom. I'll have it to you next week before the grace period is over. You know I only get paid every two weeks." Jason looked at me as I tried to remain civil.

"And what's this I hear you're getting an apartment? You would rather give some stranger your money than help out your own mother and just live at home?"

"Yeah because I'll be closer to school. And I would have to share a bedroom with Kat again, so Jason couldn't live there."

"He doesn't need to live here. You do. I don't know what you're doing with him anyway, it's not like he's going anywhere in life."

"Where exactly is he supposed to go?"

"Look at yourself Brooke. You don't dress up anymore or wear makeup. It's like you let yourself go and you're only eighteen. And for what? To be with a guy who has no future 'cause he doesn't even want to go to college?"

"We *can't* go to college at the same time Mom, one of us needs to keep a roof above our heads."

"You can do that here. That's just an excuse."

"I love Jason, Mom. I'm sorry he doesn't have tons of money and doesn't want to be a lawyer or doctor so that you'd like him better. This isn't about you, this is about what I want."

"It's always about what you want! What about me, huh? You think I chose this? You think I wanted to live like this? Now I know why women don't tell on their husbands, how are they supposed to survive?"

I gasped in a stunned silence. *Did she really just tell me that she didn't tell on Earl because of money? Would that imply that she knew all along?*

"I don't care what you think of Jason, Mom. I love him and he loves me and I'm sorry if that's not good enough for you. Maybe if you were focused on a person's character instead of their wallet you wouldn't have had a pedophile for a husband. Jason is my *fiancé* now, and I could care less what you think."

Jason reached for my hand as my cell phone went sailing across the car. "It's okay, take a second. Just calm down."

Laura's voice trailed from the backseat. I had forgotten his mom was there. "Brooke, honey, I'm so sorry. I had no idea," she said, her voice incredulous. She had been oblivious to what I had been going through, and Jason turned up the radio to try and stifle my crying.

When we got home, Jason reviewed my car insurance policy after he started questioning how much money I was giving my mom each month. I was stunned to find out that Mom had been telling me I owed her two hundred dollars more a month than I needed to give her. I had been paying for everyone else's insurance in the whole house for over a year.

Jason demanded that I confront my mom and insist I only pay what I owed for my own vehicle, so I did. It only made her hate Jason more, and I was livid that my car would have been paid off before I even started my freshman year of college had I not been giving her so much extra money each month.

"She was using you, Brooke," he said. "I'm sorry. I guess she didn't know where else to get the money since Earl is not contributing, so she just told you that your insurance was so much each month."

As I watched the relationship with my mom deteriorate in front of my eyes, I tried to reason in my head that after the trial everything would go back to normal.

Chapter Twenty-Two

"They wanted to use my journals as evidence," I said, twirling a lock of wavy hair around my finger. "But then they took it back when they realized that I probably had more damaging information in them than supportive for the defense."

"I imagine you would have been really upset. Those are personal to you," Midge said.

"Yeah. Beyond personal. I've had a journal since I was what, six? Seven?" I stared at the advocate posters littering Midge's office. Coloring pages that clients had given her with rainbows and happy faces were tacked behind her desk. The beanbag chair I squished into every week was beginning to wear at the stitching, and I plucked at a loose string.

"What's bothering you, child?"

"I just can't believe you're really leaving."

"No need to whisper. I'm movin' on I ain't dyin'. Besides, you moved two hours from here, maybe you need to find a counselor closer to where you living and save some gas. I got a good opportunity to help those kids in Colorado, it's a good thing for me."

"I know. But the trial is next week. I thought I would have you here until it was over at least."

"No telling how long those take. You've been going to court, what, well over a year now? And you just gettin' into the main arena?" Midge shook her head. "Sad, I tell you. They wonder why women give up. Drag them through the mill for justice, and a year later still nothing?"

She leaned forward in her chair. "You got Gina, you got your knight in shining armor, and your mom. Even though we both don't agree with her, she still going to be there for you 'cause she needs to be. You even got Miss Heather. That's a good support team if I ever saw one."

"Midge, did anything ever happen to you? Is that why you counsel women?"

"Would it help you any, if you knew?"

"I think so."

Midge nodded. "Mmmhmm. Get on over here close to me so I don't gotta talk loud about it, make myself all rattled up. Normally I don't tell my story, but I'm movin' on anyways." She cleared her throat.

"I was thirteen, growin' up on the banks of North Carolina when my older brother Jon came in my bedroom. He was a man now, just turned twenty-one and had a bottle of Jack in him before dinner time that day. Mama was at work, my daddy died when I was three from heat stroke. It was just Jon and me. He came in my room with that empty bottle and closed the door behind him. Turned my blood cold when I saw the look on his face. My pants were ripped off, shirt undone, and I screamed. Oh Lord, did I ever scream. He raped me for over twenty minutes before he stumbled off me, drunk as a skunk, and I took my chance and I ran."

I reached out for Midge's hand as she continued. "Ran straight through our sliding glass door I did, straight through, shattered it. All the way down to the neighbors house, about two miles. Neighbor pulled up just as I started bangin' on the door and she about fainted when she saw the blood. 'Bleedin' like a pig' she said, and 'naked as a newborn'. She wrapped me in a blanket, called the cops. They showed up, policeman Smitty. That was his name, Smitty. Took them two hours to find Jon hiding in the fields behind our house. They found him, and arrested him on the spot."

"Good, I'm glad they got him."

Midge held up a finger. "Over two hundred stitches to close me up. Jon spewed some story that I was in the shower and he scared me with a Halloween mask so I ran through the glass door all on my own doing." She shook her head. "When we went to court he spat at me, stood up in front of that judge and told me when he got out of jail he was gonna kill me."

"He went to jail right?"

"Sure he did, for all of eight months. See Jon was a bargaining man, and he found himself messed up in the wrong crowds of people, drug people. He gave over some names and they let him out in eight months."

"He plea bargained and got out in less than a year?"

Midge nodded. "That ain't even the sweetest part, child. When he got out, Mama let that fool back into our house like nothin' happened. For four months I slept with my dresser up against my door, waitin' for him to come and kill me. But he disappeared one night and we never saw him again."

"Midge, I can't believe your mom let him back in. Did you ever ask her why? Why would she do that to you?"

A hand trembled across her wet face. "Oh sure, I asked. She say, 'Because he my son, Midge, what you want me to do?' Last we heard he made his way to California, even got a woman to marry him. Wound up raping his wife's two-year-old baby. Can you imagine that? They got better laws now. They makin' sure he won't ever see the outside of those California walls again."

"I'm so sorry Midge, I am." I patted her hand as she grabbed a tissue. "I can't believe your mom let him back in the house. You're such a strong person."

"We both are, child. And you know why? We don't have the luxury of fallin' apart, for someone else to come picking up the pieces. We have a gift, you and I, we feel people's hurt and pain and take it as our own. That's what makes you protect your siblings like you do, without even being asked. It's what makes me work at a place like this, to do what I can. Ain't nobody gonna tell us it's all right to fall apart." She wagged a finger at me. "But you, you are somethin' else. You got something I didn't at your age, and I wish I did."

"What do I have that you didn't?"

"You have a Midge. And a Gina. You had a helping hand guide you to me, and make you realize that your worst fears were real. And we supported you, didn't we?"

I nodded, wiping my own face. "Then why do I feel so alone?"

"Because he wants you to feel like that. So you step down and you give up. But you look at me child and you promise me, promise me, you won't ever back down. Don't you feel sorry for him about to sit in a jail cell the rest of his life, and don't you feel sorry for your mama's money problems now that he's gone. You doing the right thing, for *you*, and anyone else he'll never be able to hurt now."

I promised Midge and hugged her close after our last session together. She was there for me when my journey started, and I hoped I learned enough to see the trial through to the end without her.

I met Heather at the courthouse that weekend. "I want to give you a tour of the courtroom and explain what will happen the day of the trial. There will be a lot more people in here than you're used to from the preliminary hearings, including a jury."

I followed her into the elevator as she spoke. "David changed his lawyer, a woman this time. Guess he didn't like the way the preliminary hearing turned out. Subpoenas are all out too."

"What's a subpoena?" I held the elevator door open for a police officer as we got off.

"It tells the person it's addressed to that they're being asked to serve as a witness in criminal court. You and your mom get one, so did Gina and Aunt Jean, and your mom's friend Ellen since David called her when you guys fled to New York."

We stopped in front of a white door with three wooden chairs lined up along the outside wall. Heather pulled a chain of keys from her pocket. "This is where you'll wait until your name is called to testify. Usually if you're subpoenaed they don't like you to sit in the courtroom listening to other people's testimony."

"Why not?"

"Everyone's testimony needs to be their own. We don't want people adding things to what they say based on what another person said. It happens sometimes, even if you don't mean it to."

"This is a big courtroom. Very white." I said, staring around at all the empty space.

"The judge sits at the front." Heather pointed to the tallest mahogany bench at the back of the room. "That door behind her bench is where she'll come in. The smaller seat to the side of her is where any witnesses will sit. If you're looking out at your lawyer, the jury will be to your left in that row of benches."

"Will I see him?"

"Yes, he'll be sitting right here." She pointed to the one desk. "Your lawyer will be right here." She tapped the other desk. "Anyone supporting you that isn't subpoenaed will be sitting behind your lawyer. Anyone supporting him will do the same. Kind of like when you go to a wedding."

"What if I don't want them to?"

"If it's anyone you know, you can let them know it's uncomfortable to have them in the room while you're testifying. That's perfectly fine. Now go ahead and sit up there on the witness stand so you know what to expect."

My sneakers echoed across wooden floor of the box and I sat, facing Heather. "Like this?"

"Yup. You can adjust the microphone when you get up there if you need to. How do you think you'll feel when you talk about what happened to you in front of people you don't know?"

"Scared. I haven't even talked to people in my family about it really, and now I have to tell complete strangers."

Heather nodded and smoothed her suit jacket. "It will be difficult, I won't lie. You'll be talking about very personal things. But you can look at your lawyer or me when you're answering a question if it'll make you feel better. You don't need to look at David at all. They'll ask you to point him out one time, just to identify him."

"How come none of my siblings are testifying? He hurt them too. Not in the same way, but wouldn't that count?"

The frown on Heather's face told me she agreed with me. "The police interviewed your siblings, yes. But they're very scared of him. We wouldn't want to make them testify if they aren't able to, we don't want to do anything that would hurt the outcome of the trial."

I was confused. "Why would anything they say hurt?"

"If a child is unsure they want to testify because they are afraid, sometimes they will say one thing when they feel safe, but when they're confronted…" Heather pointed to where Earl would be sitting. "They freeze or they recant what they said, then say it wasn't true because they feel bad like they're a tattletale. It's hard for people your age and younger to testify against someone who is supposed to love and protect them."

"Not even Adam will?"

Heather shook her head. "You have the weight of the world on your shoulders, I'm sure. You're the only one who can do it."

Heather followed my gaze to where Earl would be sitting. "There will be what's called a bailiff, most likely two of them, standing near him. They'll be in police uniforms. He won't get near you, that I can promise. There is also going to be a court reporter sitting right in front of the judge's stand. It's his or her job to write down everything that people say."

"There's going to be a lot of people in here."

"Yes, there will be. But this is a safe place. No one is here to judge you or tell you these things didn't happen. The only one doing that will be the defense."

I stepped down from the witness stand and gazed up at the fluorescent lighting that lit up the room. The bright lights and people were definitely going to make me feel vulnerable.

"What if I say the wrong thing, or don't know an answer?" All eyes would be on me. If I messed up, he could walk free.

Heather bent at the knees to be eye level with me. "There is no wrong answer when you tell the truth. If they ask you a question and you don't know, you're allowed to say you don't know. If you don't remember, then say that. The questions the defense will try and ask you are meant to trick you, but if you're telling the truth, there won't be anyone to trick."

"Okay. And you'll be here?"

She squeezed my hand. "I'll be here."

Chapter Twenty-Three

I threw up before we got in the elevator to go down to the courtroom. I hoped my stomach wasn't giving me an indication of how the rest of the day was going to go. The waiting room just outside the courtroom was packed with people I knew. They smiled encouragingly from across the room and whispered among each other as light from the early morning sun glared through the only two windows in the lobby. There was no elevator music, no self-help pamphlets, not even a fire extinguisher in sight to stare at to pass the time.

Then they called my name.

Over fifty pairs of eyes redirected their attention to the white door when I walked in. I made it to the witness stand on autopilot and recognized the familiar shape of the seat from the day before. Foggy words poured from my lawyer's mouth. My heart was in my head, throbbing and echoing, and I glanced at the jury. One man smiled. I smiled back. *Was that wrong? Can I not smile at them?*

I was sworn in, raising my right hand as my lawyer approached the bench. Rob cleared his throat, and moved his tie to the side. He was ready. "Please state your name."

I flashed back to our conversation earlier that week. "We'll start off with small questions, easy questions, and let the jury get to know you," Rob had said. "It'll build up your confidence, plus we need to establish what kind of person you are to the jury."

"What if they don't like me?"

Rob smiled. "I wouldn't worry about that."

"Brooke Nolan," I said into the microphone, answering Rob's first question. It screeched and I pulled it closer to my face, clearing my throat.

Is that really my voice? I sound so scared.

We started with easy questions, some too easy. We flowed through the storyline of my life: where I went to school, my relation to the defendant, and the dates of when I moved to Pennsylvania.

"Can you explain the relationship between you and Mr. Nolan?" Rob raised his eyebrow. The questions were about to get heavy.

"There wasn't one, really." I looked at the jury, then down at my hands.

"During the length of time you lived in New York, did Mr. Nolan ever rape, sexually molest, assault, or inappropriately touch you?"

"Yes." I couldn't look towards my supporters in the room because Earl would be right in my sightline. I didn't want to look at the jury because I was so ashamed that I wasn't sure I could hold it together. I silently begged Rob to keep eye contact with me.

"Please give the jury your details about any incidents in New York."

"He molested me. He would come into my room before bed and…"

I trailed off and looked up at the fluorescents. I didn't know if I was allowed to say the names of body parts, specifically, in the courtroom. The words suddenly seemed too vulgar to say out loud. "He put his hands down my pajama bottoms."

"Did he penetrate you?"

I looked at the judge. The wording seemed so inappropriate and foreign. All eyes were locked on me, waiting to hear what I had to say.

"Yes."

"Please tell the jury what he penetrated you with."

I closed my eyes. "His fingers."

"During the length of time you lived in Pennsylvania, did Mr. Nolan ever rape, sexually molest, assault, or inappropriately touch you?"

"Yes. Twice."

"Brooke, I know this is very difficult for you. So when you're ready, please give the jury information about those two incidents," he said, pausing to clear his throat. "In as much detail as you can."

There were more than two times. Way more. Prosecuting a pedophile in the legal system all came down to what you could prove and what you couldn't. If you didn't have a witness, some DNA, or other obvious evidence it was hard to prove. Heather told me we were taking a gamble; we had none of those things. We had my word against his, my truth and his.

"The first time was in the summer…"

I went through the motions and tried not to listen to my own voice as I recalled every painstaking and humiliating detail. I laid everything out on the open floor, darting my eyes between the jury, my lawyer, and the judge. I didn't know where to direct my voice because everyone seemed to be listening.

My lips started to tremble and bounce so furiously when I tried to say the word penis that my lawyer asked if I needed a break. Instead, I washed my face in my own tears and gritted my teeth when I was done explaining. The floorboards beneath me were sportsmanlike in not swallowing me up, like I secretly wished they would.

Rob nodded and hung his head for me. "No further questions, Your Honor."

The defense lawyer wasted no time. Her black heels paraded across the floor as she bolted out her first question. "Brooke, isn't it true that you were angry at your father for not buying you a car?"

"A car?" I didn't mean to repeat her, but the question was so out of left field I wasn't sure I heard her right.

"Yes, a car. Isn't it true you were angry because he wouldn't buy you a car when you got your license?"

"No."

"No?" She raised an eyebrow.

"Do you recall an argument the summer you claim you were raped? Where your mom wanted to put a car on your father's insurance?"

"Yeah, I think so."

"So you admit there was an argument?"

"Yeah, but not from me, my mom had an argument with my dad. I knew my dad couldn't buy me a car, so when I bought my own Mom put me on their insurance. It was easier and I just paid her the money every month."

My answers clearly were not going in the direction she wanted them to so she changed lanes. "You mentioned before that you were an honor roll student in high school, is that correct?"

"Yes. I was."

"Your Honor, I'd like to present the witness with records from the high school."

The judge nodded. "Proceed."

She whisked a piece of paper in front of me. It looked like the report cards we would get when I was in high school.

"Brooke, the highlighted section of those grades correlates with the dates you claim to have been raped. Could you please read the grades to the jury?"

I moved my finger across the page. "98, 96, 99, 92."

"Those grades would qualify you for Distinguished Honor Roll, wouldn't they?"

"Yes."

"Brooke, please tell the jury when you started your first menstrual cycle."

I could feel the heat in my face flare up as my lawyer shouted out, "Objection, Your Honor!"

"Sustained. Next question, Miss Lourdes."

"The night of the second incident which you claim you were raped, isn't it true you had an argument about sleeping at your boyfriend's house?"

"I wanted to sleep there, yeah." I felt like she was backing me into a corner, trying to unleash a motive I couldn't understand.

"So you were mad at your father for not letting you sleep at your boyfriend's house, and you coincidentally were raped that night?"

"No. It's not like that—"

She held up a hand. "Simple yes or no will suffice."

Panic rose in my chest. This lady was trying to make it seem like I was a pissed off, materialistic teenager with daddy issues. Her next question didn't skip a beat.

"Do you recall when Social Services came to your school to talk to you?"

"Yes."

"Did they tell you that anything you said would be confidential?"

"Yes, they did."

"And what did you tell them when they asked if your father ever did anything sexually inappropriate with you?"

"I told them I had a dream he did."

"Thank you. No further questions Your Honor."

Once again I panicked. She never asked me to explain why I said that they were dreams. I cringed at how easy it was for them to twist answers to fit what they were looking for.

Rob stood up at the redirect. "Brooke, please explain to the jury why you told Social Services they were dreams."

"I was scared, I never told anyone before. I thought they would put us in foster care if I told the truth."

"Did they tell you they would keep your conversation confidential?"

"Yes."

"And what did Social Services send to your house two days later?"

"A letter, saying I told them about the dreams I had and everything else I told them."

"Not very confidential, was it?"

"No."

"And didn't Mr. Nolan confront you about the letter that was sent home?"

"Yes."

Rob looked up at the jury and held up his hands as if to say, 'Good thing she didn't tell them she was being raped, huh?' "No further questions at this time."

When I was told I could step down, my legs threatened to melt into puddles beneath me. Tunnel vision masked my way out, and the jury fell behind me in a blur. My eyes were so blurry by the time I pushed open the white door that I reached out to the first person that grabbed me and hysterically fell to the floor.

**

Mom testified next. I curled up on one of the hard wooden chairs next to Gina and put my head on her shoulder. I remembered what Heather told me about my mom's testimony. "We can't paint the picture that she knew there was abuse in the house."

"But she *did* know," I insisted. "She was just in the other room when Dad would throw someone against a wall or go tearing after us up the stairs. Maybe she can say she didn't know about the sexual abuse, but she had to know about the physical abuse."

"We can't use it. If we paint it like she knew, they would deem her an unfit mother or accomplice. Your siblings would be pulled from the house, I could guarantee it."

"So what can she testify to?"

"Your father's temper, your relationship with him, things like that. The fact that she's disabled helps. It shows she couldn't intervene even if she wanted to."

"What about Gina?"

"She's a star witness. You called her to pick you up from school the day after, remember? We have school records of the time you left, and we have her as a witness that you could barely walk up the stairs when she brought you home. Plus she's seen your father's temper first hand, as an outsider, when she would drop you off."

"And my mom's friend Ellen, what can she say?"

"David called her right after you guys fled to New York. He said on the phone *'Brooke must have said'* then hung up. It's very incriminating that he pinpointed you as someone who said something when he didn't even know what was going on yet or where anyone was."

"My Aunt Jean, she was the one I told first when I went to New York. So she's going to testify about what I told her?"

"Exactly. She'll talk about how you acted when you were there, your demeanor, that kind of thing." Heather nodded. "I know I said it would be an uphill battle, because we have no DNA or witness that was right there in the room with you. It's your word against his." She closed a file that was sitting on her desk. "But you have a damn good voice, and we're gonna make it sing."

Evidence was presented for two days before both lawyers made their closing statements to the jury. Rob met us upstairs when he was finished and the jury had been given their instructions. A throbbing pulse raced through my temple and I rubbed the bridge of my nose as I fought to stay awake. Rob checked his watch. "Now, we wait. Anyone hungry? There's a pub on the corner."

I ordered a sandwich just to have something in front of me since everyone was concerned about my not eating. There was no way I could stomach food, but it was easier to listen to Rob talk to Heather as I pretended to eat.

"I hope they have an answer soon," said Mom.

"We don't want them to call us back too early, it's not a good sign," Rob whispered, munching on a chip. "Short deliberations usually come back with an innocent verdict. It's the lengthy jury deliberations that have the guilty verdicts. It takes them longer to justify sending a man to jail than it does to set them free." Heather nodded in agreement.

Rob's cell phone rang just as we paid. His raised his eyes in surprise and flipped his phone shut. "The jury is back. Verdict is in." I checked my phone. The jury had only been deliberating for three hours.

Everyone was allowed in the courtroom when they read the verdict and I sat between Mom and Gina. Heather and Rob stood in front of us and mumbled whispers continued until the jury filed into the courtroom. Two women in particular stared at me without blinking for several long seconds. They didn't smile or offer any signs of encouragement. Gina squeezed my hand. "This is it," she said when the judge walked in.

The judge never smiled or looked up. She moved her cloak over her chair and shifted papers around on her bench.

"Has the jury come to a unanimous decision?"

The foreman of the jury stood up. She towered above the podium and I thought she looked professional in her blue skirt. I targeted the piece of paper floating in her hand that revealed what twelve people thought should happen to a man they didn't even know. "We have Your Honor," she said.

Her focus remained on the judge and never once lingered to Earl sitting only a few feet from the jurors. His focus remained on his thumbs. The tipstaff handed the paper to the judge, and she looked it over. After a brief pause she looked at the foreman. "And you're sure that the jury has made every reasonable attempt to reach a verdict?"

"We have Your Honor." The foreman, for the first time, looked at me.

"Very well. It is with great regret that I inform the court that the jury has remained deadlocked and issues a verdict of a hung jury. Unable to agree upon a verdict after an extended period of deliberation, and unable to sway votes due to severe differences of opinion, it is issued from this court that the trial be classified as a mistrial and any re-trial will be done at the discretion of the plaintiff."

While the judge thanked the jury for their time and gave them their dismissal instructions, Heather and Gina rushed me from the room. I couldn't see through my tears. Even though I didn't completely understand what had happened, I knew they didn't say guilty, so for me it meant my world was ending.

"We'll do it again, we'll just have to come back at them again. It's okay Brooke, we'll do it again if we have to." Gina tried to wipe the mascara running down her face.

Heather led me into her office. "It's not necessarily a bad thing. It means the jury couldn't come to a decision. We'll regroup, patch any holes, and next time—"

"I can't do this again!" I cried. I buried my face. "This can't be happening, I can't go through all of this again."

It had been well over a year since I went to the police. I had to stand in front of countless strangers, time and time again, to tell them intimate details about my body and what happened to me. It never got easier; the same words still stuck to the roof of my mouth when I tried to say them, and the pain was always full torque.

"You can." Heather grabbed my shoulders and held back her own tears. "You can because you're such a strong person. I've never seen someone testify the way you do."

"Miss Heather, we have an issue out here." The secretary from the front room pointed toward the front of the building as she walked into the office.

"Not now, Melinda."

"Miss, but it's important. It's the jury. They're outside the courthouse and they want to talk to Brooke."

Heather met Melinda's gaze. "They want to *what*?"

As I approached the double doors leading to the front of the courthouse, I could hear Heather behind me. "My word, in the fifteen years I've been here, I've never seen anything like this."

When I stepped outside I was surrounded and hugged by twelve complete strangers. The women were crying, the men were crying, and they all took turns shaking my hand. "You are the bravest girl we've ever met," said a curly blonde woman.

"Don't think for one second we didn't believe you." A Latino man crossed his arms in front of his chest. "We believed you, okay?"

An older man with white hair and a beard to match knelt on the ground in front of me and took my hand in his. "I am so sorry, please forgive me. I had so many questions and the jury can't ask questions." He looked at the other eleven people above him. "I was the one they couldn't convince. I'm so sorry."

"I don't understand." *If they believed me, why didn't they convict him? Why were they here?*

"We're going to help. We want to meet with the District Attorney's office so next time there are no questions, no doubt in *any* jurors mind that that monster is guilty."

Heathers mouth dropped. "Really?"

Two women pushed to the front of the crowd. "Really. We want to be there when he's put away. We'll meet with the lawyer as early as tomorrow if you need us."

"Wow. Okay, well let's get your names and numbers then."

A woman who smelled like jasmine touched my shoulder. "I knew from the second I heard you speak that he was guilty, and there was no way I was going to let anyone sway me. I'm sorry we had to put you through that. I was trying to make eye contact with you without coming off as too obvious, to let you know I believed you."

"I was too," said the curly haired lady.

"That would explain the stares I was getting," I confessed. "It kind of looked like you were mad or something though."

She shook her head. "I'm Dawn, by the way. Don't worry, next time we'll get him."

Chapter Twenty-Four

A court date was scheduled for three months later, just in case I chose to testify again. I stopped answering my phone and spent the next few days hidden beneath the darkness of my comforter. Calls from my boss went to voicemail, and Cristin stopped sending texts after the fifth day.

Over a year was a long time to fight and constantly have my guard up. The nightmares had diminished a bit when I moved out of my mom's house, but they came back full force after the hung jury.

"Brooke, you failed your algebra class? Didn't you go up to pre-calc in high school?" Jason read over the sheet of paper in his hand.

I eyed the print out of my grades sitting on the floor of the bedroom and muffled my response into a pillow. "Apparently some professors have attendance rules. Don't show up so many times and they fail you, even when you ace all the exams."

"Why didn't you give him the letters from Heather? She wrote your excuse letters, right?"

"I can't do this anymore."

I felt Jason's weight next to me on the bed, but I didn't look up. He rubbed the top of the comforter that I hid beneath. "What can't you do?"

"Everything."

"What's everything?"

"College, apparently. Court. My family. You."

"Me?"

I ignored the hurt in his voice. "I can't do this anymore. It's too much."

"You think it would be easier if I wasn't here?"

"I think it would be easier if I didn't have to worry about anyone but myself. I screw everything up. Everything is just happening so fast. It's so hard all the time. When does it end?"

"You don't have to worry about me, I'm not going anywhere." His hand stroked my face and I knew he meant it. "And you didn't screw anything up. This wasn't your fault."

"Really? What's *not* my fault?"

Midge told me I would get to a point where I would feel real anger, a fury so deep about everything that I wouldn't know where it came from. It wasn't like me to be like that, so I never believed her. Suddenly it was very plausible.

"My mom can *barely* survive. There are so many kids that she's struggling to feed because of *me*. She's so money hungry all the time she's sacrificing the relationships she has with her own children just to make a buck. My older brother is in complete denial of everything that has ever happened in our life. Did I tell you that he told me he wouldn't believe the accusations I was making until a jury decided? He still keeps in contact with Earl. Can you believe that? Not to mention that he's eating himself into a stupor. My own siblings don't even believe me because 'He's their father' and it didn't happen to them, so they can't even imagine something like that going on right under their nose."

"You can't help how they are," Jason replied.

"Kat has started to cut herself. She told my mom it makes her feel good. And Thomas is in his *second* juvenile detention center in less than two years. I'm engaged but there have been so many times I've cried to you, *cried to you*, over Paul! And I don't even know why!"

I threw my hands up in the air. "How is that fair to you, Jason? I'm failing my classes, I can't even get my own fiancé to touch me anymore because you're afraid I'll start crying or that you'll do something to sexually trigger me in the wrong way, and I'm pretty sure at this point I don't even have a job." Jason opened his mouth, but I cut him off. "Ask me for a list of things I *didn't* screw up next time, it'll be shorter."

Jason reached for me, grabbing the upper part of my arm to spin me toward him. I screamed, backing into the corner of the room like a feral animal. "Don't *ever* touch me there! Don't you ever grab my arm like that!"

"I'm sorry! I'm sorry, did I hurt you?" His voice cracked as I placed a hand over where he had touched me.

There was one time, only one, where I had tried to escape from Earl and fight him off. There was a small window of opportunity where I actually had a chance to run; a surge of adrenaline and desperation insisted I try, so I did. Earl's grimy hand seized the upper part of my arm and he was able to pin me back down on the bed like a ragdoll. Jason couldn't have known that, but I was past any form of rational thinking at that point.

I took the ring off my finger and slammed it down on the desk next to the bed. Jason looked at it, terrified. "Baby, you're upset, I know, but—"

"But what? You'll never understand. No one will ever understand. I don't even understand!" I blindly searched for my car keys.

"You can't drive like that, Brooke. You stay, I'll leave. Please."

"I need to get out of here."

The door slammed behind me as I pulled on a jacket. My accelerator touched the floor and I reached for the phone in my purse. "Gina!" I cried when she picked up, "I need you."

***

"So, you finally got angry huh?" Gina filled my glass with wine for the second time. "I was wondering when that was going to happen."

"I was horrible to him, Gina. He won't take me back. I wouldn't take me back." I pivoted my wrist and watched the wine flow off the sides of the glass like Lou had taught me.

"Oh, he'll take you back. That's not even a question. Question is do you *want* him back?"

"I don't know. I don't know anything anymore."

"You still think about Paul?"

"I have dreams about him sometimes. I've cried to Jason about missing Paul. Isn't that screwed up? But Jason just tells me he understands, that he was a part of my life and he wouldn't expect me to forget he existed. Then I remember how he treated me when we broke up and I just...I don't know. Can you love two people at once?"

Gina raised an eyebrow. "You were both so young, ya know?"

I knew Gina wanted me as a daughter-in-law. She always hinted that she thought there would be a day that we would rekindle our relationship, and when we did, she would be anticipating lots of grandbabies.

"I know. I know Jason and I won't get married anytime soon anyway, I'd lose my financial aid for college."

Gina and I were three glasses of wine in when she approached the next topic. "You know the jurors are trying to meet with the D.A.'s office this week. They can tell Rob exactly what he needs to clarify next time. There's no way he'll walk next time, no way."

"How am I supposed to do that all over again? I've been a wreck. I can't even remember the last time I didn't have to schedule a day of court into my life. I throw up before going in to see him. The nightmares just won't go away."

"Don't rub your face like that, you'll get wrinkles. And you *will* do it again, because you have people there to support you. Would you rather him out on the streets, finding other little girls and boys to molest? I don't think so."

"Little boys?"

Gina silenced herself with a gulp of wine.

"What little boys?"

She looked away from me.

"Gina, tell me."

"Oh God." She covered her mouth. "I promised I wouldn't say anything. It's the wine."

"Gina!"

"Please don't tell anyone I told you. Please don't. There's a reason why the defense won't bring up the fact that you would sometimes pass out when he raped you. They can't open that can of worms."

"I don't get it."

"You had a witness. Your brother, Thomas, he walked in on it."

My mouth dropped.

"He went into your parents' room to use their bathroom because someone was in the hallway one. He saw you passed out on the bed and tried to leave the room before Earl saw him. Oh, the wine." She pinched the bridge of her nose before continuing. "Earl ran after him, chased him into his bedroom and pinned him up against the wall, asked him if he liked what he saw." She waved her hand in front of her mouth like her tongue was on fire. "He was raped too. I'm so sorry. I'm sorry no one told you, we wanted him to tell you when he was ready."

"No, Gina. Oh my God. No…"

She pulled my hand away from my mouth as she wrapped her arms around me. "I'm so sorry. I shouldn't have told you."

"Why isn't the D.A. doing something about this?" My voice carried louder than I expected it to. "Why can't we let Thomas testify too?"

"He's been in and out of detention centers. He's having trouble passing his classes and is in trouble all the time, he's lashing out. He's a textbook example of what an abused child acts like."

"Exactly!"

Gina handed me a tissue. "He doesn't have the credibility you do. He didn't get the help like you did. Do you really think he could sit up there and have a lawyer tell him he was making it up? Or imply that what he was saying was a lie?"

I shook my head as I blew my nose. "Thomas would jump over the stand and kill him."

"Exactly. Your testimony alone is enough to put him away for a great length of time, Brooke. And if and when he's ready, there is a long statute of limitations. He can be thirty when he decides to press charges. He's not there yet."

Suddenly it all made sense.

Thomas was always asking when and if Earl would be coming back home. He wasn't asking because he missed him or because he didn't believe what I was saying. He was asking because he was terror-stricken that he would have to live under the same roof as him again. Thomas and I shared the same nightmares.

Gina bent down beside me. "You have a chance to get justice for you and your family. You can put him away, I know you can. You're smart and you're ready. If you can do it one time, you can do it again and again. You won't let him beat you, not like this."

She was right. The goal was always about keeping my siblings safe. I failed to do that when I sacrificed myself to Earl. It was the smoke and mirrors I let myself believe to justify that I was protecting them. He would win if I backed down now, and everything I had gone through up until that point would have been for nothing.

I nodded at Gina. "When can we meet with the jurors?"

Chapter Twenty-Five

Two of the jurors met with the D.A.'s office for over a week. They hashed out what they thought needed clarification: Was my grandmother in the bedroom, like the defense suggested at one point? Where exactly was my mom during all of this? Why didn't I tell anyone, and when I did, what brought me to do that? Why *were* my grades so high? They assured Rob that once he clarified those questions, there would be no room for reasonable doubt among the jury and a guilty verdict would be imminent.

I had some questions of my own for Heather and Rob. "Who do I look at when I'm answering a question? I want to look at the person who asks but I don't want to look at David. I can feel the jury looking at me, so I don't know where to look."

"Talk to the jury," Rob said. "They're the ones that need to understand, not myself, and not David's lawyer. It's a tactic they use, actually. The defense lawyer will purposely stand in front of his client when they ask their questions because it forces you to look at David. It's meant to intimidate you."

"And you can always look at me," Heather suggested. "I'll be sitting with the previous jurors and family members who are supporting you."

"And it's okay to use words like penis and rape? Can I say that? I always feel like I shouldn't, like it's inappropriate or something."

"You can use whatever words you need to give the jury as much detail as you can. There's no right or wrong way, you won't get in trouble in that courtroom. Not even if you curse, or cry. It's expected. There's a lot of emotion," Rob said.

"Don't feel like you need to answer a question right away either," Heather chimed in. "If you need to think about it for a few seconds then do that. There are a lot of dates and specifics that they'll try and confuse you with. Listen to the question carefully, and ask them to repeat it if you need another minute to think." She smiled. "You'll be okay."

"I didn't want to do this again."

"We know." Rob rubbed the scruff on his face. "But we're really glad you are."

When I walked through the white door of the courtroom several weeks later, it wasn't any easier. I knew what to expect though, so the stares from the jurors were not so intense and I managed to completely ignore Earl when I took my seat on the witness stand.

Rob started first, and we channeled through his questions like we were old pals catching up on each other's lives. We established that I bought my own car, and anything else I needed, from working part-time. He clarified that I wanted to sleep at my boyfriend's house because I was scared to go home, not to be rebellious. "Brooke can you please explain to the jury, in detail, what happened during the two incidents you were raped."

Too ashamed to make eye contact with any of the jurors, I spoke to the wall behind them. My eyes burned when I tried to explain how I was grabbed and pinned down on the bed. By the time I started to explain the second rape, an unfamiliar warmth shot across my chest.

I was angry.

I gripped the edge of the witness box, the tone in my voice articulate and betrayed, not caring about the tears that soaked my face. When I finished, I glanced up to monitor their reactions. I caught sight of an older black man with a bald head. A hand covered his mouth, his brow wrinkled in fury.

I steadied myself for the defense to start. Earl had a new lawyer, again. The man struggled to get out of his seat, and he smoothed his jacket over his protruding belly.

"Brooke, I'm Mr. Solak." He approached the witness stand, his eyes hinting that he wasn't going to be easy on me. This time, I was ready.

Okay Brooke, here we go. Be precise. Be strong. Be truthful. Be yourself.

Mr. Solak edged his way around a poster board he had on display in front of the jurors. "Brooke, on this diagram of the

upstairs of your house, could you please tell me what room this is?"
He pointed to my parents' room.

Be precise.

"That's the room I was raped in."

He nodded at first, undoubtedly not expecting to hear my response. Then he frowned and glanced at Rob, who was painfully trying to hide that he was smirking.

"Please tell me who *slept* in this room."

"Oh, my parents."

"And what room is this alllll the way down here." He dragged his finger to the other side of the hallway, stretching out his words as if to say '*See how much distance is between each room?*'

"The room I would hide in. My bedroom."

The corners of his mouth dropped. "So you expect the jury to believe that Mr. Nolan *carried you* all the way to his bedroom?"

Be strong.

I looked down at my diminishing figure and then up at the jury. "Yep. All ninety-five pounds of me."

On cue, the jury glanced across the room at Earl, studying his stocky and more than two hundred pound body. Exhilarated that they got my point, I positioned myself for more.

Mr. Solak placed my grades from high school in front of me and asked me to read them out loud. When I was finished, he turned to the jury with a smug look. "So your grades actually *increased* during the time you claim to have been raped."

It wasn't a question, or even directed to me, but I spoke up. "Because the only time I was allowed to keep my bedroom door locked was when I was studying. So guess what I did all the time?"

I knew I didn't fit the classification of what everyone thought a sexually abused child acted or looked like. My coping skills just happened to be funneled into productive outlets instead of destructive ones.

Mr. Solak didn't even have the patience to object. Instead, he fired off another question, one he thought would corner me for sure. "Miss Nolan, if this was going on for so long, why didn't you tell anyone?"

Be truthful.

"I thought I was protecting my brothers and sister." For the first time, I made eye contact with the jury members. I needed them to understand my intentions. "I thought that if I let him hurt me, he wouldn't hurt them. It turns out I wasn't protecting *them* though, I was protecting *him*. I thought that what happened in my house was normal because I didn't know anything else, he molested me from the time I was a little kid. But when I found out…"

I shook my head, still in disbelief that I had been so naive. "When I knew that my house was different, I knew it had to stop."

"And what is it you'd like to see happen to David?"

Be yourself.

The defense lawyer wanted me to show a malicious side, Rob had told me earlier. The truth was, it didn't matter to me if Earl ended up in jail. I didn't care if he was subjected to strutting around in anklets, never seeing the outside world again. It wasn't about that. It wasn't about revenge or control. No amount of jail time would help me regain the innocence that was taken from me for so many years. There was really only one response I could give.

"I just want to make sure that he can never hurt anybody ever again. It doesn't matter what happens, I just don't want to see other people get hurt."

"No further questions, Your Honor," said Mr. Solak. He waddled over to his table and huffed as he sat down.

Rob had one more point to prove. "Brooke, you testified earlier that the reason why your grades were so high was because you studied a lot?"

"Yes."

"So when Mr. Nolan was trashing the house, or abusing your brothers or sister, you coped by distracting yourself…with studying?"

"Yes."

The tone in his voice was disbelief. I got uneasy about what he was trying to say. Didn't he believe me? Wasn't he supposed to be my lawyer? Wasn't he on my side?

"So you can tunnel your stress, your worry, and forget about everything else except what you're trying to memorize?"

"Yeah."

"Brooke, could you please empty the contents of your pocket for the jury?"

"Objection Your Honor. Relevance?" Mr. Solak didn't want any more surprises. He shook his head at Rob and waited for the judge to make a call.

The judge looked as surprised as I was.

"I assure you, Your Honor, the relevance will be revealed momentarily."

The judge eyed Rob. "I'll allow it." She leaned forward on her bench to get a closer look.

Three index cards emerged from my pocket and I placed them on the stand in front of me. I realized what Rob was trying to prove and grinned, ever so slightly.

"Brooke, please tell the jury what the contents of your pocket are."

I picked up the note cards and turned them over in my hands. "They're chemical reactions for my organic chemistry class. I have an exam in two days."

"You're here today to testify against your father for *raping* you, and you have organic chemistry equations stuffed in your pockets?" His grin was ear to ear.

"Yes."

The jury digested my explanation, nodding their heads in unison.

I had testified for over three hours with the defense. Every direction his lawyer tried to pull me in, I had changed it around. I hated that I cried so many times in front of strangers, but as I sat in one of the wooden chairs outside the courtroom after I was dismissed, I realized I wasn't ashamed anymore. I felt hurt and betrayed, but I was not ashamed.

The trial lasted two days, just like the first one. Both lawyers gave their closing arguments, and the judge charged the jury with instructions on how to come back with a verdict beyond a reasonable doubt.

"What does that even mean, beyond a reasonable doubt?" I asked Heather.

"It just means that we have the burden of proving he did it. He doesn't have the burden of proving he didn't do it. They all need to believe that without a doubt, based on what we told them, he's guilty."

I considered what she said, feeling uneasy since verbal testimony was the only evidence for both sides, and automatically there would have to be doubt. It was my word against his.

The same pub we frequented after the first trial was just getting ready for dinner hour as I crammed in next to Aunt Jean and Gina. Rob loosened his tie, while Heather repeated the parts of Earl's testimony that she could remember.

"David said, 'As soon as Brooke mentioned sexual abuse, Aunt Jean just took it and blew it out of proportion' so Rob says, 'She blew the sexual abuse…out of proportion?' and David said 'Yes'."

Aunt Jean gasped, insulted that she was being accused of overreacting. "I absolutely did not—"

Heather held up a finger. "Hold on it gets worse. So Rob says 'So she made the sex thing a big thing?' David says, 'A really big thing.' Rob turned to the jury with a look of surprise and goes 'That should have been kept small I guess?' I never heard a lawyer call out objection so fast!" Heather shook her head as she laughed. "By saying that the whole thing was blown out of proportion, he incriminated himself on the stand. He was actually trying to convince everyone that what he did was not a big deal. Unreal."

"Yeah, well there are a lot of charges against him. It would carry out a heavy sentence, so the longer they deliberate, the better it looks for us." Rob bit into a corned beef sandwich as his phone rang. "Excuse me, long day. Probably my wife."

"How are you doing? You doing okay?" Gina stroked my head, eyeing the bar. "I think I'll order some wine. I need a drink."

"No time." Rob shut his phone and pushed his plate away in disgust. "The jury came back. They have a verdict."

"Already?" Heather sounded panicked. "It's been forty-five minutes, Rob."

It was too soon. Everything about her face told me that the jury had come back from deliberations too quickly.

"I know." He grabbed his briefcase and we shuffled out of the booth.

Everyone tried to keep their composure as we scanned through security in the lobby, but there was a sinister cloud of doubt that followed us down into the courtroom. Since the jury had come back from deliberations so quickly, we could only assume that they did not decide on a guilty verdict.

We were the last ones to file into the courtroom and I slid into a bench closest to the door. When the jury walked in and took their place, the room slowed like a movie scene as the judge asked the foreman, the bald black man, if the jury had reached a verdict.

"We have, Your Honor."

"Very well. On the count of rape by forcible compulsion, how do you find the defendant?"

Gina fell to her knees on the floor, sobbing as the foreman read out the first guilty.

"On the count of incest, how do you find the defendant?"

"Guilty."

"On the count of corruption of a minor, how do you find the defendant?"

"Guilty."

Cries of joy and pain rose from the benches where I sat. Gina, Mom, Heather, and Aunt Jean all tried to squeeze me as I hung my head, relief washing over me like the parade of guilty verdicts.

"On the charge of indecent assault without consent, how do you find the defendant?"

"Guilty."

Judge Wilkin interrupted the verdict process and pointed to a bailiff. "Could someone please remove that woman?"

Gina refused to hold back her sobs. "Oh you did it, Brooke. You did it." The bailiff approached and Gina stood up voluntarily. "I'll go. I'm sorry, I'll go."

"Now then." Judge Wilkin cleared her throat, "If we can continue. On the count of endangering the welfare of a child, how do you find the defendant?"

"Guilty."

In total, when the foreman sat down, they had found him guilty of nine felonies and twelve misdemeanors. There had been twenty-one charges in all, and he was found guilty on every single one of them.

Not one time did Earl flinch, yell out, or otherwise change his expression. I watched him stare straight at Judge Wilkin as if she were telling him his shoelaces were untied. Unfazed, barren even, he must have finally realized that his facade was compromised. His secret was out, and the jury had believed me.

It was over.

Judge Wilkin thanked the jury and spoke to Earl as the officers bound him in handcuffs. Chaotic chatter filled the elevator and Rob smiled and nodded to me. "No, no don't thank me. She's the one who blew this thing out of the water. I've seen grown men crack under the pressure that defense attorney put on you." He winked at me. "You're gonna be just fine."

While everyone crowded around Heather's office, I reached for another tissue. "Mom, I need to go home. Someone has to tell Thomas he's not coming back." I paused until Gina looked at me, scared that I would say too much. "I need to see Adam and Kat, too. I need to hug Ethan. They need to know he's not coming back."

We exited the courthouse, and Gina offered to ride along in my car. "Me and you kiddo, we did it!" Gina rocked all over the car as we sped away. "Oh, I am *so* happy for you. Thank the Lord, thank God you got the justice you deserve."

I pushed a CD into my stereo system and Dixie Chicks vocals filled the car. Gina turned it up when she realized what song it was and started to sing along, "'Cause Earl had to die na na na na naaaa naaa naaa."

Lights disappeared behind us on the highway as the county jail, just off the main interstate, came into view. It would be Earl's new home-away-from-home for a short time until he was transferred to another permanent location. I beamed at Gina and stuck my hand out the window as we passed, passionately giving the jail the middle finger.

Chapter Twenty-Six

Court was over but there was still a two-month wait to find out how long of a sentence Earl would get. Each charge carried a minimum and maximum amount of time, and since there were twenty-one counts, the time he would spend in jail would greatly vary. I tried to bury myself in college courses and work until the last court date.

"You, everyone in your family, and anyone who knows you should write an impact statement." Heather's voice broke up as I walked across campus so I pressed the phone to my ear, attempting to drown out the voices of students surrounding me.

"What are they for? Like what should they say?"

"Victim impact statements are just letters written by people who know you to say what they think should happen to David, based on what they know of the situation. The judge takes them into consideration for sentencing. If you get a lot of people to vouch for you and insist he be put away a long time, it'll just be better for you. It doesn't mean it will definitely help, but we encourage people to write them. You need to write one too."

"All right. I'll let everyone know."

Over several weeks I collected more than twenty-five impact statements, even more were emailed directly to Heather. Mine was the last to be added to the pile. Exams and projects piled up as the end of my sophomore semester came to a close. Jason offered to go grocery shopping so I could finish up my letter. Two hours later, I sat cross-legged on my bed to read it one last time:

I do not think of myself as being heroic for telling on my father. I didn't tell to make our lives harder. I simply wanted him out of our lives so we could live, and grow, like children are supposed to. Not in fear. I don't think it's fair that I lost my 'virginity' to my father.

I thumped my pen anxiously on the paper and looked away. Even after two years of court, that thought still screamed in my head.

I also do not think it's fair that my siblings and I had to grow as much as we did not knowing a father's love. Without him in the home, a drastic change has occurred. We never stop laughing with each other, we joke around, and are loud and carefree, not nervous and timid. It was not until I started dating my very first boyfriend and met his family that my views about my dad started to change. At my boyfriend's house there was no yelling or screaming. I remember one time when his little brother spilled a glass of milk at dinner, and I gasped and jumped up from the table. Everyone looked at me so weird, because I expected his father to go into a rage like mine would have done. But he never did. It was unusual behavior to me, to see him act so calm, and the more I was surrounded by it, the more I realized that it was MY house that was unusual.

My mind flashed to how many times my brothers had flinched at the sight of Earl's hand being raised, even if it was just to stick a fork full of food in his bearded mouth at the dinner table. Who knew that Adam could tell such hysterically funny jokes instead of being so quiet? And that Kat wanted to be a cheerleader instead of hiding in her bedroom closet, etching new scars across her wrists? The first time Kat showed me her scars, she was almost proud of them. "I wish they would just…go away," she would mumble now, rubbing her pink-polished fingers over the damage.

There is, however, the constant fear that he will someday return to our home, and everything will be back to the way it was. I fear the day I am in a public place and see his face in a crowd. I do not ever want to feel the heart dropping dread I have for this man ever again.

I bent my head down and read the finishing words to my letter.

Your Honor, I am requesting that you serve David Nolan with the maximum amount of time allowed by law. If there is one decent thing that he has ever done for his family, it was that he left our lives. And now that he has, please do not let him come back.

I examined it two more times and flipped the pages over to make sure everything was perfect before tucking it into my book bag.

"Hey, how's it coming?" Jason pushed the door open, carrying a pizza box and two plates. He moved a pillow aside and put the box down between us. My stomach growled in response.

"Good. Finished." I pulled two slices apart and handed him one. "Can I ask you something?"

Jason grunted between bites.

"I'll take that as a yes. I know I didn't want you to come to the trials and stuff. You know, so you didn't have to listen to those things," I said.

"Yeah, that's okay. I understand."

"I know. But can you come with me to the sentencing?"

Paul had started the journey with me. His mom offered me support the whole way through, inside and outside the courtroom.

I couldn't imagine Jason not being there for when that chapter of my life finally came to an end, especially with how understanding and supportive he had been the entire time. Jason welcomed me back with open arms after our fight, just like Gina told me he would. He was the steady and consistent presence I had come to love and need in my life. His dedication was unwavering, and I wanted him to witness what his support had helped me accomplish.

He bent forward and planted a greasy kiss on my lips. "If you want me there, I'll be there."

***

I didn't have to point out Earl when we entered the courtroom since he was the only one there in handcuffs. Jason had never seen him before. All of my childhood pictures were devoid of his face, due to some skillful scissor work.

"Not what I expected," he whispered, as the judge was announced into the courtroom.

"What'd you expect?" I whispered back.

"I don't know. He just looks... normal."

Judge Wilkin addressed the court to say why we were there. After a few formalities, she spoke about the impact statements.

"There were thirty-two in all, and I read every one. But I must say…" She glanced at me sitting in the back row of the courtroom. "I find it unbelievable that a glass of spilled milk is what gave one little girl more strength and poise than I have ever seen in this courtroom."

She shuffled papers in front of her. "With that being said, it is the court's decision that David Nolan spend no less than eight years with a maximum of sixteen years in a correctional facility."

Heather's mouth dropped and Rob's head shook back and forth. Disbelief was portrayed on everyone's face. David was sentenced to the maximum amount of jail time allowed by law for his crimes.

I was tackled by almost everyone as I buried my face deep into arms, tears, and hair. Everyone was crying, smiling, and nodding their heads. A few of the jury members looked over at me as I mouthed, "Thank you". A surge of relief encouraged me to smile for the first time inside the courtroom. Finally, Earl was going to a place where he couldn't hurt anyone else.

I would be almost thirty-five years old by the time he would be released, if he served the maximum time. I knew parole and other factors went into what his actual release date would be, but right in that moment, my face lit up the courtroom as Earl was escorted away in handcuffs.

Jason squeezed my hand three times, our way of saying 'I love you' in private, and I squeezed his back. We made our way to Heather's office. "I can't believe I am leaving this courthouse with a smile," I said.

"It's amazing. I never doubted you, don't get me wrong. But, wow, you must have made quite an impression." Heather pulled me off to the side as we approached the front lobby of the courthouse. "Brooke, can you come to my office for a minute? I want to show you something."

I looked at Jason and nodded, "Go ahead, I'll be right there in a minute." He nodded and kissed my cheek, following my mom outside.

Heather pulled a file from a tall oak bookcase on the back wall of her office. She flipped through some papers and pulled one out. "I wanted you to read this. I thought you should know."

"What is it?"

"An impact statement we got. For you."

The letter was typed and I didn't recognize the name at the top.

"I'll give you a minute." Heather's weak smile and quick shuffle to the door made me feel like I didn't want to know what the letter said, but I started reading anyway.

Dear Honorable Judge Wilkin,

It is with deep regret that I write this letter nineteen years too late. When I was twelve years old, and coming from Molly's side of the family, I was asked to babysit Adam and Brooke Nolan from the time they were three and four years old.

I glanced up at the name again, and it still didn't look familiar.

It was great money, and I loved taking care of them. When Molly's shift at the hospital changed, David Nolan started to drive me home from babysitting. I'll never forget the first time he walked into the living room naked, touching himself. I was terrified. He told me that he could teach me how to feel good, but that if I told anyone he would make sure that everyone knew about our secret. For eight months I was trapped. I was asked

to do unimaginable things with him and to him, while Brooke and Adam played in the next room. I finally told an older cousin what was going on; I wanted help. That cousin told me to never repeat what I told him, and that it would put our family to shame if I did. My father's relocation for a job is the only thing that saved me since we had to move away.

I never told anyone else what happened during that time in my life. I never sought counseling or help as I got older. I moved several states away, putting thousands of miles between me and my past. When I heard about what happened to Brooke, I blamed myself. I attempted suicide, and wound up in a mental health institution for over a year. I thought that if I had been a braver boy than I was, if I had told 'just one more person', or done something more, this never would have happened to her. I blame myself for the years of torture I am sure she had to withstand, and I can only hope that she gets the help she needs to grow into the healthy and successful woman I know she'll be.

I didn't speak up then, so I'm speaking up now. I owe it to Brooke, Adam, Thomas, Kat and Ethan. I owe it to myself. I am asking that you issue the maximum sentence to David Nolan. Please do not let my failure to act repeat on generations to come.

I stared at the letter for a long time until I heard a soft knock on the door. Heather appeared and she leaned against the desk, taking the letter from my hand. "The statute of limitations for him to press charges against David ran out years ago. You got justice for more than one person in that courtroom today, Brooke. You should be so proud of yourself."

I nodded, stunned. "Yeah, but that means someone in my family knew what kind of person he was, even back then. And they did nothing about it?"

My heart ached. Who could leave two little children in the care of that monster, knowingly? I didn't even recognize the name on the letter. Whoever he was, he was obviously so ashamed of what he went through that he couldn't even bring himself to be around family anymore. Was a family's reputation so important that children needed to be sacrificed?

Heather nodded. "The important part is that you knew what kind of person he was and you did something about it."

"How many more people Heather? Who else's life did he ruin?"

Heather shrugged. "I don't think we'll ever know, honey. But he's in a place where he can't hurt anyone anymore. Including you. Your life is far from ruined, it's just starting."

"I wish I knew who it was so I could thank him."

"Thank him?"

"For his letter, for coming forward so many years later. It's not his fault that he told someone and they didn't listen. I don't blame him, but I don't regret what happened to me either. I don't think I'd be the person I am right now if I didn't go through that. Maybe I would have just run off to college, ran away from everything like he did."

Heather cocked her head to one side. "You're the exception to every rule, you know that?" She reached out for a hug. "Now go, you have some celebrating to do."

Chapter Twenty-Seven

A Saylorsburg man was found guilty of raping a girl at his Kunkletown home twice on two separate occasions. David Nolan, 48, was found guilty after the jury deliberated for more than an hour following a two-day trial. Nolan, who had no prior criminal record, will be sentenced at a later date.

I pushed the headline away after reading it for the hundredth time. There was so much missing information and emotion intertwined in those three unimpressive sentences of the newspaper.

I suddenly grabbed it and hovered it above the trashcan as I looked down at the print, carefully considering if I wanted to keep it. Grabbing a pair of scissors I snipped out the small article before I could change my mind, folding it in half. Maybe I would need a reminder every once in a while that he really was in jail, and that it really was over.

Two weeks later, I was proven wrong in the form of a panicked phone call from Mom. "Brooke, did you get an unmarked letter in the mail?"

"No, why?"

"Your brothers did. And your sister. I got one too."

"What is it?"

"Maybe you should come read it."

When I opened the front door at my mom's she was on the phone. "I know, I know everyone got them. Just throw it out, if you want. Hey, Brooke is here, let me go." She hung up the phone and pointed to the end of the table. A cigarette dangled from the corner of her mouth.

"What's going on?" I looked at Jason who had picked up one of the envelopes on the corner of the table.

He turned it over in his hand. "They used labels to mail it, no return sender. It's stamped from a postal office in...Jersey?" He slid his finger under the sealed encasement and read the sheet of paper that was inside. He frowned and I walked over to him, reading over his shoulder.

Brooke denies that she ever told anyone that her father sexually abused her. She denies that the allegations are true and states that he never touched her or sexually abused her.

She tells me that her dream was during this past summer and she dreamt about a time when she was laying on her father's bed and her father was asleep on the bed as well.

She tells me that she told her boyfriend's mother—Gina—about this dream a month or so ago. Brooke continued to deny allegations and denies that anyone—never mind her father—has ever sexually abused her.

Safety has been assessed; Brooke appears safe at this time. Sexual assault has been unsubstantiated.

"Is that the interview Social Services did with me at the high school? How did anyone get this?" I grabbed at the white envelopes sitting on the counter. "Who else got them?"

"Everyone!" Mom flung her hands up in the air. "Aunt Jean, your cousins, grandparents..."

"They sent this to Grandma and Grandpa?" I screamed.

The lone page from the interview Social Services conducted at my high school made it seem like Earl's conviction was an oversight. It was completely out of context, with no explanation listed as to why I had initially come forward talking about the abuse as dreams. Except for the core family members who were subpoenaed to court, I didn't tell anyone about all the details. *Jason* didn't even know all the details. No one would know why I told Social Services they were dreams at first; we had clarified my reasoning in court. Now, I had over twenty people in my family opening their mail that morning to a letter they never should have seen. The letter painted myself as a liar and Earl as a victim.

I was mortified. "Who sent this? How can we find out who sent this?"

"I don't think we can, baby," said Jason.

The single addressed label on the front gave no clues. The stamp showed the date the letters were mailed, and the location of the post office was Kilmer, NJ. Jason was right. Someone made it a point to make sure the letters didn't get traced back to whoever sent them.

"Mom, how am I supposed to explain this to everyone?"

"I don't know, maybe we can start calling everyone and—"

"No!" Jason's voiced boomed. "You're not calling anyone."

His outburst startled me. "What do you mean, Jason? I have to—"

"If anyone in your family is going to question whether or not this really happened based on some shady attempt to embarrass you, then you don't owe them any explanations. It's not your place to explain to every family member the details of what happened. They know what happened, and if they don't believe you because of some stupid letter then screw them."

I put my hand on his back as he turned away and ran his hand through his hair. "I mean what kind of sick person is *still* trying to control the situation from the other side of a prison wall?"

I'd never seen him upset like that, but he was right. I didn't need to give explanations. Not to them, not to anyone. The details of what happened to me were already exposed in abundance over the last two years to the people of the courtroom, and I never had to see them again which made it easier. I didn't need to traumatize myself by calling everyone in my family on top of it.

"He worked in Jersey," Mom said, suddenly. She eyed Jason as he settled down. "He must have sent the letter to a buddy he worked with, and had them send it out so it wouldn't get back to him."

"Maybe, but Jason's right. He just wants to prove he's still in control. I still want to call Grandma and Grandpa though. I can't stand them thinking I lied about anything. They'll understand."

The phone rang twice as I twirled my hair around my index finger. The front porch gave me some privacy while I made the call. When Grandpa picked up, I asked him if he had gotten any strange mail with information about me in it.

"Oh uh, yeah. We got that." I opened my mouth to start talking and was cut off. "Don't worry, I um, threw it out. Didn't need your grandma reading that garbage."

"Thanks, Grandpa."

Jason smiled at the look on my face as I hung up.

"He didn't buy any of that, did he?"

"No, he didn't."

The front door flung open, and Adam stormed toward me waving a newspaper in my face. "What's this?"

"Oh, it's okay Adam—"

"It's okay? It's NOT okay!" He shouted.

"No it's fine, I already saw—"

"Yeah, you and the whole town saw. Or read. Or whatever." The newspaper hit the ground with a loud thwack as he looked up at me. "I'm tired of this, tired of being talked about and having our business in the paper all the time. All the damn time!"

"Stop yelling, Adam. Who's talking about you?"

"Everyone! Not everyone is straight-A, superstar, Miss Popular like you. We all didn't have friends that would back us up about this. I had to listen to the names and the rumors about you and our family. People are sick, they're twisted."

"People *are* sick, you can't let it get to you though. Come on, you really think people didn't say things to me?"

"I don't care. It doesn't matter anymore." He turned on his heel and headed for the front door as I looked at Jason, who looked as confused as I was.

"And you know what?" He stopped at the door, a shaking hand on the knob. "You always got what you wanted. You were always the favorite. I'm *glad* that stuff happened to you. You deserved to have your perfect life flipped upside down for once."

"Hey!" Jason lunged after Adam as he disappeared inside. "Don't you dare say that—"

"Jason, stop!"

He skidded to a halt at the tone in my voice. "Are you kidding me? Did you hear what he just said?"

"Yeah, I heard."

"You're gonna let him get away with that?"

"He's hurting, Jason. Just leave him." I pinched the bridge of my nose and sank into the porch swing. "We're all hurting."

***

Heather was enraged when I told her about the letters. "How did he...? I mean where...?" She grunted into the phone. "All right look, can you bring me one of those letters? I'm getting to the bottom of this."

"Yeah, I can, but Heather you don't need to. I know you're probably swamped. I just wanted to let you guys know about it."

"Nonsense. Bring me a letter or two."

When I hung up, Jason was sprawled across the couch in his boxers, flipping through channels. "Can we just *try* and pretend we're normal for one weekend? Maybe barricade the doors shut or something?"

"You wanna do that to keep other people out or me in here?" I teased.

"Both." He grabbed my wrist and dragged me onto him, kissing my neck.

"Yeah that's what I thought," I said, laughing. "Okay so here's some normal life for ya. What bills are we going to pay next week, because we sure don't have the money to pay all of them."

He dragged a hand across his face. "Ugh, okay well rent is paid. Groceries are done?"

"Yup."

"Okay. I guess pay the cell phone, we need to communicate with the outside world somehow."

"So, no electric?"

"They can't shut it off anyway. Wintertime laws, remember?"

"Yeah." I moved off of him, perching myself on the cushion to his right. "Have you thought about what we talked about?"

He raised an eyebrow. "Not much to think about. You have a stripper college friend who's recruiting more stripper college friends to dance at their club and you think it'd be a good idea."

"The *money* would be a good idea. And not stripper, really, go-go dancer. We can't be naked since they serve alcohol in the club."

"Well then, that makes all the difference."

"Your sarcasm is noted."

"Really though, it's up to you." He leaned forward and put his chin in his hands. "Your body, your call. If you think it'll be worth it, go for it. You know I'll support you."

"I don't think we have a choice." I pointed to the stack of bills piled across the room. "You can't do more than the seventy hours a week you already work. I can't work more than thirty with my full course load. My mom needs two hundred dollars, and—"

"Can you explain to me, again," he said, touching the side of his head, "why we can't even pay our own bills, but you're paying your mom's?"

"She needs it. It's my fault he's not there anymore."

I went to get up off the couch and Jason reached up and pulled me back down. "Come here, I didn't mean it like that. I just, ugh, I wish you didn't have such a big heart sometimes."

He tackled me to the ground and smothered me in kisses when I stuck my tongue out at him.

It turned out I wasn't the only one giving my mom money every month. My aunts and uncles had pooled together to ensure most of her bills were covered. After a short while *life* kicked in and their own families, understandably, became their priorities. Mom started to look for money in other places, namely my brothers and sister.

Since I was the only one who had moved out of the house, I wasn't aware that she had started charging them a hundred dollars a week for rent. I was putting myself through college, and my siblings' retail and manual labor jobs only went so far. I started working at Twisters as a dancer to make up the money Mom fell short on.

I was terrified the first night I walked into the dressing room. A lot of the girls walked around naked as they changed their outfits and I immediately noticed I was the youngest one there. "You got I.D.?" A red-haired and scrawny woman with a mole on her left cheek eyed me up and down. "I need I.D. before you can start."

It was simple enough. Get up on the stage, dance around, walk through the lounge and talk to the guys there between dances. Some guy paid me fifty dollars to talk to him—and only him— for half an hour. Another guy gave me a twenty to sit and have a drink with him. I always requested an energy drink when guys offered to buy me something, to hide the fact I wasn't old enough to drink alcohol yet.

The back room is where I made most of my money. Every guy had a story: Divorced, mid-life crisis, bachelor party, or hated his wife. The back room was a rounded, purple domed nook with submissive lighting that bounced off plush couches that lined the wall. Mirrors framed the remainder of the space. A beefy security guard stood at the doorway to enforce the hands-off policy.

The first time I saw the room was when a guy paid the hundred-dollar fee to take me back there, since I was insisting I had no idea what I was doing. I didn't know a thing about lap dances, which was the overall expectation of going in the back, and none of the other dancers looked like they wanted to teach me. The guy was young, maybe late twenties, clean cut, and I liked his cologne. He had come in with two other guys his age, and they were floating money around to all the girls like it was candy.

I straddled him and rocked my hips at first, pushing off the couch to stand and awkwardly ask him what he thought I should do next.

"Jesus, you've really never done this before?"

I shook my head and he patted the couch next to him. "Me either. My buddies are regulars, but I appreciate my money too much to throw it away. No offense. Sit, talk with me."

"None taken."

"So uh, your eyes are pretty clear." He studied my face, taking a long swig of his beer. "That means you don't shoot up before your shift like the other girls. Your body is way too hot to have had any children and you look like you're about to cry when guys call you over. What's the deal?"

The bodyguard gave me a confused look as precious time the guy had paid for ticked away.

"College. Need the money," I lied.

"Ah, I see." He sipped his Corona. "You don't belong here."

"Huh?"

"You don't belong in here. You seem different."

"You're telling me? But the money's good."

"How good?"

"Almost four hundred a night."

"Four hundred a night?"

"Five, now that I got you back here."

We laughed and the guard pointed to a neon clock above the door. "Time's up pal."

"Ah. Yeah, well," he said, standing up, leaving his beer bottle behind. "Money well spent. I'll see you again...?" He trailed his voice, inviting me to tell him my name.

"Brooke."

"I know that's what they call you but what's your real name?"

"Brooke."

"You don't use a stage name?"

"I think I would just get confused when they called my name to dance." I shrugged. "Seems easier to use a name I actually respond to."

He had a great smile. "Unbelievable. Well, nice to meet you Brooke."

Two weeks later I unloaded my sack of cash onto the bed when I woke Jason up after my shift. "Wow," he said, rubbing the sleep from his eyes. "You rob the place?"

"Kind of. The other girls don't really like when I work."

"I can see why. What time is it?"

"Three in the morning."

"Have any friendly back room chats?"

"Clearly," I said, pointing. "You wouldn't believe how many guys are desperate just to have someone to talk to. Can you believe I still haven't done a lap dance? Not one. The bodyguard keeps asking if I'm a dancer or a counselor."

"They want to take you into the back room and talk?"

"Don't roll your eyes I know it sounds weird. They all say the same thing too, that I don't belong there and I should quit. Maybe they think I'll run off with them if they be gentlemen," I said. "It makes sense, really. They all just want me to listen to them. I think their lives kind of suck."

"Mine doesn't." Jason rolled me into bed on top of him. "I have a hot, stripper girlfriend who comes home and saves all her energy for me."

The environment of the nightclub was wearing on me, though. Guys weren't always perfect gentlemen. A lot of them were older or had hygiene issues. I once sat and talked to a guy who told me it was his last night of freedom before he went to jail. I didn't have the nerve to ask why. Some other guy moved me to the end of the bar so he could ask me if I thought it was weird that he painted his toe nails pink.

The more I worked, the more I felt uneasy about it. The last night I worked there was when a Latino male insisted I meet him for breakfast after the club closed. He wouldn't leave, or take no for an answer, and the bouncers had to usher him out the front doors.

"I just can't do it anymore. I have to pep talk myself every night before I go in. I'm just sitting there thinking, 'I can't believe I'm doing this'."

"So then why do you?" Midge called once a month to check in. I had sent her copies of the newspaper clippings when the trial was over. She sent me a card with a heartfelt message inside, telling me I was her hero.

"Everything is just so messed up. I had this idea in my head that once the trial was over things would go back to normal."

"Which is…?"

"Exactly, no one in my family knows because I'm the only one who ever bothered to go to counseling. They all went to a few sessions because the court basically made them, but once the trial ended they wanted nothing to do with it."

"Does that surprise you?"

"Kind of. I mean, once I knew that our lives weren't *normal* I couldn't wait to make it healthy, you know? Jason and I don't raise our voices to each other, we never argue or get hostile because it's not something I'll ever allow in my life again."

"And they do?" Midge asked.

"Yeah. They scream at each other, at me, at themselves. They all seem miserable, yet no one does anything about it. My mom will call me crying about money, or something Kat did, or something Ethan did and she wants *me* to talk to them. Last time I checked I wasn't their mother."

"Maybe not literally, no, but you protected them like a mother would. They come to you for advice, they cry to you, and ask you for help. They don't go to her, and maybe she knows that."

"They trust me."

Nothing fell into place like it was supposed to. There was still so much anger, but it was being channeled in the wrong ways. Anytime I brought up counseling I was told it didn't work, or they didn't have time. There was always an excuse. Poor Ethan was standing in the eye of a storm, looking to me for stability while starting to question the craziness that surrounded him at Mom's house.

"I don't know Midge, I feel like I'm going crazy. My mom seems so different, like I don't even know her anymore."

"Lemme ask you somethin'. You's standing in the middle of a field and two things are happening. It's rainin' and there's a tornado off in the distance. I mean, it's a twirling, killer tornado, coming right toward you. You can feel the rain soaking you as you watch this tornado. Which one of those things you gonna notice first, the rain or the tornado?"

"The tornado," I said.

"Why?"

"I don't know. It's scarier? It can hurt you."

"Now let's assume that tornado goes away. The threat is gone. Now are you gonna notice the rain?"

"Yeah."

"Why?"

"'Cause I'd probably be getting wet and cold, I would notice that."

"You had somethin' in your life so powerful and frightening it took your full attention. It was more threatening, and could hurt you worse. That tornado was Earl. Now that the tornado has gone away, your focus shifts. See? The rain was there all along, your mama always was the way she is now, you just didn't notice it."

"So you think everyone was always this way? I just didn't see it until he was out of the picture?"

"You were in survival mode, Brooke. You did what you did to survive. You cleaned your mama's house, and you looked after them children like they was your own 'cause she was too high to be bothered herself. She used you, honey, because she could. Now that you got rid of her means of living, she's got a whole lot of responsibility that's new to her. The manipulation she tries to pull on you, that selfishness, it was there all along child. You just had bigger things to worry about, and she never had to use it before."

What she was saying made sense. When I was younger, my brothers and I would have to give Mom all the money we would get from holidays and birthdays. She told us she put it in the special savings accounts she had for us. We did this for years, and sometimes Adam and I would talk about the things we would buy when we got older.

When I got to the age that I wanted to start buying things, she told me that there *was* no savings, that she had four kids to raise at the time, and that I should be thankful we had a roof over our heads. We had been tricked into giving her our money for safe keeping from the time we were five years old. It seemed reasonable that she would continue to make us feel sorry for her and take our money as adults too.

"Thanks Midge," I said.

"You're welcome, sweetheart," she said, lowering her voice in warning. "Just remember, rain doesn't seem all that threatening at first, but too much rain can turn into a flood."

Chapter Twenty-Eight

Halfway through my sophomore year of college, I realized that a degree in medicine was out of reach both in time and money. Jason and I struggled to keep our utilities on and food in our cabinets. A few times we cuddled close under piles of blankets when the oil tank was drained and we became creative in making dinners out of the remnants of our fridge.

I had to graduate quickly so I could start working full time and stop playing Russian Roulette with what bills to pay. After the first day of taking a developmental psychology course as a prerequisite, I marched down to the registrar's office to officially switch majors to Psychology. It was a wildly interesting field and surprisingly easy to load up on courses to graduate quickly.

"Professionals don't know what gives some people a resilient personality," Dr. Russ said, pacing the classroom. "You can have four people go through something exceptionally traumatic, and one of those people will have a higher resiliency to coping. They won't turn to drugs or rebel against society, they'll seek the positive in any given situation. Now the interesting thing is the argument whether resiliency is nature or nurture. Are we born with it, or is it taught to us?"

I hung on his every word, half expecting Midge to bound through the door and tell me she had told the professor my life story. He rattled on. "These children usually have strong mentors from a young age that they can build their strength on, they have some kind of talent or outlet they use to channel their frustrations or stress, and they're intelligent." He tapped the side of his head.

"Scientists and psychologists have been studying the phenomena for decades. Just what makes one child so susceptible to crumbling under situations another one simply rises above?"

The nightmares became more bearable as I learned to explain them to Jason. I was also getting better at identifying what triggered the flashbacks or memories of Earl. Most of the time, a lot of the time, it was the people I surrounded myself by that reminded me of a life I wanted to forget. Those people trickled out of our lives.

The nightmares came in waves. Jason would shake me from my sleep as I clawed at him drenched in sweat. Other times I would mumble, scream, or hysterically cry until I woke myself up. When I *would* have those rare nights of deep, uninterrupted slumber, Jason would get anxious and wake me up just to make sure I was still breathing.

"You got permission to take twenty-four credits a semester?" Jason raised an eyebrow. "You're also starting an internship and you work. Are you trying to get away? Is it me?" He lifted up his arm with a smile. "I must smell."

"Nooo. Full time is twelve credits. I mean, I'm doubling the recommended course load but psychology isn't exactly hard, it's just time consuming. We have to write a lot of papers. Very interesting though."

"You seem happy about it."

"I *am* happy about it."

I interned at a facility called Children's Hope and Promise, or CHAP. It was an alternative school and boarding facility for children who had severe emotional disturbances and behavioral issues. They paid me for the length of my internship, which was unheard of, and they even offered me a job—if I wanted it—to start after I graduated.

Tackling my piled up course load allowed me to graduate an entire semester early, which was perfect timing, because Jason and I found out I was pregnant. We stood in the bathroom for hours watching the blinking pregnant signal, hugging, and bursting at the seams to share the great news with everyone.

When I had the miscarriage, it was two days before graduation. The picture of the pregnancy test we had taken nine weeks earlier was still the background picture on my phone. We had told most of our family at that point about the pregnancy, even some of our closest friends. "Looks like I'm the one getting a graduation present," Jason had teased. He kissed my belly and told me that as soon as I graduated, we would start planning a wedding.

I must have peed every two hours in those first few weeks. So when Jason woke me up in the middle of the night thinking I had wet the bed, he was not expecting what he found. When he turned on the light and saw that I was soaked in blood, he carried me down the stairs and floored it to the hospital. No ambulance would have traveled faster than he did that night.

I was zombified after coming home from the hospital, and I had no intentions of walking at graduation. After getting the okay from the doctor, Jason insisted. "You've worked too hard and sacrificed too much to not go. You owe it to yourself."

So I walked with my graduating class, painfully and slowly. No one there would have assumed I was anything other than tired from a week full of finals looking at my graduation pictures. I smiled and went through the motions, shook hands with my professors, and then disappeared into a cloud of mourning for the next two months. With no classes, and since I didn't technically accept the job offer from my internship at CHAP, I had ample time to sit around and think.

So that's exactly what I did.

After gaining fifteen pounds and wearing out my bathrobe to the stitching, I called around and applied to a job in the town where my mom lived. Jason was ecstatic that we were moving back to the Poconos. I just needed a change. I needed to get out of that apartment and start over.

So we did.

Chapter Twenty-Nine

I pulled up to the familiar house with the white sign on the front lawn and put the car in park. Taking my time, I gathered my things and headed inside. The same ceiling high posters still littered the walls, and it still smelled the same. There was a receptionist I didn't recognize sitting behind the counter in the lobby. "Hi there, can I help you?"

I smoothed my suit jacket and nodded. "I'm Brooke Nolan, I have an interview with Anne for the Community Advocate position."

"Oh very good, I'll let her know you're here. Have a seat." She pointed to the waiting room and picked up the phone.

I sat in the same chair I did almost eight years prior. A jumbled up puzzle and some coloring books were scattered on the floor. I wondered how many children had passed through the waiting room. How many children told? How many of them went on to lead prosperous and fulfilling lives despite what happened to them?

A woman with glimmering dental work rounded the corner and stuck out her hand. "Brooke? I'm Anne, so glad you're here. Come, follow me back to my office."

I tailed behind her, catching a glimpse of her pin striped suit and stocky pumps. Her silver hair was pinned in a bun at the top of her head and she smoothed a wrinkle across her forehead as she sat down. "Whew, I am swamped. Sorry for the wait. So you're *the* Brooke Nolan huh?"

I laughed. "Well I guess it depends on what you've heard."

"Nothing but great things, don't you worry." She stirred a spoon into the sides of a mug on her desk. "Midge certainly had nothing but great things to say about you."

I blushed. "Good to know."

"So there are quite a few people applying for this position. You understand what a Community Advocate is?"

"Yeah, someone who educates the public about domestic and sexual violence through community events. I would be mainly targeting youth though, right?"

"You got it. We really want to push towards a more modern approach for getting youth's attention. They're into technology and computers, honestly I don't know much about it." Anne raised her eyebrows. "Old lady like me needs to know when to take a step back and let the younger generation step up."

"Yeah, we can be complicated," I agreed.

"I have over fifty applicants." She patted a stack of papers next to her. "Why you? Why are you the best for the job?"

When I applied to the job ad Midge sent me for the Women In Crisis center, it stated that personal experience was respected. I knew Midge had probably filled Anne in on the majority of what my life was like, and if she didn't, all Anne had to do was pull my file from when I was a child receiving services there when Midge was my counselor.

"I think it takes a certain personality to comfortably talk about topics like domestic violence and sexual assault in the limelight. I've been there and I've seen it firsthand, so I have an insider's perspective. But I've also grown from it, and came out above it I guess you could say."

"Yes. It is important, the way we overcome," Anne said, scribbling on a pad in front of her.

"I don't want to educate youth after the fact though," I continued. "I want to impact the community about these topics from as young of an age as possible. I want to teach prevention, so they know the signs and what to do about it before it effects their lives. They need to know their options."

"I see," she said, putting her pen down. "So as a victim, you think you have what it takes to get into these kids' heads?"

I smiled. "No ma'am. As a survivor I have what it takes."

***

Gina met me after my interview so we could catch up. "I'm so glad you moved back. We can do tea now and I can see you more."

"I know. I hope I get this job though."

"You'll get it. They'd be crazy not to hire you. Is that your phone?"

"Yeah, one second," I said. The number didn't register a name on my cell phone.

"Brooke? This is Anne. Have a second?"

"Oh sure, sure. Go ahead." Gina squinted her eyes at me.

"Well, it didn't take much deliberation, and we'd like to have you join our team as Community Advocate, if you'll take us."

I gasped. "No kidding! It's only been a little over an hour."

"Is that a yes?"

"Oh, yes. Yes, I'd love to. Thank you!"

"Great. I know you said you could start as soon as possible, so if you want to come in on Monday, we'll get you set up. See you then."

"I got the job!" I cried as I hung up the phone.

Gina wrapped me in a hug. "I told you! Oh, congratulations! You'll do great there."

I got Jason on the phone to tell him before I got back to our conversation. "So anyway, you need me to let your dog out while you guys go on vacation, right?" I asked.

"Yeah, you're okay with it? Paul's still living out by college and I'd hate to ask the neighbor, she's not really a dog person."

"Yeah it's not a problem. When are you leaving?"

"Next Thursday."

"And you told Paul? Just in case he shows up and I'm here?"

"Umm…" She swirled her spoon. "You know, I think I mentioned it. Yeah."

I eyed her. "Maybe I'll let him know, just to make sure. And hey, I need to tell you something. Promise you won't get mad?"

"What is it?"

I slipped the ring onto my finger and held it under Gina's nose. "Jason and I eloped last week. We're married!"

Gina covered her mouth, half happily surprised and half upset. "Oh, Brooke. Jason is such a great guy, he really is. We really love him. Congratulations, honey!"

Her eyes watered and I considered how much she had wanted me to be a part of her family. I knew she had secretly hoped Paul and I would rekindle an old flame and give her some grandbabies.

"Thanks," I said.

"Have you told anyone yet?"

"Our family, some of our friends. We had it in this beautiful outdoor garden nearby, and I even had a dress. It was just really intimate and sweet. I wish you could have been there but we just wanted something discreet, you know?"

"I don't blame you. I think it was the perfect idea and I'm so happy for you guys. Now make me some grandbabies! You'll always be a daughter-in-law to me, no matter who you're with."

I smiled at Gina's kind words as I signed into Facebook that night and messaged Paul. I didn't expect him to get back to me as soon as he did. I told him I was going to be letting the dog out while his parents and little brother went on vacation and I just wanted him to know I would be at his house. For a while after we broke up he didn't want me to visit his mom at all, which I understood. He finally realized that we would indefinitely be a part of each other's lives and stopped caring when I would go there, as long as it wasn't when he was home. I didn't need any drama, so I wanted to give him a friendly heads up that I would be helping out his parents.

We hadn't talked in years, and anytime I tried to extend an olive branch he would scoff at it. An alert on my phone went off and I read the inbox message twice to make sure I had read it correctly:

Id love to stick around and see u ill take you to dinner we can catch up if youd like unless im crossing some sort of line then ill just see you at the house

My heart skipped a beat. He wanted to catch up? Dinner? Those two words were never a part of his vocabulary. There were so many years between the last few times we spoke, so much left unsaid. I wasted no time replying.

That actually sounds really nice, unless you want me to cook something and we can watch cartoons for old times sake

He wrote back:

Lol you mean ill cook u something you forget who my mom is not saying u wouldn't cook something amazing but dinner is a better idea so we can appreciate the moment

Now all of a sudden we had moments? I instinctively looked down at the ring on my finger, drumming it on the screen of my phone for a minute. I nodded as I typed back a more casual response:

True, your mom is the best cook I know. Whether you want to whip something up or go out, I think I'd just like the pleasure of your company.

I hit send. Message clear— just two platonic people having dinner to catch up on heavy emotional baggage. The next alert didn't even finish going off before I grabbed my phone again.

I could care less either way as long as we get to catch up and I get to see your pretty face lol and my company isn't too pleasurable but youre putting me on the spot I have to come up with a surprise now

I waded into unknown territory, letting the words *pretty face* obsessively repeat in my head before another message popped up.

If calling would make your life easier, it would make mine I hate talkin on facebook

He left his number and it took most of my will power not to pick up the phone and call immediately. I hated that he suddenly sprang up out of nowhere, talking about moments and dinners after all these years, suddenly having things he wanted to catch up on. I waited a full ten minutes before I added him as a contact in my phone. Another five minutes passed while I thought about what to say before starting a texting war.

I've always enjoyed your company actually

His reply was just as coy.

Yeah I always enjoyed your company we went well together lol

I cringed. What was all this *we* stuff? I grabbed a wine glass out of the cupboard before I responded. Jason wouldn't be home for another couple of hours and I needed to see where this was going. I texted back between gulps:

Guess I'll have to try extra hard to make sure we have a good time then, don't wanna disappoint you

I sounded so fake, but I couldn't think straight. Paul was being civil with me for the first time in years and I desperately wanted to hear what he had to say.

You don't have to try hard Brooke I'm sure ill have a great time with you just being you. I just need to see your pretty face again plus you scared me back then

The conversation turned a corner where I'd hoped it wouldn't but I found myself texting back, needing to know exactly what he meant. I sipped my wine, aware of the silence that filled my living room. Of course he was reaching out to me now—now that I was married, starting a new job, and overjoyed with life in general. Why is it that guys had a way of know exactly when you're at your happiest to come parading back into your life? I opened my phone to respond.

What does that mean Paul...?

I don't know maybe that's why I acted like a hard ass and I do apologize for not being there when u really could have used my help. I admit I was selfish and a jerk but at the time it was hard to deal with, finding someone I love have something so horrible happen to them was too much for me. So I did what I did and took off thinking it was best for myself but being selfish in the process and also throwing away one of the best things that happened to me. So with that said ill leave it alone and maybe now we can be friends at least

As I read his book of an apology, I finished my second glass of wine and leaned over my phone with my mouth dropping to my knees. In a single text message he had said everything I had waited years to hear. He apologized, told me he was wrong, and that he shouldn't have walked away. I answered back.

I need a minute to process everything you just said. I've never stopped thinking about you, so this is kind of a huge deal to me right now and ive had too much wine, need to think before I respond.

You're probably mad, I understand. And you can just blame it on the wine if you want to lash out at me lol

I'm not mad at you Paul, I'm sad for you. I wanted you to be happy, and I thought I could do that for you. I knew where my heart was at the time and I thought you deserved nothing less than that.

To be honest u were probably the only one that would have made me happy but what I thought I needed was to get away when really I let go of the one person who knew exactly how I felt. I've been with other girls and they

were nothing compared to you. I threw away a great girl who cared a lot about me, my loss and my loss only ill take the humiliation of conceding that you were right and I was wrong

I threw my hands into the air in praise, "Ladies and gentlemen, we have a winner!" My cheeks hurt from smiling as I replied, trying to keep my composure.

Well im excited for dinner itll be nice to see you and talk face to face

Yeah I haven't been with anyone since last May just trying to get my life on track tired of getting my heart broken in meaningless relationships by girls with no substance. Not saying I haven't been a jerk at times

Well im glad you're on the right track. Need to go for now but im looking forward to seeing you.

I switched my phone to silent as I heard Jason's car pull in the driveway. I fanned my face and waited for him to come into the living room while I tried to regain my composure.

"You'll never guess what just happened," I said, not giving him a chance to take off his shoes. Beyond already having Jason as my best friend, I cherished that I could tell him anything. Even if it was something he didn't want to know.

Jason studied my face. "You okay?"

"You know how I'm watching Gina's dog?" I explained the Facebook and text messages in one breath. I handed him my phone, letting him interpret the conversation at his leisure as I finished. Jason shifted his weight on the couch and clasped his hands together.

"So, what are you going to do?" he asked.

"What's wrong? Why do you look so sad?"

"I used to ask what you would do if he ever apologized, remember? I asked what would happen to us if he ever said he was wrong and wanted you back. I used to ask all the time if you would go back to him."

I nodded, "Yeah?"

"And what did you always say?" he asked, twisting his wedding band in circles around his finger.

When I didn't respond after a minute he finished his own sentence. "You always used to tell me that he would *never* apologize, so it didn't matter for you to answer the question." He rubbed his knees and smiled. He was so brave sometimes. "Well, you finally got what you wanted. So now what?"

My heart battled my head over the same question while I waited for our reunion. There was so much history between us, even at such a young age. I had wanted his family as my own. I loved all of them so deeply.

But Jason was there for me when he was supposed to be, when it mattered the most. He never walked away, even when I would have understood if he did. I was in love with Jason. He had become the exact thing I never knew I needed.

When I pulled into Paul's driveway and saw his car, I had to catch my breath. There were so many things I had to say and I wasn't sure I knew where to start.

I knocked.

When he opened the door I almost didn't recognize him. He had a full beard traveling down his face and neck and he towered over me. I reached up on all toes to give him a hug and planted a kiss on his cheek.

"Come in." His voice was gruff and he pulled the hood from his sweatshirt up over his head. He kicked his feet up on the coffee table and sat down on the couch. I sat on the adjacent couch and crossed my legs.

"How are you?" I asked. The wavering in my voice intensified the awkward silence.

He nodded in response and flicked a crumb off of his sweatshirt.

Both of us stared at the blank TV for what seemed like hours. I crossed and uncrossed my legs and cleared my voice several times, but nothing ever came out. He looked at me at one point, raised an eyebrow, and then continued to study the remote sitting next to him.

We had shared a common beginning. At fifteen years old we thought we knew what love was and ran with the feelings that were new to us. I had loved him, but it always seemed like we would be on different chapters in life. At that point, I doubted our lives would ever be parallel. It seemed like no benefit would come from going backward in time, and in all honesty, I was a little angry that it took him comparing me to several other failed relationships before realizing I was what he needed. Jason always knew right from the start that I was special.

It was unfortunate, the way we parted ways when we were so young, and I guess I would always wonder how my past played a part in the outcome of our relationship. I couldn't go back in time to change anything, and we weren't the young teens we were back then. If the good pieces of our relationship weren't enough to keep us together in the first place, maybe they wouldn't be enough to keep us together a second time. Maybe love wasn't enough, if that's even what we had to begin with.

Paul stood up, looking at his phone. "I have to get back to college. Roommate needs his key."

"You're still taking classes?"

"Yeah. Failed a few."

I nodded and stood up. We had absorbed each other's presence in total silence for over half an hour, neither of us completely sure why we were there in the first place. I wrapped my arms around his neck to say goodbye and buried my cheek into the side of his face.

He didn't move and we dragged out the embrace. When he pulled away and looked down into my eyes, all I could do was fake a smile to keep myself from crying. He walked out the front door and I resumed my position on the couch to listen for his car to pull away. As the familiar sound of his muffler disappeared into the distance, I took a deep breath and exhaled. I was finally able to let go of Paul.

I was happy in my marriage, more than happy, and that's where I wanted to stay. I was sure that somewhere down the line Paul would meet someone and she'd be lucky to have him, but I didn't know him anymore. I knew Jason, and I loved him. I thought back to the night Paul told me that I would never find anyone as good as him. He was right about that. Jason was so much more.

Paul and his family would always have a special place in my life. It seemed like a pattern of wrong time, wrong place with Paul. Thinking back, I doubted that he had the ability to support me emotionally when we were younger and I needed him, not because he didn't want to, I just don't think he knew how. He wasn't obligated to give me the closure or any explanations for his behavior from when we dated, but he finally did anyway.

I was so grateful for that.

Chapter Thirty

My old professor from college, Dr. Russ, saw me on the news one night working an event for Women In Crisis. He called to ask if I would accompany him to a meeting at the local courthouse where I used to go to college. "I was asked to speak to the domestic violence policy group, and I thought you would be perfect as a guest speaker."

"Okay great, what exactly do you want me to talk about?" I asked.

"There will be a lot of judges there, lawyers, courthouse personnel, that kind of thing. I want you to give them an inside look to what it's like to go through the system. Tell them what was right, what was wrong, and offer any procedural changes or give any ideas to help children cope within the system."

I was impressed with the idea. "That actually sounds great, I'd have a lot to say. Do you know how many people will be there, so I know?"

"Not too many. Maybe around ten, fifteen max. I'll send out a memo that you'll be there as a guest speaker to see if we can get more people to show up."

The room was packed with over forty people when I showed up weeks later. Court personnel made up the majority of the population but there were also social service workers, some politicians, and even a funeral director. The room encompassed all types of people whose jobs were impacted by domestic violence. The empowerment in the room was electric, and I folded several note cards into the palm of my hand as Dr. Russ introduced me.

Involuntary jitters that started from my core made their way to the surface, and my hands danced with adrenaline. "First I'd like to thank Dr. Russ for bringing this meeting to my attention. I think it's great that a domestic violence policy group exists and I'm more than happy to help everyone here understand what it's like to go through the system as a child."

I cleared my throat. "This is actually the first time I'm talking about these things out loud, to people who aren't jurors or a judge. I've never talked publicly about my own experiences before."

Everyone's eyes were locked on mine. I addressed some of the latest statistics on domestic violence and how so often children become silent victims when they witness a parent being abused. "My mom was never physically abused by my dad but I was, along with my siblings."

I told them that more than half of teen relationships were domestically violent. "It's just in a different way. Boyfriends control who girls talk to or who they text and they think that's okay. Girls think it's okay to punch a guy, scream in his face, or scratch him. It's normal to call each other names that are degrading or hang up on each other in the middle of a conversation. Teen dating is a breeding ground for adult relationships and if they don't realize that what they're doing now is wrong, they'll carry that over into their relationships as adults. It only escalates from there. Even though the majority of reported rapes are from women, I'd be willing to bet it's just as high for men." When I saw a few of the men in the audience crinkle their noses in disagreement, I explained.

"When some of my peers found out in high school that I was being sexually abused, they came to me with their own trauma. I think they thought I was the only one in the world who would understand them. One guy told me his father, from the time he was six, had raped him. Another guy told me his female boss was sexually harassing him at work. A cousin of mine was in a relationship where his girlfriend would scratch his back during arguments until he bled. I also found out that another family member had fallen victim to my dad as well, but when he told an adult no one believed him. I was young at the time, and had someone believed him I wouldn't be standing here today, telling you that I am a survivor of incestuous rape by my dad."

A woman in a gray suit widened her eyes in surprise and another man scribbled things down on a pad in front of him. Dr. Russ had told them a survivor of sexual abuse was going to be the guest speaker, and I know I didn't fit the mold of what people expected. Most people want to believe that they would know if someone they knew was being abused just by looking at them, but that was rarely the case. Men especially carried an immobilizing burden when they were abused.

"Just because men don't report it doesn't mean it's not there. Men carry more shame with their situations than women do because they think people will label them as gay, or that they weren't manly enough to stand up and fight the perpetrator off. I wish more of them *would* come forward so that they can get the help they need to not carry their hurt into their adult lives." Talking about male victims had captured their attention. No one wanted to believe that men were susceptible to the same fears and nightmares as women.

"Eight out of ten times, the victim knows their rapist. It's not like on TV where there's a dark alley and someone is waiting in the shadows. Yeah, it happens, but not nearly as frequently as when the victim knows the perpetrator."

"Why not?" someone called out.

"Who better to know your schedule? Who else knows when you leave the house and when you come home? They know exactly what your child likes and doesn't like. They know what candy they'd do anything for, and what rooms in the house no one can hear them in. Children get groomed, won over, and that takes time and patience. Children get the things they want, special privileges, and then touching body parts turns into a game that's fun and expected."

A woman raised her hand. "Why don't they tell an adult about what's being done to them?" Several people shook their head in agreement.

"You don't know something is wrong if it's all you know," I explained. "If a child is groomed from the time they're three until the time they're twelve, they don't know that life is supposed to be any different. Then by the time they realize it's wrong, they're threatened, blackmailed, or shamed into keeping quiet. While my brothers suffered physical violence from my dad in a way I could never fathom, I suffered through sexual violence to an extent I never want them to know."

Dr. Russ laid a hand on my shoulder as I choked over my last words. "And don't be fooled by the non-textbook red flags for sexual abuse. I was on the honor roll in high school and I was a cheerleader. I held a job, had a boyfriend, friends, and I never in my life got detention. Yet my brother was in and out of juvenile detention centers three times during the time I testified. When my dad was finally sentenced and sent away for his crimes, he thought it would be a good idea to send my already emotionally distraught brother a handmade birthday card from jail. He became so re-traumatized, that he got doped up on every drug he could get his hands on and went wandering into neighbors' homes, looking for things to steal so he could buy more drugs. If he hadn't been caught, he would have died of an overdose." The stares I was receiving were sympathetic.

"Not all children cope the same," I continued. "Some channel their energy positively, like I did. On the outside no one would suspect a thing. Some children channel their energy negatively, they are rebellious and in trouble with the law. Make no mistake, there is no *one* example of what a child looks like or acts like when they're being abused."

A man in the back raised his hand. "So how do we get a child to tell us when they're being abused if we can't pick them out? How do we know?"

I smiled. "You can't, and you don't. Not until that child is ready to tell. And I mean one hundred percent, fed up with their life, ready to tell. You can't make a child tell you anything, but what you *can* do is cultivate an environment where *if* they told, they would be taken care of. Social Services came to my school and I could have told them, but I didn't. My boyfriend's mother suspected that I was being abused but I didn't tell her either. I didn't tell my best friends, and I didn't tell my boyfriend. You know who I told? My aunt and uncle. And do you know why?"

The audience shook their head as I held up my hands, holding an imaginary basketball. "Because of this."

They stared at my hands with raised eyebrows and curious eyes. Some turned their heads to try and figure out if my hands were contorted into any given shape or letter. I smiled.

"It's a bubble. A safe, protective bubble. My uncle showed this to me when I went to his house. He looked at me and said 'Brooke, our family has this bubble over it. No one hurts anyone in it and it's safe in here. We can help anyone who is in trouble, and we wanted you to know *you* are protected by this bubble.' I passed the pretend bubble to the woman sitting across from me and everyone laughed as she instinctively brought her hands up to catch it.

"I needed three things," I said, holding up my fingers. "I needed a safe place, my bubble. I needed someone to talk to, a mentor, and I had my boyfriend's mom and my counselor. I also needed my breaking point, a final straw." I reached into the folder I brought and showed the audience a picture of Ethan when he was two. "I realized that if I left my house when I graduated high school, my little brother was going to have to face my dad alone. I was not about to let that happen, not while I knew what kind of torture and pain I had to go through."

Heads nodded from all around the table. "Now, you're all here because you deal directly or know someone who deals directly with the process of the court, correct?"

Nods again. "Okay everyone, here's what they don't tell you in the textbooks."

A few of the men smiled as I proceeded. "First of all, Social Services..." I shook my head dramatically and a few people laughed. "Please do not ever, EVER, tell a child that what they tell you will be in confidence if it is not. Don't lie to us. If it *is* confidential, do not send a letter home to that child's parents telling them what they told you. Do you have any idea how *dangerous* it was for me when my dad opened up a letter from Social Services saying that I had talked to them?" One woman to my left covered her mouth.

"He could have killed me if I had actually told them what was going on. Also, when you do your follow ups, why would you ask a child how they're doing right in front of the parent? If anything is new, they're not going to say something with the perpetrator right there. And even if they aren't there, bring the child out of the house. Bring them outside or to your office. Their home is a constant reminder of the hell they're living in, so don't make them talk about it in an unsafe place if you can help it.

Law enforcement and police. When I went in to do my interview I was mortified. I couldn't look the police officer in the face and there was nothing to help me cope with the weight of what I was saying out loud for the first time. People will be embarrassed, they'll be scared, and they will be blunt. They'll say things like 'He touched me'. Let us know right away that it's okay to say the names of body parts. *Lie* to us, please, and tell us you've heard this before. If it's a girl victim, get a girl cop. If there isn't one available, tell them that you have talked to lots of little girls about bad things that have happened to them. We need to know our bodies are safe to talk about to a male in a police uniform. Give us a piece of paper and a pencil so we can scribble as we talk to avoid watching your reaction as we walk you through our horrific details, or let us write it down instead if we can't quite find the words. Also make sure your departments know the laws about fleeing a state with children and Protection From Abuse orders."

I shuffled my note cards and moved on. "For anyone working in the District Attorney's office. My victim advocate was the best thing that happened to me during my trial. I never had to ask what was happening before, during, or after any court hearing and everything was explained to me in a way I could understand. Tour the courtroom before the hearing, tell the child that it's okay to show emotion, and say who they can look at when they're sitting on the witness stand. I was shy at first and couldn't bring myself to say the words penis or rape, but let us know that those words are expected and we won't get in trouble for saying them. My advocate also signed me up to receive alerts when my dad was transferred to a different jail or if anything changed in his status. It's a relief to know where he is at all times."

I looked around. "How many mental health or social service type agencies do we have in here?" A few people raised their hands. "Listen, confidentiality is everything. I had kids come up to me in school and apologize for what happened to me because they had mothers in the front office of my school who knew all about it. That's unacceptable. Counseling is what made the difference in how I coped with the trial, both during and after. I am the only one of my siblings who sought help, the only one who doesn't still live at home in the same toxic environment, and I actually have a *healthy* relationship. My mom and siblings refused counseling after a few sessions, they didn't want it. But then they wonder why they have so much tension and anger in their lives. They wonder why they have nervous breakdowns and call me in the middle of the night with the latest drama."

Since I was in the presence of people who potentially had the power to change things, I wanted to throw an idea out at them. "Programs need to be established with required participation from all family members. Just because I was the one testifying didn't mean that I was the only one who needed help. I know my triggers and what upsets me and now, I know how to handle those things. My siblings are depressed and go in and out of promiscuous or unhealthy relationships. They abuse drugs or alcohol and turn to food for comfort. Sometimes I feel like I sacrificed two years of testimony for nothing. My dad is out of the house and they still treat each other horribly. They didn't want to deal with it, and they haven't. For years after I first came forward, I felt like the black sheep in my family for wanting a better life, a calm life. I don't want to believe I set my expectations too high when it comes to moving forward. That leads me to my conclusion. You can't change someone who does not want to change."

I held up a finger because I needed my point to stick. "If a child does not *want* to tell, they won't. If a family does not *want* to heal, they won't. I wanted to heal, I wanted peace in my life, and I wanted to tell. So I did. I thought my family would want the same, and it kills me that they have such great potential to thrive but they don't. I lost a lot of sleep over that. I cried a lot over that. But at the end of the day, the only person I can make changes to is myself. No matter how much I tell them how liberating it feels to finally be as happy as I am, they'll never understand if they don't *want* to."

I looked around the room. "I was hesitant to come here today, I'll admit. I asked my husband, 'What would it matter that I came in here and exposed myself and my story to these people? What'll that change?' Well, maybe it won't change anything, but maybe it'll inspire some of you to make changes in what you do. Maybe next time you're faced with a young boy or girl and they're about to turn their lives upside down and inside out to testify against someone that should have loved and protected them…"

I shook my head, absorbing the moment. So much had happened since I came forward. I never imagined I would have the strength to inspire other people with my story. "Maybe you can tell them that it's okay, that it's worth it, and that you'll help. Thank you."

The audience jumped to their feet in applause. The conference room boomed with excited mutters of enlightenment. I scanned the room and hoped, I prayed, that *one thing* I said made a difference.

I knew how important it was to have one moment of clarity, one seemingly unimportant glass of spilled milk at a dinner table, for a child to break the cycle of abuse in their family. After my insight somebody in that room would undoubtedly become someone else's glass of spilled milk, their only hope, and their one fighting chance.

For that reason alone, everything that had happened was worth it.

Chapter Thirty-One

Gina moved the probe over my swollen belly and shrieked. "Two little babies in there, that's for sure. One for me and one for you, right?"

I laughed. "Of course! Who knows, maybe there's a third one hiding in there somewhere?"

"Hope not." Jason looked down at me and smiled. "Besides, you're already more than four months so I think we would have seen it by now."

"Ah everything looks great, just perfect. Okay, okay." She squinted at the screen one last time. "Want to know what they are?"

Jason's face twisted into a goofy grin. "Yes, but no."

"We want it to be a surprise," I said.

Gina's mouth dropped open. "So I'm the *only* one who knows? Ah this is perfect, baby shopping time!" She clicked a few pictures and set down the probe. "Oh I can't wait to meet them, the little bambinos."

She grabbed a rag and helped me clean off. "So that means you'll have to pick out two boy names *and* two girl names. Just in case."

"Yeah, double the everything," I said.

Jason helped me sit up and he stroked my belly. "Time to go home, kids."

We held hands as we cruised through town and pulled into our driveway. The due date was set for Jason's twenty-fifth birthday, and we joked about how easy birthday planning would be for the next couple of years.

A blue envelope was sitting on the table when we walked into the house. "What's this?" I asked, reading the front.

"I think it's from your brother. He's getting out in a month or two isn't he?"

"Hmm," I said. I slid my finger underneath, pulling out a thick card. 'Sister' it said at the top. I traced the laced inside as I read his handmade card.

Hey Sis, how's life? Jail is fine. Actually it sucks and I can say with complete confidence I am never coming back. I've had a lot of time to sit in here, and think. Truth is, you're my big sister and I can always go to you with anything. You're extremely smart, beautiful, and so funny. You're gonna make a great mom because you're loving, caring, and pretty much would do anything for anyone without anything in return.

You went through hell to make sure I was safe growing up and made sure Ethan and the rest of us would be loved. You're strong willed and go to the end of world and back for the people you love. You're the best sister I could ever want. I miss you extremely and hope someday I show you how grateful I am for what you did for me and our family. I don't know where I'd be without you Brooke, I love you.

Thomas signed it with his signature smiley-faced logo and drew a comical picture of a large lady holding her belly. An arrow pointed to it that said '*You*'. I laughed as I wiped away a tear and stuck the card to the bulletin board in the kitchen.

"He 'misses you extremely'?" Jason said, raising an eyebrow.

"He barely graduated high school, give the kid a break."

Jason cracked open a beer and pointed to the living room. "I might watch the game, want to join?"

"Oh sure, drink a beer in front of the fat lady."

"You're not fat." He grabbed me by the waist and pressed his lips into mine. "You're my beautiful, very pregnant, somewhat chocolate addicted wife."

I rolled my eyes and whacked his butt as he walked away. "You go ahead, I want to write for a little while."

"All right baby, but don't work our children too hard. There are labor laws you know."

"Speaking of labor laws, you know you can't invite Ethan over to watch movies and then convince him that working on your truck is cooler. That's an awful bait and switch if I ever saw one."

"Oh, he loves it. Did you see his face when he tightened a lug nut by himself?" He smiled at me. "He's doing pretty good now, huh?"

"Yeah," I smiled. "Pretty good."

I thought about Ethan and Midge as I made my way down the hallway. Midge had passed away of pancreatic cancer six months earlier. She would never get to meet my children but I kept her picture on my work desk and planned to tell them all about her one day.

One of our last conversations played in my head as I sat at my computer. I had asked her what she thought about me going to confront Earl, to finally close that chapter in my life. I didn't know what I expected from the conversation we would have, but I did know I wanted him to show some kind of remorse or to admit to what he did to my face.

"Child, you ain't ever gonna get it," Midge said. "And if you go there, you still giving him all the control. He can get up and walk outta that room if he wanted. He'd make you feel like *you* the one that did something wrong by coming to see him."

"Yeah, you're probably right. He just had no emotion, no reaction when he was sentenced. Like he had nothing to say."

"Maybe he don't. But I'll tell you what. You ain't ever gonna forgive that man, and you ain't ever gonna forget. I know you. You'll put it behind you and you'll move on, that I'm sure of, but I think he needs to know he didn't ruin your life. You're out here with a fine husband, job you love, and you can remind him that he's in there because of what he did to himself, not what you did to him. Best way to do that is to write a letter. Can't walk away from a letter. He can't interrupt you none, and I am sure willing to bet he will read it front to back. So if you feel the need, you go ahead and write him what you feel."

It was the last conversation I had with Midge. A co-worker called to tell me that she had passed, and Midge had left me a small amount of money that she wanted me to use to take some time off of work and write about my experiences so that maybe it would help someone else. I owed that to Midge.

Maybe I owed that to myself.

I powered up my laptop and waited for the humming to slow before I opened Microsoft Word. My fingers traced over the keys. I thought about the day I drove to New York when I told my aunt and uncle what was going on. So much had happened since then. I had so much to say in my letter and I wasn't sure how it would end, but I sure did know how it should start.

Hi Earl,
I bet you're wondering why I'm calling you Earl...

Discussion Guide Questions

1.   What do you think about Brooke's choices in the book (keeping her father's secret, etc)? Were her choices justified given the circumstances she faced? What would be some other options she could have explored?

2.   Despite only being a teenager, Brooke seemed mature beyond her years. Did her character change throughout the story? How?

3.   What was the most difficult challenge faced by Brooke? Do you think you would be able to make such decisions? What would you have done differently?

4.   What role does Midge and Gina play in the story? How might Brooke's situation have turned out without them in her life?

5.   Brooke kept secrets from the family and friends in her life. What kind of advice would you have given to Brooke to come forward?

6.   Do you agree with the judge's decision to give David the maximum sentence? Why or why not? What other consequences (if any) should David have received?

7.   Do you agree with Brooke's decision about Paul that *love is not enough*? Why or why not?

For more resources, including inquiries to SKYPE with the author for a Q&A session for you/your classroom, please email the author at:

authorklrandis@gmail.com

ABOUT THE AUTHOR

K.L. Randis, author of bestselling novel *Spilled Milk* and the *Pillbillies* series, started journaling at the age of six and had short stories and poetry published by the time she was thirteen.

She is a graduate of Pennsylvania State University and a certified expert in the field of domestic violence. She has since written numerous local publications that brought awareness to domestic violence and child abuse. K.L. Randis engages audiences on a local and national level to raise awareness about child abuse, serving as a frequent commentator to media outlets. She has developed local high school presentations on teen dating violence, was named Community Woman of Distinction by East Stroudsburg University, and was invited to the Pentagon several times to speak to the department of defense about child abuse.

Spilled Milk is her first novel, which grabbed the #1 bestsellers spot in the genre of *Child Abuse* on Amazon for eight consecutive months only 24 hours after its debut. She resides in the Pocono Mountains of Pennsylvania with her family.

Contact the Author:

Website: www.klrandis.com
Email: authorklrandis@gmail.com
Facebook: facebook.com/klrandis
Spilled Milk Fan Page: facebook.com/spilledmilkrandis
Twitter: @KLRandis
Instagram: KLRandis

ALSO BY K.L. RANDIS

Pillbillies
(Pillbillies Series Book1)

When paramedics discover three-year-old Lacey floating in the bathtub and Jared Vorcelli barely conscious in his parents' living room, his drug addiction is put into the limelight and his pill-pushing days as a Kingpin of the Pocono Mountains come to a screeching halt. A chance meeting with a man named Dex opens a can of worms only Jared can close, as following a trail of red-speckled pills and green-tinted heroin become the only way to avenge his sister's death.

Laced
(Pillbillies Series Book 2)

Exiled from his past life and plagued with the responsibility of a broken empire of Pillbillies, Jared Vorcelli dives into the underbelly of an addict's world to avenge the ones he loves and pull them from the wreckage of his choices. Targeting a dangerous ex-drug kingpin and his own father, Jared needs to learn who to trust, who to kill, and who to forgive when their respective paths collide.